Kate Wilhelm is the author of more than three dozen novels, and her fiction has been translated into many languages. She lives in Eugene, Oregon.

THE DEEPEST WATER

Abby Connors's father, Jud, was a successful novelist and the most important man in her life (much to the chagrin of her husband). Jud's murder suddenly overturns everything in Abby's life — she must rediscover who she is, who her father was, and who the people around her really are. Fortunately, she has an unlikely guide to help her on the path towards rediscovery — her late father, whose last novel might just point the way . . . if she could only see through the fiction to get at the truth. Does her father's novel reveal his own murderer?

Books by Kate Wilhelm
Published by The House of Ulverscroft:

THE GOOD CHILDREN

KATE WILHELM

◆

THE
DEEPEST
WATER

Complete and Unabridged

ULVERSCROFT
Leicester

First published in Great Britain in 2001 by
Robert Hale Limited
London

First Large Print Edition
published 2003
by arrangement with
Robert Hale Limited
London

British Library CIP Data

Wilhelm, Kate, *1928 –*
   The deepest water.—Large print ed.—
   Ulverscroft large print series: mystery
   1. Fathers and daughters—Fiction
   2. Children of murder victims—Fiction
   3. Psychological fiction 4. Large type books
   I. Title
   813.5'4 [F]

   ISBN 0–7089–4850–2

Published by
F. A. Thorpe (Publishing)
Anstey, Leicestershire
Set by Words & Graphics Ltd.
Anstey, Leicestershire
Printed and bound in Great Britain by
T. J. International Ltd., Padstow, Cornwall

This book is printed on acid-free paper

1

Afterward everyone said the memorial service had been poignant yet beautiful, exactly what Jud would have wanted. But not yet, Abby protested despairingly, silently, not at forty-eight years old! For days she had said little or nothing, as if her vocal cords had frozen, she had lost the power of speech. People held her hand, embraced her, patted her, and she understood that they were trying to express something, but she could feel herself adding layer after layer of protective, invisible shielding against every touch, removing herself in a way that kept her numb and rigid, unresponsive to their sympathy, unable to stop adding to the cocoon that might keep her safe. Shock, they said; she was still in shock.

Exactly what her father had ordered, the funeral director assured her, even to the box that Jud had provided along with his instructions. He placed the box in her hands deferentially, then walked away with his head bowed until he had cleared the crematorium chapel, when he straightened and walked more briskly.

'Honey, we have to leave now,' Brice said at her elbow. He took the box from her, held it under his arm, and put his other arm around her shoulders, guided her toward the door. People were waiting. Jud's parents from California, Lynne — Abby's mother from Seattle — Brice's parents from Idaho, friends, strangers ... Lynne had said the family would have to go back to the house after it was over; everyone would expect coffee, wine, something to help ease them back to the world of the living. She would take care of things, she had promised, that's what she had come for, to help Abby; then she wept. Abby had looked at her in wonder. Her parents had been divorced for so many years, why was she crying now?

'Mrs. Connors?' Another stranger, another outsider.

She paused, expecting him to hold out his hand, kiss her cheek, something.

'I'm Lieutenant Caldwell,' he said apologetically. 'State special investigations. I need to talk to you — '

Brice's hand tightened on her shoulder. 'You can't be serious!' he said. 'Not now!'

'No, no,' he said quickly. 'Of course not now. But tomorrow? Around ten in the morning?'

Abby accepted this as numbly as she had accepted everything else. She nodded.

'We've already told the police everything we know,' Brice said. He tugged at her shoulder; she started to move again.

'I understand,' Caldwell said, still apologetic. 'I'll explain in the morning. I'm very sorry, Mrs. Connors.' Then he was gone, and they walked out into a fine light rain.

There were a lot of reporters, a camera crew, others waiting. After years of struggling, Judson Vickers had become an overnight bestselling author; his death by murder was news, at least today it was news. Abby walked past the crowd blindly.

That night, after the mourners had gone, and only her mother remained for one more night, Lynne said almost pleadingly that she didn't have to go back to Seattle yet if Abby wanted her to stay on a few days.

Abby shook her head. 'There's no point. In the morning the police are coming to ask more questions, and in the afternoon Christina Maas is coming. There are things we have to talk about. That's how it's going to be for a while.' Her voice sounded strange, as if muffled by layers of cotton.

Lynne looked at Brice, and he shrugged helplessly. 'It's been a tough few days,' he said. 'We'll be okay after we've had a little rest. I'll take you to the airport in the morning.'

Her mother was going to cry again, Abby thought guiltily, and she still didn't know why, and couldn't ask. Not now. And Brice ... She knew she was shutting him out exactly the way she was closing out everyone else, and she knew it was unfair, even cruel, but she couldn't help that, either. He wanted to hold her, to comfort her, to wait on her, do whatever he could, and she was like a stick in his arms. Silently she began to gather plates, cups, and saucers ... Her friends Jonelle and Francesca had brought food, she remembered; it all looked strange and unfamiliar.

'Honey, please, go take a long bath, try to relax,' Brice said. 'We'll take care of this.'

With the unquestioning obedience of a good child, she left the room to go take a long bath. She could hear their voices as she went up the stairs; talking about her, the state she was in, she thought distantly. The house was usually spacious feeling, with three bedrooms, two baths, stairs with a plush, pale green carpet, a nice Aubusson rug in the living room, a carpet in the den, drapes throughout; room enough, with sound-deadening furnishings, so that voices carried no farther than from one room to another, yet she imagined she could hear them all the way up the stairs, through the hallway, the bedroom, on into the bathroom, even after

4

she turned on the water. She went back to the bedroom for her gown and robe, and came to a stop holding them.

The voices were not her mother's and Brice's, she realized, but her mother's and her father's, or her father's voice talking to her, telling her something important. That's what he would say: 'This is important, listen up now.'

She took a step and staggered, and only then recognized her fatigue, that she was reeling, maybe even hallucinating from sleeplessness. Tonight, she told herself, tonight she would take one of the pills her doctor had prescribed. She would give herself half an hour and if by then she was still wide awake, she would take a pill. Dimly she remembered that she had made the same promise the previous night, but instead had sat huddled in a blanket on the couch in the dark living room, dreading today, the relatives, the memorial service, remembering Jud, denying his death, willing him not to be dead, willing it not to have happened, afraid of the pill that promised sleep, because it seemed to offer a kind of death to her.

★　★　★

Later, while Brice was getting ready for bed, Abby went to tell her mother good night, to

5

thank her for coming. She felt awkward, as if in the presence of an acquaintance, not her mother.

Lynne was in the guest room, the room Abby called her study. She stood in the middle of the room, wearing her robe, holding the dress she had worn earlier, and for a moment they simply regarded each other. Then Lynne dropped the dress and took Abby in her arms. 'I wanted to be with you,' she said softly, 'but I didn't know what to say, how to act with you. Abby, baby, please say something, talk to me. Yell at me. Anything!'

Abby gazed past her mother silently and offered no resistance to the embrace, but neither did she return it. People had always said she looked like her mother, and she had denied it, had seen only the differences, not the similarities; they were the same height, and Lynne was only a few pounds heavier, her hair was as dark as Abby's and, out of the chignon she had had it in, hung straight to her shoulders, like her daughter's. They both had dark blue eyes and heavy eyebrows, bold and thick, without a curve, much less a peak. The likeness, remarkable as it was, appeared superficial to Abby. The image of her mother that rose in her memory was of a face contorted with anger: a mouth pinched in fury or downturned in resentment; glaring, red-rimmed eyes; her voice loud and shrill, out of control in her rage or whining in self-pity.

She disengaged herself and drew back, picked up her mother's dress and took it to the closet, placed it on a hanger.

'I can't talk right now,' she said, her back to Lynne. 'Not right now. I'll come visit you in a few weeks.'

'No, don't come up to Seattle. Call me and I'll come down here. We'll go to the coast for a day or two. Will you do that?' She was pleading again.

Abby closed her eyes hard for a moment, then opened them and turned around. 'Yes. I'll call you when things settle down again. We'll go to the coast.' She didn't know if she was lying or not. But they both had known she wouldn't go to Seattle; she didn't like Lynne's husband or her own half brother, Jason. 'Good night, Mom. Sleep well. I'm glad you came. Thanks.'

Back in her own room Brice was already in bed. They had twin beds pushed together, his mattress not as firm as hers, but he was on her side, waiting for her.

'I need a little more time,' she said, taking off her robe. 'I'm sorry, but I need a little more time. I took a pill and I think I'll sleep okay tonight.'

'I just want to hold you,' he said. When she got in beside him, he held her tenderly, stroking her shoulder, demanding nothing. She stared dry-eyed into the darkness of the room.

Later, when he kissed her cheek and moved to his own bed, she pretended to be asleep and listened to his breathing change. He had a little snore, one that she was used to and sometimes even found comforting, but she felt herself go tense when he snored now. She waited longer, then silently got up, felt for her robe, and left the bedroom.

The third bedroom had been turned into a study where Brice often worked at home. She entered and closed the door. There was no need for a light; his computer monitor was enough. An endless stream of aircraft flew silently by: zeppelins, the Wright brothers' first plane, SSTs, 747s, biplanes, helicopters, all forever flying from the void, going nowhere. Their ever-changing light flowed over the top of the funereal box, which Brice had placed on his desk.

She had seen the box before; it was mahogany so dark, it looked black, finely carved all over with intricate patterns of flowers and birds — a souvenir from his R&R on Bali, Jud had said.

'They carve everything,' he had said that

afternoon at the lake. 'They'll start carving a living tree while it's still standing, the damnedest thing you can imagine — demons, birds, gods, snakes, flowers . . . And they carve it for eight feet up, ten feet . . . They carve the undersides of stairs, where no one will ever see the art. They carve the concrete walls at the airport . . . '

'Why?'

'I think it's a religious act,' he said thoughtfully. 'Nothing else quite explains it. They're expressing their religion through art. Little boys, four years old, five, they're already artists. They do the traditional things the same way their ancestors from the beginning of time did them, and then they do their own thing on the back of stairs, on boxes, whatever is at hand. In that climate nothing lasts very long except stone, and when the paint fades, gets washed away, or eaten by mold, they repaint it exactly the way it had been before. If a wooden object or building crumbles, they rebuild it exactly as it was before. You can't tell by looking if anything was made that morning or a hundred years ago. They're preserving the past, keeping the faith, but here or there, hidden away, they express whatever it is they need to say through their art.'

She had felt the box all over, the delicate

tracery of flowers and stems, and thought that it was a magic box, that it contained secrets no one would ever decipher, except the boy who had carved it.

'Honey,' Jud had said that day, 'this is important, listen up. When I die, I want my ashes to be buried in this box, here by the lake. I might never ask another thing of you, but this is important. Will you do that for me?'

She had nodded solemnly. At ten years of age, she had not yet believed in dying. It did not occur to her to ask why he was telling her, not her mother. The divorce came two years after that. Perhaps he had already known Lynne would not be around to carry out his wishes.

She touched the box on Brice's desk and again felt the mystery of the carved wood, the unknown, unknowable mystery of the artist who had carved it.

She felt the mystery of the man whose ashes were inside it, her father, unknown, unknowable forever now.

2

She ended up taking the sleeping pill that night and slept until Brice shook her awake at nine.

'How do you feel?' he asked.

Human, she thought, human monster with a watermelon for a head and leaden legs; that's what sleeping pills did to her. But feeling anything at all was an improvement. She said, 'Okay,' and pulled herself up and out of bed.

'You should have gotten me up,' she said in mild protest at the kitchen table when Brice said he already had taken her mother to the airport.

'Honey, you were a walking zombie, out on your feet. I just wish that idiot cop hadn't said ten this morning; I would have let you sleep until noon, or even all day.' He was opposite her at the breakfast table, studying her face anxiously.

She drank her coffee, and when she started to rise to get the carafe, he jumped up and hurried across the kitchen; in passing, he kissed the top of her head.

'Let me wait on you for just a little while.

You don't know how I've felt, wanting to do something, anything. I watched you sleeping,' he said, pouring the coffee, 'and I wanted to sit there and not even breathe, just watch you.'

'I'm . . . I'm sorry,' she whispered, not looking up at him.

'Oh, Christ! I didn't mean to dump a guilt trip on you. I've just been so goddamn helpless.'

'I know.'

She did know. They had been married for four years, and it was a good marriage; he was a tender and passionate lover; he brought her unexpected presents, listened attentively when she talked about the museum, her work there, her dissertation that was going nowhere; he, in turn, talked about his clients, the others in the office, his plans. They were lucky, she knew, especially when her friends talked about this couple or that, or their own failed marriages or affairs, or when she remembered her first marriage, she realized again how lucky they were. She understood and cherished what they had, but this week she had not wanted anyone to touch her, not her mother, not friends, not relatives, and not him.

He touched her hair now, a fairy touch, light and tentative; although she willed herself

12

not to flinch, not to stiffen, something was communicated, and he drew back. 'Well,' he said in a strained voice, 'that cop is due any minute now. After he leaves, I have to check in at the office for a few hours. Will you be okay?'

She nodded, aware only then that he had on a suit and tie, dressed for the office. She couldn't remember if he had gone in at all that week. Had he gone in to report on the weekend meeting? He must have, she thought miserably; his world hadn't caved in the way hers had. She simply hadn't paid any attention, like now, not noticing that he was dressed for clients, dressed for business in a good gray suit, maroon silk tie, shirt dazzling white. At thirty-four, he was even more handsome than when they married. Marriage agreed with him, he sometimes said jokingly. She wondered if his folks had left town yet, if they were driving home to Idaho, the potato farm. His father's hands had been spotlessly clean, she thought, and her mind skittered off in yet another direction.

That was how she had been all week, unable to focus on any one thing for more than a few seconds and left with no memory of what she had been thinking. A persistent thought recurred: if he had had a fight with his father, he had to make amends now,

13

before it was too late.

Just then the doorbell rang. She had forgotten that the policeman had said he would come at ten, and she glanced down at herself in dismay; she was in jeans and an old sweater.

'Finish your coffee,' Brice said. 'I'll take him to the living room.'

She left the coffee and followed him to the front door, where he was admitting the policeman and a woman with short brown hair so curly, it was almost too frizzy.

'Lieutenant Caldwell, and this is Detective Varney,' the policeman said politely, as if aware that she had no memory of their names.

She nodded, and Brice said briskly, 'Well, come on in. Do you want to take off your jacket and coat?'

Caldwell was wearing a windbreaker; Detective Varney had a long dark green raincoat. She pulled it off, then held it, but he shook his head. 'It's okay. Beautiful day out there, just right, not too hot, not too cool. And not raining,' he added, making a leisurely examination of the foyer, of Brice and Abby, everything. He was a stocky man in his forties, heavy through the shoulders and chest, with dark hair turning gray at the temples, and dark eyes. Everything about him seemed too deliberate, too slow, as if he never had rushed in his life and would not be rushed now.

'This way,' Brice said, steering them toward the living room, where he and Abby sat on the sofa, and the lieutenant and detective sat in identical tapestry-covered chairs. The detective did not relax, but Caldwell settled back, crossed his legs, and examined the living room with the same methodical scrutiny he had given the foyer.

'Nice house,' Caldwell said finally.

Abby could feel her stomach muscles tightening harder and harder. The house was nice, with good, maybe Danish furniture, good original art on the walls, even if not very much of it. There was a grouping of netsuke on the mantel; the lieutenant's gaze lingered on it as if in appraisal.

Expensive, she wanted to say. Too expensive. Brice had brought home two of them from a trip to Los Angeles, her first anniversary gift, startling her. Take them back, she should have said; we can't afford them. But they were so beautiful . . .

'Well, we're not selling and you're not buying, so let's get on with it,' Brice said, glancing at his watch. 'I already told you we've given statements to the local police. What more do you need?'

Lieutenant Caldwell faced Abby and Brice then. 'You see, Mr. Connors, that place where the crime happened is sort of in a no-man's-land, the lake and all. Part in one county, part in another, it makes for confusion. In cases like this they often call in the state investigators, and that's what happened this time. And just to keep things straight in my own head, I'd like to go over your statements again, get it firsthand, so to speak.' He shrugged, almost apologetically, it seemed. 'And, of course, you might have remembered something during the past few days that you didn't think of when the sheriff talked to you.'

'I can only repeat what I said before,' Brice said wearily. 'On Friday I drove to Portland for a business meeting with associates from my company. We had dinner together and talked until about ten-thirty. I went to bed around twelve. I had to make notes about the meeting; it took a while. On Saturday morning I checked out, drove down to Salem and had breakfast there, and then drove home. I gave the sheriff copies of the log of my trip and my receipts. And they already took our fingerprints, they said for elimination purposes. That's all I can tell you.'

Caldwell had been listening intently, consulting a notebook from time to time. He

16

nodded. 'Your firm is Hartmann and Fine Financial Services?'

'Yes. The head office is in Bellingham; there's an office in Spokane, one in Olympia, in Portland, Salem, and here in Eugene. A representative from each office attended the meeting.'

'Your company in trouble?'

'No. It's not like that! If you read the newspapers, you know how the market's been for over a year, crazy swings up and down. We have clients who get antsy when it gyrates like that. We've been having these meetings once a month over the past year. Purely routine.'

'You always go?'

'No. There are three of us here in the Eugene office; we take turns. They aren't exactly pleasure jaunts, Lieutenant. It happened to be my turn.'

Caldwell nodded, as if everything Brice said checked out with the notes he had. Then he said, 'I understand that some of the associates share rides. Do you do that?'

'No,' Brice said stiffly. 'Dave Fulton is in Salem, and I would have stopped and picked him up, but I planned to stay over Friday night, and he didn't. So we drove up separately.'

'Do you usually stay up there overnight?'

'That was the first time,' Brice said. 'The other times I went I didn't get home until

17

after two in the morning. We never know when the meetings will end, and no matter when I go to bed, I'm awake by six-thirty. I decided to stay and get some sleep this time since Abby would be gone.'

'Did you check in at your office here in town before you drove up to Portland?'

Brice's impatience was clearly strained almost past endurance. 'I already told them. No. Abby didn't have to go to work until nine, and we lazed about that morning. I left when she did.'

The lieutenant asked more questions: where he had stayed, the names of his associates, where they had met, had dinner, where he had had breakfast. All things Brice had gone through with the sheriff, all things already in his notebook, Abby felt certain. Brice's tension was almost palpable; she took his hand and held it. At first he was as stiff and unresponsive as she had been all week, then he squeezed her hand and she could feel his tension ease. They were both like that, she thought fleetingly, coiled so hard and tight that a word, an expression, a breeze might make either of them erupt in some unpredictable way.

'Okay,' Caldwell said at last, and turned to Abby. 'Mrs. Connors, you want to tell me about Friday?'

She moistened her lips and released her hand from Brice's grasp, which had grown increasingly hard. 'I was at the coast with friends.'

He smiled at her. 'In just a little more detail, maybe?'

'Jonelle, Jonelle Saltzman, picked me up when I got off work at about two, and we drove out. To Yachats. Emma Olson and Francesca Tremaine came out a little later. We walked around, ate dinner, and talked until very late. On Saturday the deputy came to tell me. Jonelle brought me home.'

'This is something you do often, go spend the weekend with your pals?'

'Once a year, sometimes twice.'

'Who made the reservation?'

'I did. At the Blue Horizon Cottages.'

'Why that weekend?'

'Since Brice would be away, and the others could make it, it seemed a good time.'

'When's the last time you folks were at the lake, Mrs. Connors?'

She moistened her lips again. 'August.'

'I understand your father called you on Friday morning. Is that right?'

She nodded.

'What did he say? How did he sound?'

'He asked if I could come over for the weekend, and I said I couldn't.' She realized that the other detective, the woman, was watching her hands, and she glanced down and saw them clutching each other almost spasmodically. She flexed her fingers and spread them, then let her hands rest in her lap. 'If I'd gone, it wouldn't have happened,' she said in a low voice. 'I could have gone there instead of to the coast. If I — '

'For God's sake, Abby! You might have been killed, too,' Brice said. 'You couldn't have stopped the maniac who shot him. You would have been killed with him.'

'Do you remember exactly what he said that morning?' Caldwell said, ignoring Brice.

She nodded. 'He was happy and excited. He said, 'This is important. I have something to tell you.' He was laughing and happy. And I said I couldn't.'

'Did he say what was important?'

She shook her head. 'I asked if he could come to town on Saturday, that we could all have dinner Saturday night, and he said he'd just stay put and work.'

Brice put his arm around her shoulders, squeezed her shoulder lightly. 'Lieutenant Caldwell, tell her she couldn't have prevented what happened out there. It wasn't her fault.'

Abby avoided glancing at him; he sounded desperate, pleading. A glance now might be the cue that would make her erupt into tears.

And she was determined not to cry, not now. Get through this, that was all that mattered.

'Tell me about the dog,' Caldwell said, paying no attention whatsoever to Brice.

Brice squeezed her shoulder harder.

'Spook? What about her?' Abby asked.

'Mr. Halburtson said she barked during the night, all the next morning. Did she bark a lot?'

Coop Halburtson was the nearest neighbor to her father's cabin; he always heard Spook when she barked. Abby shook her head. 'No. Just if a raccoon came around, or a cougar, or a stranger, something like that.'

'Did the dog stay out every night?'

'No. Sometimes there are bears, or cougars . . . He kept her inside. She has a dog door and can come and go when she wants to, but he always locked it at night.' She added, 'She, Spook, tangled with a skunk once and he said . . . he said he never wanted that to happen again.' She looked down at her hands; they were clutching each other hard.

'Mrs. Connors,' the lieutenant said then, 'from all we've been able to find out up to now you're probably the one who was closest to your father. You lived with him for years after your mother moved to Seattle; you kept in touch. Did he have enemies? Did he ever tell you about anyone who might have wanted

21

to harm him, kill him even?'

She shook her head.

'Do you know where Matthew Petrie is?'

She looked up, startled. 'No. I haven't seen him or heard from him since . . . since we were divorced eight years ago.'

'Why did your father give Petrie a check for fifteen thousand dollars the day after you divorced him?'

Caldwell didn't look menacing, merely puzzled, but suddenly Abby began to feel as if he had been building a trap, luring her toward it gently, effortlessly even, but knowing exactly what he was after, where he intended to lead her. She shook her head again. 'I don't know anything about that. Dad didn't have that kind of money back then. Who told you that?'

Caldwell shrugged. 'You see, when it comes to a murder investigation, we have to go through a lot of history — records, bank records, things like that. It came up. Did your father and Petrie have a big fight before Petrie took off?'

'Not a fight. Just yelling back and forth. But Matthew wouldn't have a reason to come back, to hurt him.' Then she whispered, 'You've been going through all his papers, his private affairs, everything.'

'I'm sorry, Mrs. Connors, but it's part of

22

the routine. We have to try to tie up some loose ends.'

Abruptly Brice stood up. 'I think this has gone on long enough, Lieutenant. The sheriff summed it up. Some psycho, probably high on meth or something, went to the cabin and shot Jud. The dog barked and the guy got away. It has nothing to do with Abby or with the past.'

Caldwell eyed him speculatively, then nodded. 'You're probably right. Occam's razor, the simplest solution is most often the right one, but we're stuck with routine, like most people. We just have to follow up if there are a lot of loose ends.' He looked at Abby once more and asked, 'Do you know why your father got cashier's checks a couple of times a year for the past seven years, who they were for?'

'I don't know what you're talking about.'

'See? A loose end. Was he giving you an allowance, paying for your schooling?'

'Yes. He said it was his job, to see that I got an education even if it took a lifetime to do it.' She blinked rapidly, then ducked her head again. 'But not cashier's checks, just a regular check every month.'

Brice was still standing, his face flushed with anger. 'People get cashier's checks for a lot of reasons. He traveled a lot; maybe he didn't like to use credit cards or carry cash with him. What's that got to do with his murder?'

'Over a hundred thousand dollars, walking-around money? And he did use credit cards, you see. So, a loose end.'

'A hundred thousand?' Brice sat down hard.

Caldwell nodded, then said, 'More, actually. One hundred forty-five thousand. Just one or two more things, and we're out of here. I talked to Harvey Durham, your father's attorney and executor of his estate, and he said you weren't aware of the codicil your father added to his will years ago. Is that right?'

Abby nodded.

'Do you have any idea why he added it?'

'No.'

'Strange thing to add. You inherit it all, act as his literary executor, continue to get your monthly allowance, but you can't touch the principal or sell anything for six months. He never mentioned that to you?'

'No. Harvey told us on Monday.'

'But you knew you were his heir?'

'Yes. After my mother remarried, he told me he had changed his will. We . . . we laughed because he didn't have anything to leave except the cabin and his papers.'

'Did he tell you about the designation with the thirty-day contingency clause?'

She shook her head. 'No.'

'Did he confide in you at all about his finances, the sales of his work, how much he was making in the past few years?'

'No. Lieutenant, he never talked about money, not when he didn't have any, not when he did. It just wasn't important to him. He began to travel, and he bought me a new car, a Toyota Supra, two years ago, and bought a van, a sports utility van, but even that wasn't really important to him. More like a necessity, living back in the mountains, as he was. I don't know how much he was making, or what he was doing with it.'

She had a flashing memory of the time Brice had suggested that his company would be happy to advise Jud about stocks, mutual funds, whatever.

Jud had laughed. 'There are three people that, if you use their services at all, you should make sure are not related to you. Your doctor, your lawyer, and your money manager. But thanks.'

Caldwell had asked something else, she realized, something she had not heard. 'I'm sorry,' she said.

'Did he stay here with you when he came to town?' Caldwell repeated.

She shook her head. Jud had never spent a single night in this house.

'Did he stay with Willa Ashford?'

'I don't know,' she said faintly. 'You'll have to ask her.'

Finally Caldwell stood up. 'Just one more thing, Mrs. Connors, then we'll leave you in peace. As I said, we've had to go through his papers, records, all that. But the problem is, you're the only one we know who can look over the cabin and make sure nothing's missing, that things are pretty much like he kept them. Can you go out there with us tomorrow?'

'Jesus!' Brice snapped. 'For God's sake, can't you see what this is doing to her? That's too goddamn much to ask!'

Caldwell kept his gaze on Abby. 'The crime lab technicians have gone over things, there's nothing left to see. It's been padlocked ever since the sheriff got there, but we need someone like you to have a look around before anyone takes a notion to break in or something. How long a drive is it from here?'

'Two hours,' she said. He was just doing his job, she thought bleakly. That was all it meant to him, another job to get over with, move on to something else. Then she thought, that was what she wanted, too. To find out who shot her father in the face on Friday night. She nodded.

'Good. Nine? Is that okay with you? We'll pick you up at nine.'

She nodded again. She remained on the sofa, with her hands clasped tightly, when Brice took them to the door.

'I just don't think you should come,' Abby said to Brice after the officers left. 'There won't be anything for you to do, and you must have a ton of work to catch up on.'

'I don't want you to go off with them alone. Let's take the box, give your father his burial, then close up the place for now. We can drive Jud's van home.'

'No!' She took a breath, then said calmly, 'I'm not ready yet, and not with them along. Not with police watching. It . . . it has to be private.' She realized that she had already decided to bury her father's ashes alone, not with anyone else present. It had to be private. She was not aware of having thought it through before, but the idea was firmly implanted in her mind. Maybe she had known ever since the day Jud had told her his wishes, an implicit part of his instructions, unstated but communicated.

'Okay,' Brice said. He looked almost rigid, his mouth tight with frustration. 'We'll leave that for later, but I should be with you when you go back the first time. I don't care what they've cleaned up, it's going to be hard for you to go back.'

The doorbell rang, and he glanced at his watch. 'Christ, it must be that agent. We'll talk about this when I get home, okay? Call me if you need anything. I'll be at the office all afternoon.' He went to admit Christina Maas.

Abby met Christina in the foyer, surprised to see the woman enter with a roll-on suitcase and briefcase, dressed in a black pantsuit with a silvery blouse, ready to travel. Or to move in?

'I have a five o'clock plane to L.A.,' Christina said. 'So I checked out of the hotel already. I can get a cab from here, can't I?'

Brice said sure, call for a cab when she was ready to go; he blew Abby a kiss and left the two women in the foyer, where Abby regarded her guest with suspicion and even hostility. Christina had been one of Jud's women, she knew with certainty, and she didn't know how to act with her. How to treat her. Clearly Christina had not shed many tears over Jud's death; her makeup was too perfect for that, untouched by human tears. She was tall, five feet ten, almost too thin, with what Abby thought of as big-city style, New York style; her hair was pale, nearly

28

platinum, beautifully coifed and moussed, her nails manicured, ivory, a heavy gold chain her only jewelry.

'Is there someplace where we can spread out some papers?' Christina asked, glancing into the living room, dismissing it.

Abby nodded and led the way to the breakfast table, where she began to pick up the coffee cups. Now, in a better light, she realized Christina was older than she had first appeared. Tiny lines around her eyes and mouth betrayed her in spite of the makeup. Forty-something, not pretty at all, just smart looking.

'Abby,' Christina said, watching her wipe the table, 'we might clear the air before we start. Jud told me you suspected that we'd had an affair, and that you didn't approve. I'm sorry. I cared for him very deeply, but it was over a long time ago, and afterward we became good friends as well as business associates.' She sat down and placed her briefcase on the floor.

'The police questioned me yesterday about Jud's work, how he got paid, how much, when, everything. I told them exactly what I'm going to tell you. Better to tell them up front than wait for a subpoena.' She was brisk, businesslike, as if to say there should be no doubt about this meeting; it was purely business. 'You're the literary executor. That means you have to approve any deals I make, or reject them. It means that you can choose to have a different agent handle his unpublished work, if you want to go that route, but I'll still handle everything I handled in the past — foreign sales, for instance. The movie deal I'm negotiating now. I can make the deal, negotiate, do it all, but you have to approve and sign the contract.'

Abby listened to her mutely, hardly able to comprehend the meaning of her words as Christina continued to talk about the agreement she and Jud had reached, and what it meant now that Abby was the literary executor, the contract that Abby would have to sign agreeing to the arrangement with the agent.

Then Christina began to spread papers out on the table, and presently she asked if there was any coffee. Later, when Christina began to talk about a tax attorney, Abby shook her head.

'Stop. I don't understand the contract you're talking about, the Hollywood deal you're talking about, subsidiary rights, any of this.'

'What it means,' Christina said slowly, 'is that if these various deals go through, if you approve and sign the contracts, you're going

30

to make a hell of a lot of money. Not all at once, and not until the terms of the will are satisfied about the six-month waiting period, but over the next few years, perhaps a lot of years.' She regarded Abby through narrowed eyes. 'Jud and I kept in close touch. He said he was wrapping up a new novel, that it would be finished almost any day now. I think he meant it, that the new work was either completed or nearly done. Do you know if it's done?'

'No.' Was that what his call had been about, the completion of the new novel? He was always happy when he finished; he always wanted to celebrate, and she had said no, she couldn't make it.

'You have a decision facing you,' Christina was saying. 'Do I handle the new work, or do you get a new agent?'

Abby had not even thought of getting a new agent, and wouldn't know how to start. 'He trusted you,' she said. 'He wouldn't want me to change anything.'

'Good. But you're right, this is too much all at once. I made copies of his files, the royalty statements, our correspondence, and notes about our telephone calls concerning the movie deal I'm working on. I'm going down to L.A. from here to try to get a final contract we can all agree to. I'll leave all the copies with you. Go over the material and whatever you don't understand, jot down questions. I'll give you a call early next week, and then, Abby, if you're up to it, I'll want to look through his past work. He said he had a lot of stuff he never even showed anyone. I want to see it. And I have to read the new novel. He said it was all in the cabin. Can we go there together, go through his papers together, see if there's anything else publishable? The policeman I talked to said there are file cases, and boxes and boxes of papers. We'll have to sort through everything.'

Abby nodded. 'I'll take you there.'

After Christina left, Abby returned to the table and stared at the many file folders the agent had prepared for her. It wasn't fair, she thought. All those years with nothing, no money, no job, nothing, and now, too late, all that money. Jud had never held a job longer than a few months; he had written advertising copy and detested doing it, had written a lot of technical things, manuals, computer documentation, even programs, but only when things got truly desperate, only long enough to pay the electric bill or pay rent for a few months . . . When Lynne finally could take it no longer, the uncertainty of a paycheck, or of having heat in the winter, never knowing if there would be enough food next week, next month, she had left him, after years of holding jobs herself, years of bitter fighting.

Jud's first novel had been published in 1989 and had not made him very much money, but the next one in 1991 had made money, and the last one four years ago had made a lot of money and would be making much, much more, according to Christina.

And if the new novel was finished . . . Abby whispered, 'It's not fair.'

She gathered up the file folders and took them to the guest room, the room she used for her schoolwork and her dissertation, the room her mother had stayed in. She could still smell Lynne's perfume lingering in the air. She put the folders in the desk drawer; no more for now, she thought. She didn't want to discuss any of it with Brice, not yet, not until she had grasped what it all meant. He would take over the management of the money, she knew; that was his specialty, managing money. The thought of making plans for investments, purchases, travel, all the things he would want to discuss, repulsed her. Not yet, not so soon.

She went to his study, picked up the mahogany box and carried it to her room, and placed it on her own desk.

Standing with both hands on the box, she knew that she would find a way to prevent Brice's going to the cabin the following day. She did not want him to go through her father's papers, not until she had sorted them all out. She didn't want him to read her father's short stories, his novel, which might be completed by now. First she had to read the new novel, and then she might decide to bury it with her father's ashes.

3

Brice came home late, looking tired and harried. 'The market goes up, they want to sell; it goes down, they want to buy. Those who aren't on the phone yelping are in the office yelping. Buy at ten, sell at noon, buy again at two . . . Stacks of unanswered calls to get to . . .'

She put her fingers on his lips, aware that he had to talk about the office; he was trying to put the past week behind him, behind them, trying not to think of the coming visit to the cabin. 'We have to start getting our lives in place again,' she said. 'You have to take care of your clients, or they'll do their yelping to the head office, and I have to go to the cabin tomorrow. I'll drive the van home and bring Spook with me. Then we'll have the weekend to get some rest.' She began to tell him about Christina Maas, the Hollywood contract she was negotiating.

'I'll tag along tomorrow,' he said, interrupting her.

'You'd just be in the way,' she said. 'There's nothing there for you to do. I'll be safe enough with a couple of cops at my elbow.'

His grin in response to hers was weak, but he agreed.

* * *

Now, driving on Highway 58, with Caldwell at the wheel, Abby in the front seat, and Detective Varney in the back, they were passing through the small dying town of Oakridge. They had not yet reached the high mountains, but the road was curvy and there was a lot of traffic, people getting an early start on a weekend outing, logging trucks, RVs, commercial trucks. It was one of the most dangerous routes across the Cascades, with fatal accidents year after year; today it would take longer than the two hours Abby had predicted.

'How did your father stumble across such a remote cabin?' Caldwell asked, picking up speed again outside the town, along with everyone else on the road.

'It was his father's. Grandfather was transferred down to Santa Rosa, and he was going to let it go for back taxes, I guess, so Dad bought it for what was owed the state. He spent every summer and most weekends up there when he was a kid. I did, too.'

Caldwell muttered a curse as an oncoming driver pulled out to pass; there was nowhere to move over, no room to pass, either. The idiot driver pulled back in line.

Abby had hardly noticed. She was remembering the scene when Lynne learned that Jud was taking over the cabin. 'You're paying his taxes! What with? We can't even afford to get our own place.'

'I told you, I took the job with Aaronson. Dad will carry a loan for a few months.'

'For a lousy cabin you'll get a job! Look at that bathroom! Look at that kitchen sink! We live like dogs, and you want to buy a cabin in the woods!'

'Wait till you see it. You'll love it as much as I do. And Pudding Face here will, too. Won't you?'

Abby had nodded. 'Why is it called Two-Finger Lake?' She was coloring pictures.

'Make a fist,' Jud said. 'Here, put your hand down on the paper first. Now, trace around it with your crayon, all around.'

She traced her fist, then looked at him. She was four.

'Okay. Good. Now stick out your first two fingers.'

She put out her little finger and her ring finger, and he laughed. 'Wrong two. This one, and this one.' He touched her forefinger and middle finger, and she extended them, keeping the rest of her hand fisted on the

37

outline she had traced. Jud took the crayon and drew around the two fingers. 'And there it is! Two-Finger Lake. See?'

She studied the object they had drawn and shook her head. 'It's a rabbit,' she said.

Jud laughed. 'Damned if it isn't. Okay. It's Rabbit Lake, and our cabin is right here, on the lower ear.' The setting for all his novels had been Rabbit Lake.

She had loved it already that day, with as much fervor as Lynne hated it. Neither of them ever changed her mind about the cabin on Rabbit Lake.

'Did he actually live out there, or just hang out between other things?' Caldwell asked, bringing Abby back to the present, back to the reality of her father's murder.

'For years we just went up for weekends and summers. After I graduated from high school, he moved all the way out.' When she married Matthew Petrie, he moved all the way out, she should have said, if she had been more literal about the facts. He had taken an apartment for her sake, so she could finish high school in Eugene, and as soon as she was out from underfoot, two weeks after her graduation, one week after her marriage, he was gone. Within a month he had finished his first novel, and a year later it had been published.

Traffic was slowing now as they climbed into the mountains. There were no more villages, nothing but the road with all-too-rare passing lanes and the mountains from now on. Somewhere up ahead, she knew, there would be a camper laboring up the road, with a line of impatient drivers crawling after it, darting out to pass whenever they thought they could chance it. Caldwell seemed content with the slow going, she thought with relief. Jud had always been a patient driver, too.

The mountains were beautiful at this time of year; sumac, vine maples, poison oak all blazed scarlet, and the cottonwoods were golden against the perpetual dark green of the fir forests with their deep shadows. There had been enough rain that the fire hazard was not high this year, but not enough rain and wind to denude the trees early. Not enough soaking rain to bring up the mushrooms.

Remembering again. Jud had shaken her arm to wake her up early one morning. 'Time to go hunting, princess,' he said.

She had been sleepy and fearful. Hunting? They had been at the cabin two days, and that night they had to go back to Eugene. Lynne had refused to go with them that weekend. 'It's been raining all week,' she had snapped. 'It'll be cold and wet. I'll wait here, thank you.'

But at the lake the sun had come out, and the following day Abby and Jud had gone hunting, carrying mesh bags they could sling over their shoulders, and they had filled them both with mushrooms. Then they went out in the rowboat and fished, and that night they ate lake trout and mushrooms with rice. They had taken mushrooms back to town with them, but Lynne had refused to touch them.

'You wait for a good soaking rain,' Jud had said, 'and two days after it stops, the mushrooms pop up like magic. They like to hide underground, but they know exactly when to come up for some fresh air.'

They crossed over Willamette Pass, and there was the sign for the ski resort off to the right, and another one for a recreation area, also on the right. Abby said, 'The turn to the state park road is just up ahead on the left.' It was a dangerous turn; the traffic speed had increased again going downhill, but there were still cars, trucks, campers climbing up from the east. The problem now was not the oncoming traffic as much as the traffic behind them; stopping and waiting for the opportunity to make the turn invited a rear-end collision. They had been driving for two hours and ten minutes when Caldwell entered the road that led to the state park.

'Halburtson's driveway is on the left, just up ahead,' Abby said. This road was narrower than the highway, but a good road with pine forest pressing in closely on both sides; it was easy to miss the entrance to Coop Halburtson's place.

'I know,' Caldwell said. 'We crossed over the lake from there last time. Today I thought I'd drive up, see what that's like.' He glanced at her. 'The road's passable, isn't it?'

'At this time of year it's okay, unless it's snowed recently. Later you'd need a four-wheel drive, but it would be crazy later even then. We never drove up in the winter. In fact, we hardly ever drove up at all. We used the boat to go across the finger unless we had big things to carry. You'll add another forty-five minutes to the trip.'

'I thought we might,' he said. He drove past Coop Halburtson's property, and soon after that turned at the entrance to Two-Finger Lake State Park onto a winding lava-rock road with smaller lanes that led to campsites hidden among trees on the right. He passed them and drove to the boat-launching area, where he pulled in and parked. There were canoes, rowboats, even a kayak or two on the lake, nothing motorized. Motorboats were forbidden here.

'Let's stretch our legs,' he said, 'before we attack the mountain. Why is the water so black?'

It looked as black as ink, but that was deceptive. From another vantage point it would appear to be almost as blue as Crater Lake. 'It's underlain with basalt in places,' Abby said.

They walked to a rail and stood gazing at the water, at the surrounding cliffs, the boats. Like most of the state parks, this one was well used year-round; there were a lot of people in the area that day.

'One of the things bothering us,' Caldwell said, watching the boats, 'is how the killer approached the cabin. Can you see it from here?'

Abby shook her head. 'You can see part of the finger, but not the cabin. It's only a couple of miles from here, actually, but the cabin is set back a bit; trees block it from view.'

'Two miles,' he said musingly. 'Why couldn't someone have launched a boat down here and paddled up?'

She had rowed across to the state park many times, and occasionally someone did row up the finger to the end, but only in daylight. She pointed. 'See that cliff over there, the basalt rimrock? It goes into the water, just below the surface mostly, but there's a place where it's actually above the water level. You can spot it from here. But just barely. There's a break in the rocks there, at the left of the basalt. At night you'd need a powerful light to find your way through without grounding. There's another break over by the cliffs, and you can't see it at all unless you're out on the water. They're both hard to see in daylight, and invisible at night.'

Caldwell was peering at the lake, frowning, but Detective Varney exclaimed, 'I see it. A little island, a little black island.'

Abby nodded. Siren Rock. Jud had rowed her out to it one hot summer day; about four feet long and half that wide, it rose from the water no more than six inches, black and shiny, as smooth as the back of the Loch Ness monster. She had said, 'It's a Siren rock, isn't it? Calling you to the deep water where the fish are.' She had been reading a lot of mythology that summer, and Siren Rock the island had become. Jud's first novel was titled *Siren Rock*.

Their finger was quite shallow, no more than eight feet at the deepest point, but at this side of Siren Rock the basin plunged down eighty or ninety feet, and the water was many degrees colder than in the finger. They always fished in the deep water, and swam in the

43

warm shallow water.

There were no boats visible in the finger, and never any boats in the north finger, which was a spring-fed creek that had spread out fifty feet or more and was hazardous with boulders and blowdowns, unnavigable. It was good for finding crawfish and pretty rocks and places where she used to slide down slippery, moss-covered boulders and splash into tiny pools.

She turned her back on the lake and looked instead at the high mountains.

'Let's move on,' Caldwell said. 'We brought sandwiches and things. We'll eat when we reach the cabin. I suspected there wouldn't be much in the way of edibles along the way here.'

They drove out of the parking area and came to another intersection. 'Where does that go?' Caldwell asked.

'East, over to Highway 97, about ten miles, another couple of miles up to Bend. That's where people out here go shopping, rent movies, things like that. The other way goes to the cottages on the north shore of the lake. Mostly summer places or weekend retreats.'

He kept driving. Another dirt road angled off to the right, and she said, before he asked this time, 'That goes up to a hot spring. It's pretty popular, but tough to get to.' It was a deeply rutted dirt road. Most visitors hiked up. The forest service road they were on, only marginally better at the start, became much worse; it went up and down, back and forth, climbed steeply, then dropped just as steeply. It was sixteen miles from Highway 58 to the cabin, and it took at least forty-five minutes to drive there. She had called this the rolly-coaster road and had loved it. Remembering. Looking out the back window, she had seen a cloud of dust billowing after them, and she had decided it was helping out, pushing them up the mountain.

Detective Varney made a soft sound in the back seat and Caldwell slowed even more. Ahead, it appeared that the road vanished into nothingness, another outside hairpin curve.

'I sure wouldn't want to drive this at night,' Caldwell muttered. Now and then the lake came into view, but he didn't look down to admire the changing scene, sometimes blue water, sometimes black.

'This is why we use the boat to go back and forth,' Abby said.

They came to a one-lane bridge over the north finger, in deep forest now, with no sign of the lake or the cliffs they had traversed.

'It's only a little farther,' Abby said. 'It's

hard to see the driveway until you get right on it.'

When they reached the gravel driveway, Caldwell was making the turn before she could tell him *now*. The cabin was fifty feet lower than the road, with a steep approach. He stopped the car and looked at Abby. 'You ever drive up here by yourself?'

Surprised, she shrugged. She had driven up many times, and down, she told him. She thought her mother had come by road only that first time; after that she had refused, although she also had been afraid of the small rowboat. 'I've never been on the road after dark,' she admitted. 'I doubt that my father ever drove it after dark.'

They got out and started toward the cabin door. There was no landscaping here; pine trees, alders, and mountain laurel pressed in close to the driveway, and only the basalt shelf that held the cabin kept the dense growth from enveloping the structure.

The cabin was made of logs, with a shed roof that sloped down low on this side, making the building appear smaller than it was. The basalt formed a walkway from the door, around the side of the cabin, down to ledges that made steps to the water, ten feet lower than the cabin.

Someone had come here around the turn

of the century, her father had said, and cleared some forest, used the felled logs, and built himself a hideout. The last of the Hole-in-the-Wall Gang maybe. Or a miner looking for gold. Or a runaway Chinese railroad man, or an escaped convict. Over the years improvements had been added: insulation and knotty pine paneling installed, electricity brought in, appliances and furniture trucked in over that incredible road. But none of that had ever mattered to Abby; this was the hideout.

She watched in silence as Caldwell opened the padlock the police had put on the door. It probably was the first time the door had ever been locked.

Her father had added a loft, an aerie, he had called it, cantilevered out over the back, with stout supports anchored to the basalt. 'What's an aerie?' she had asked.

'An eagle's nest, or a fort on a mountain, a house on a high point. That's where I'll work.'

And the space under it, she had decided, was hers, a fairy cave.

They entered the cabin; it looked exactly the same as always. Knotty pine paneling aglow on the walls, Indian rugs on the floor, throws of many colors on the sofa and an easy chair, a rattan chair. The living room and kitchen made up more than half of the first floor; the rest consisted of two small bedrooms with a bathroom between them, and the staircase to the aerie. There was a television and a CD player; for years all they could watch were movies, then he had installed a satellite dish. Bookcases overflowed, more books stacked on the floor, on tables ... The table that divided the living-room area from the kitchen had a bowl of candy bars on it, just like always. Abby caught her breath and then moved to the middle of the room.

She realized that she had braced herself, had expected to see the chalk outline of a body, bloodstains, something. But there was nothing unusual to see. Everything looked natural, the same as it had been in August, the same as always. But too still, too empty. And the carpet, the stair runner, had been removed.

'I think we should have our lunch,' Caldwell said behind her.

She spun around. 'Not yet. Where was he? Where did it happen?' She was trembling, and her voice was harsh.

'How we reconstructed it,' Caldwell said evenly, 'goes something like this. He had been up in the loft. When he came down, he was shot at the bottom; he fell backwards, partway up the stairs. It probably was

48

between one and two in the morning. Halburtson said he got up to go to the john during the night, and his wife roused enough to hear the dog barking. Mrs. Halburtson said he usually gets up between one and two, and the coroner said that's about right. She thought that maybe a cougar or a bear had come nosing around on this side. Their dogs didn't bark, so she didn't pay much attention. It was a cold night; Halburtson closed their window, and they couldn't hear the dog anymore. Not until the next morning when they got up. Then they heard it again. And they could see it from their ramp, running around the house, jumping at the windows, things like that. They tried to reach Mr. Vickers on the phone and got no answer. Finally Halburtson got his boat out and came over to investigate.'

Abby was staring at the steps to the aerie. Someone came in and stood about where she was standing now, in the middle of the room, and when Jud reached the lowest step shot him in the face. She jerked away from the spot and she felt the floor tilting, the walls moving inward . . .

Detective Varney grabbed her, put an arm around her shoulders, steadied her a moment, then took her to one of the chairs at

49

the table. 'Put your head down, all the way, to your knees,' she said calmly.

★   ★   ★

A few minutes later, sipping coffee from a thermos, they all sat gazing out the back window at the finger of water. From here it looked blue. Across the half mile to the other shore, they could make out a patch of white, Halburtson's house, and closer, the dark weathered wood of the boat shed.

'What was the arrangement with Halburtson?' Caldwell asked.

Abby was no longer light-headed, and her hands were steady now, but her voice was different, duller, when she answered. 'Dad rents — rented — space in the shed for the rowboat. We'd drive out, leave the car, and cross over in the boat. You can see his boat ramp from here. Dad would put the boat in the shed if he planned to be gone more than a day, and we both just tied it to the tree stump to go shopping in Bend, or something like that.'

'So theoretically anyone could have driven to his place, launched a small boat, and come across late at night,' Caldwell said, still gazing out over the water.

'Not really,' Abby said. 'He has two dogs,

Spook's mother and a littermate, and they're pretty fierce, really good watchdogs. You couldn't get near his ramp at night unless they knew you well. Dad could, and I could, but no stranger, no one else I know.'

'There must be other places on that side where you could put a boat in.'

She shook her head. 'Not up here. This and Coop's place are the only two. You can see how the cliffs rise all around the lake and the woods . . . How could you even get a boat through the woods?'

'Don't know,' Caldwell said. 'I say it's time for a sandwich.' He began to unpack a cooler chest and very matter-of-factly handed a sandwich to Abby, then one to the detective.

After a moment Abby began to eat. Coming here, having the lieutenant recount their reconstruction of what had happened, made it real to her. Nothing had been real for the past week; she had felt trapped in a dream, felt nothing real, tasted nothing real, but now it seemed that she had been released from a spell. Someone had come in during the night, had shot and killed her father, and she would do whatever she could to help the police find out who the killer was.

After they had finished the sandwiches and packed up the thermos and cups again, the lieutenant said, 'The sheriff found a rifle up

51

in the loft, and Halburtson said your father had a handgun, too. Do you know where he kept it?'

'In the drawer by that end table,' she said, pointing.

'Not there now,' he said. 'Do you know what kind of gun it was?'

'A forty-five. I don't know the make or anything.' Then, without prompting, she said, 'We had another dog before Spook. Mindy, a border collie. A cougar killed her, and he said he would get the guns, one for downstairs, to have handy, one for the loft that he could shoot from the window if he had to.'

Then she was remembering again. He had wrapped Mindy in a sheet, handed Abby a shovel, and said, Let's go. That was all. He led her on a search for deep enough ground for a grave; it had been hard to find a place because it was so rocky and tree roots were everywhere. He carried Mindy in his arms like a baby until they found a spot, then he had dug the grave and they buried the dog. She had helped him pile rocks on the grave so bears or cougars wouldn't dig her up again. They had made a funeral cairn of rocks. They both had cried the day they buried Mindy. Abby had been thirteen.

That was where she would bury his ashes.

'Okay,' Caldwell said. 'What I'd like to do

is just walk through the house, each room, and have you look around, in closets, drawers, like that, and tell us if anything is out of place, or missing, whatever you notice out of the ordinary.'

They spent an hour at it: downstairs first, both bedrooms, his closet, her old closet that still had a toy box, then up to the loft, his desk, computers, some fifteen years old, one very recent acquisition . . . Detective Varney had a notebook out and made notes as they moved through the cabin; Abby couldn't imagine what she was finding to note.

'Why so many computers?' Caldwell asked in the loft. There were seven or eight against the walls, on tables.

'He used to write manuals, and he kept them all in case the codes changed, or needed modification, patches. He said obsolete computers were worthless, and he might as well hang on to them. I think he just liked them all.'

'You know much about computers?'

'A bit,' she said cautiously. In fact, Jud had taught her a lot about computers; she had copy-edited text for him now and then, had learned to read his code, tried out new programs — his first beta tester, he had called her.

'Maybe you can explain something,' he

53

said. 'I noticed that those pages, maybe the last ones he was working on, are numbered Chapter A-three, one through nine. But there's a big stack, and they don't seem to be in any particular order. Is that his new novel he was working on?'

'Yes, I'm sure it is. That's how he worked. He rarely started with chapter one, page one. He was back and forth all over the place. A-three means chapter A, the third revision. It's not necessarily the first chapter; it could go anywhere. He could have written the first draft months ago, or just recently. You can tell more by looking at the directory, when the sections are dated, but even that won't be conclusive if he was doing a lot of rewriting, backing it up, rewriting again.'

Caldwell shook his head. 'He worked toward the beginning and the end all at once?'

'I think it was the only way he could work.'

He looked dubious, then asked, 'Did he always back up to a floppy disk?'

'Always.' He had drilled it into her head: *save, save, save.*

'Okay. Another item, another loose end. No floppy disk was in the computer. We made copies of his hard drive, and I understand that you and his agent, Christina Maas, will be going through his papers. When you do,

54

will you let me know how near finished he was with this project? If you can tell,' he added, as if that would be impossible.

'Why?'

'I don't know,' he said with a shrug. 'Our computer guy says he didn't save or print out what he was working on the last time he used the computer, probably Friday night. At least, the top pages in the stack don't match up with the last file he had open. Our guy found material in the automatic backup file before anyone messed around with the computer. But if your father didn't save and exit properly, who turned the machine off, removed the floppy disk, and why?'

Abby stared at him. 'You don't think it was a random act, do you? A hiker or camper, someone like that who came in?'

'Of course not,' he said, leaving the loft, starting down the stairs.

After a moment she followed. She had assumed someone had come in from the forest and shot her father, a drug-crazed someone looking for money, for something he could sell, or even just a crazy who saw the light and walked in. The door would have been unlocked.

'So you can't see that anything's been disturbed?' Caldwell said, back in the living room, looking about unhappily.

'No.' There were things of Willa's that never used to be there, a painting, a hairbrush, a mirror with a silver frame and handle. She didn't comment on any of those things, and neither did Caldwell, but she suspected that Detective Varney was making careful notes about them all.

'Okay, what I'd like to do is have a little row around the lake, out to the black island, along the opposite shore. You up for that?'

She started to ask why again, but since he never really answered her questions, she simply nodded. 'But we should leave by four-thirty, or you'll be on the mountain road in the dark.'

'Oh. See, what we figured is that Varney will go ahead and drive out, and you and I will cross over in the boat and take your father's van back to Eugene. And the dog.'

Abby looked quickly at Detective Varney, who nodded.

'We probably should clean out some of that stuff from the refrigerator,' the detective said, female and practical as well as police professional, Abby thought.

'I saw some paper bags over there,' Varney said, pointing. 'Want me to haul the perishables out and bring them to your place later this evening?'

'No,' Abby said quickly. 'No. Just . . . drop

it all off at the Halburtsons, if they want it. Or keep it. Or . . . dump it somewhere.'

It didn't take long to pack things up and carry them to the car, but then Abby said, 'Wait a minute.' She hurried back inside and picked up the bowl of candy bars and took it out. Caldwell and Detective Varney were at the driver's door, speaking in low voices. He came around the car and took the bowl.

'I'll be a minute,' he said.

She understood that she had been dismissed and returned to the cabin. She had never felt lonely in this cabin, never afraid, or even aware of the silence, but suddenly the little building seemed filled with silence and emptiness. She walked to the kitchen counter and gazed out the window. Two bottles of champagne were on the counter. He had planned a celebration. She closed her eyes.

Soon Caldwell came back. 'One more thing,' he said, and went up the stairs to the loft.

Outside, the car engine started, tires grated on the gravel driveway; it sounded very loud. Proving a point, Abby thought distantly, tracking the progress of the car as it climbed the steep ascent to the forest service road. Caldwell didn't come down until the silence had returned.

'Okay. We'll lock up again and go for a boat tour. I'd like to keep the key another day or two, then I'll hand it over. You finished in here?'

She nodded. Finished.

4

They walked around the cabin to the natural basalt deck, where the rowboat was moored to a rock on the lowest ledge, inches above the water. The oars were in the boat.

Caldwell examined the ledge carefully. It was above water now, but in the winter rains the water rose to cover the first ledge, and with the spring runoff it came up another foot to the second ledge. He turned his attention to the rowboat; it was ten feet long and lightweight, old but sturdy. Every fall Jud had repainted it, repaired anything he saw amiss. The plank seats had been worn satin smooth.

'If you want, we could get the cushions,' Abby said. 'We never used them unless we planned to stay out and fish.' Or if she drifted out on the water, pretending she was on a cloud high above the earth; or when Jud was drifting and claimed to be writing. He had said he did most of his writing out there on the water.

'It's fine like this,' Caldwell said. He was peering at the water now. 'How deep is it here?'

'About four feet.'

'Looks bottomless,' he said.

She began to pull the boat into the water; he watched and didn't offer to help. He was listening, she realized, to see how much noise she made launching the boat. It made a scraping sound that she had never paid attention to, a sound that now seemed very loud. The basalt was smooth, but this was the reason Jud had had to upend the boat year after year and retouch the paint. She unhooked the mooring rope from a rock, coiled it, then tossed it into the boat. 'You want to row?'

He shook his head. 'No way. I'd just take us in circles, or run us aground.' He pointed to a light low on the back side of the cabin. 'Did he keep that on at night?'

'It's automatic. Dusk to dawn. He stepped off the end once, and the next day he went to Bend and got the light. Coop has one, too. Same reason. It's hard to see the surface at night against all this basalt, especially if it's raining.'

'So it wouldn't be much of a problem to cross over after dark. Just head for the light. Any other lights on up here in the finger at night?'

'No.' She stepped into the boat, settled on the narrow seat, and took up the oars;

gingerly he followed, evidently uncomfortable as the boat rocked with his weight. She started to row as soon as he was seated.

Abby rowed around the far end of the finger, then down to Siren Rock and the other break in the rimrock to show Caldwell the two places boats could pass from the deep water to the shallow water. She was getting tired, she thought in disgust. This little bit of rowing was using muscles that had gone soft and lax.

'Okay,' Caldwell said, gazing at the cottages along the north shore. 'You up for just a little more?'

'Yes. Where?'

She assumed he wanted to go to the state park ramp or the cottages, but he seemed to have little interest in either. 'Along the shoreline over there,' he said, 'on up to Halburtson's ramp. Close in, as close as you can.'

He was examining every inch of shoreline, looking for a place a boat could have been put in the water, she realized, and she knew there was no such place. She rowed toward the shore silently. On this side the lava had flowed in narrow streams, and between them the soil was much deeper than on the far side; trees grew close to the water here, some with roots that jutted out over the lake.

'It's only about three or four feet up to land,' Caldwell murmured a bit later. 'Can you stop here?'

She stopped their forward motion and looked at the roots he was examining. 'If a boat was already in the water, I guess you could get into it from there,' she said. 'But look at those trees. How would you get a boat of any size at all through them?'

'Trails and such up there?'

'Yes. You can hike from the cottages all the way to Coop Halburtson's property; it's shorter than going by the road, actually. Up there the trail merges with the road.'

Caldwell made a noncommittal sound, then said, 'Okay, onward.'

He had her stop once more, another place where, if there was a boat already in the water, a person could come down the side of the shore and board it, but it would be impossible to get a boat up there in the first place. After that she headed toward the ramp.

She remembered the year Jud and Coop Halburtson had built the ramp. For years it had been simply a dirt incline, but winter rains kept eroding it, guttering it, and they had built a new one of logs. It had taken a year of weekend labor to fell the right trees, cut them the right lengths, peel off the bark, and get them to the shore. She could see Jud digging, smoothing dirt, then gravel, using a sledgehammer to drive long metal bars into the ground to hold the first log at the edge of the water. That one was ten feet long; they had borrowed a horse to help move it into place. Jud called it the anchor log, the one that held all the others back. The rest were six feet long; Jud and Coop had placed them carefully, sinking them just enough, filling in between them with more dirt, tamping it down. She had been their water girl, trotting back and forth to the house above, bringing them water or iced tea or lemonade from Florence's kitchen. For the first several years she had been afraid the ramp would sink so far into the ground that it would disappear, but Jud said it was just settling in, getting comfortable, and it had been years now since there had been any change. When it was rainy, the ramp was slick and it was easier to pull the boats up, but it was treacherous underfoot. Today it was dry.

The second the boat touched the ramp, three very large dogs began to bark.

'Spook!' she called. A gray dog appeared ready to jump into the water to meet them, nearly manic with excitement, and the other two dogs stopped barking.

When they got out of the boat, Caldwell helped her pull it up the ramp, all the way to the shed. Spook danced around her the whole time, not jumping on her, but too excited to sit still as the others were doing. After the boat was put away, Abby knelt down and hugged Spook, and the dog licked her face, licked her hands, making a soft whimpering noise.

When Abby stood up, her eyes were hot with unshed tears. Softly she called, 'Here, Sal. Come on, Bear.' They came to her, and she petted them both as they greeted her with licks on her hands.

'Sal is their mother,' Abby said then. 'Coop always said she went out and mixed it up with a bear, and these two were the result.' Sal was also large, but sleek, a gray, short-haired dog of no particular breed; her offspring were both much bigger than she was, both shaggy, one black and brown, Bear, the other gray and black, Spook.

'Do you have to check in with the Halburtsons, anything like that?' Caldwell asked as Abby rubbed her hands on her jeans.

She shook her head. 'I called and told them I'd pick up the van and take Spook home with me. I told them I'd be with the police. They won't expect me to pay a visit today.'

She couldn't face them again so soon, she thought. Florence had wept so hard before the memorial service, she had become faint, and Coop had not been much better, the shock of discovering Jud's body still making his hands shake, his voice quavery. Their grief was too intense, their sympathy too hard to cope with now. And it was too hard on them, too, she added to herself, justifying not going up to see them. They were both eighty and had lost their best friend. It was too hard on all of them.

It was obvious that Caldwell had seen all he wanted to see of the boat shed; now he led the way to the carport, where the van, a pickup truck, and a two-year-old Taurus were parked. There was enough graveled space to turn, to maneuver a boat to the ramp, release it, and then go park. The three dogs trotted with them to the van.

'In, Spook,' Abby said, opening the back door. The dog jumped in instantly, then sat down on the backseat.

'Mind if I drive?' Caldwell asked.

She shrugged and handed him the keys, walked around and got in the passenger seat.

'One more thing I'd like to do before we call it a day,' he said, starting the engine. 'I'd like to have a look at that trail.'

He drove out the driveway and turned toward the state park, driving very slowly, examining the woods on both sides. Before they reached the entrance to the park, he pulled over to the side of the road.

'Who'd see a car stopped about here late at night?'

She looked at him in surprise. They weren't hidden by trees or bushes or anything else. 'Whoever came along,' she said.

'It's one or one-thirty in the morning,' he said. 'Who'd be coming along?'

'Maybe a late arrival. Or someone from one of the cottages getting in late. I don't know.'

'Let's get out and walk a couple of minutes.'

Resignedly she got out. 'Stay, Spook.' She opened her window a few inches and closed the door. 'The trail?'

'You can get to it from here, can't you?'

She nodded.

'Not at the deep part yet, are we?'

'No. We're still west of it.' They couldn't see the water, but she knew exactly where they were. She led the way across the road; then, weaving in and out around trees, they came to the trail and stopped. 'This is it.'

Caldwell grunted, and she wondered what he had expected: a neatly groomed, bark-mulch trail with rails and signposts? She turned and began to follow the trail until the water came into view. Now they could see the cabin; they were about six feet above the lake, but the trail was not straight for more than a few feet at any place. It wound among the trees, around boulders, skirted the lake, then back into the woods once more. And it was rough with roots and rocks.

'Imagine doing this at one or one-thirty at night,' she said sharply. 'I'm telling you, the idea is insane.'

'Hold up,' he said. 'If you used a flashlight, who would notice?'

'No one,' she had to admit. The campsites were too far away, in deep woods, and no one in the cottages had a view of the finger at this point. 'But when you get near the water, if anyone on shore happened to look, you'd stand out showing even a candle up here.'

'Who'd be up looking at one or one-thirty in the morning?'

She shrugged helplessly and started to walk again. Now he had someone lugging a canoe or small boat and holding a flashlight at the same time. He called a stop again in just a minute; they were at the place where the roots afforded access to the water, only three feet down. She watched him examine the rough ground, the tree, the roots. He didn't touch anything and didn't get close to the roots, but looked them over carefully.

Then he said, 'Onward.'

She knew they would not get much farther

before Sal and Bear would set up a clamor, but silently she led the way. The trail took a sharp turn toward the road, then angled back, and Sal and Bear began to bark and came leaping through the forest.

She called their names, and they stopped, not wagging their tails, just watching.

'Coop's property,' she said.

'Would they cross over his line, come after anyone on this side of it?'

'No. He trained them. They know his property.'

Caldwell nodded. 'Right. And the trail leads back to the road now?'

'Yes. A couple hundred yards, but it's like the rest of it, zigzags all the way.'

'Let's have a look.'

She sighed and followed the trail, back and forth among trees, around rocks, over roots and blowdowns, to the road. 'See?' she said tiredly. They caught glimpses of Sal and Bear now and then, pacing them.

'Okay,' Caldwell said. 'Wait here and I'll bring the van.' He began to walk down the road.

She hurried after him. 'You can't get it alone. Spook wouldn't let you.'

'Even after we've been together the way we've been?' he asked, looking surprised and a little offended.

'Not even. Coop trained her, too. She knows her job is to guard the cabin, the rowboat, the van, me.'

The lieutenant stopped moving and regarded her soberly. She realized the implication of what she had just said. But Spook had let someone enter Jud's house, someone who had put her out and closed the door on her, locked the dog door on her, someone who had killed Jud and left without being attacked. If she had attacked anyone, there would have been signs; Coop would have seen signs, or the police investigators would have seen them.

'Just how savage can she get?' Lieutenant Caldwell asked softly.

Abby swallowed hard and shook her head. Spook was big and strong; she could get savage enough to frighten off a bear or a cougar. No stranger would have dared to try to get past her.

They started to walk again, not speaking now. At the van Spook whined softly. 'I was going to say, Why don't you drive,' Caldwell said, 'but I think you're too beat. I'll do it.'

Not just beat, she thought. Shaken, stunned, frightened . . . Something else, not just beat. It had been someone Jud had known, someone Spook had known well enough to let in without attacking.

5

Felicia Shaeffer had always thought of the basalt ledge out in the lake as the break until Jud wrote about it and called it Siren Rock; it had become that in her mind as well. Standing at the rear window of her cottage, she watched Abby row a man close to Siren Rock, then along the other side of the ledge, as if to demonstrate that there really were no good passages through, except the two narrow ones that only a suicide-bent fool would try to navigate after dark.

Florence Halburtson had called to tell her that Abby was coming with some more police officers, and she expected that now Abby would come through the break and deposit the policeman on the park side, let him question the people over here. But they didn't come this way, and soon were out of sight again. They shouldn't dawdle much longer, Felicia thought worriedly, or they would have to drive down that damned road in the dark, and while she didn't care a fig about the police officers, she did not want Abby in a car coming down the mountain at night.

She gazed about her cottage distractedly.

When Herbert, her husband of forty-two years, died, she had completely remodeled the building. Walls had come out, a woodstove put in, a skylight cut into the ceiling, rugs and carpets junked, and good, washable vinyl put down, and then, finally, at sixty-nine years old, she had a real studio. That had been four years ago, and she loved her studio with a passion that had not diminished a bit. She had sold the big house in Eugene and bought a condo unit, big enough for one, she had told her four grown children. Her daughter Sara had suggested that perhaps she and her husband and three children could share the big house, so Felicia would not be lonely. She had no intention of having any of them move in on her, or to move in with any of them. Besides, she had her two beautiful dogs, Daisy and Mae, snow-white, curly-haired poodles, who had more sense than all her kids put together. She had never said that out loud, but she certainly thought it. None of her children had come to the lake in years. They had no idea of all she had done to the cottage, and expressed their bewilderment and dismay again and again at her eagerness to stay out here for extended periods. She had told them to butt out.

After years of working at the kitchen table

when no one else was using it or in the bedroom when Herbert was not sleeping, she had a real workroom. Easels were set up; a long table held many clay figures, some fanciful, some realistic; pots and tubes of paint and brushes were arranged so that she could find exactly what she wanted at any hour of the day or night; there were shelves of books and manuscripts, a television, CD player, and a computer with an excellent oversize monitor. She liked to museum-hop on the Internet, as well as keep in touch with an ever-growing network of friends from all over the world, many of them beginning artists who valued her comments on the digitized art they e-mailed her. Her illustrations were everywhere in the cottage, on the walls, in frames leaning against the walls, on the worktable. She illustrated children's books and was good at it, and had no intention of retiring and entering a community where she would have company, organized recreation, competent medical attendants around the clock if needed. She suspected that her dutiful children conspired to ease her into such a place every time they got together.

During the past week, since Jud's murder, they had taken turns calling her, urging her to go into town, where she would be safe.

'You're all bugging the bejesus out of me!' she had exclaimed to Junior the last time he called. 'I have work to do. Leave me alone.'

Her husband was an accountant, she had told Jud years ago, and unfortunately all four children were accountants also. Not in fact, but in spirit. Jud had laughed delightedly, and they had spent the afternoon labeling people: four categories, they had decided. Accountants, bureaucrats, beasts of burden, and artists.

'Oh shit,' she had said. 'We need another one. What about scientists?'

'Artists,' he had said without hesitation. 'Some of them, anyway. Surrounded by pencil pushers, grant writers, Bunsen burner igniters, and computer data tabulators.'

Felicia was sitting at her kitchen table, her two dogs at her feet, her gaze on the lake, but she was no longer seeing it, thinking instead of the many times she and Jud had sat here, talking, joking, companionable in a way she had not known with anyone else. No need to explain things with him, or explain herself or try to. Of course, when Herbert died, she had missed him. You have to miss someone you've lived with for more than forty years, but this missing was different. She missed Jud in a way she had not expected, had not been prepared for, and could not quite understand.

It wasn't as if he had been with her all that much, a couple of times a week, then gone for weeks sometimes, but she had always known he would be back, that they would sit and talk while she made fantastic figures out of clay, her models. Or he would sit while she painted or sketched. Often he would bring fish or something, and they would share dinner and drinks. Or he would pick up an order she had placed at a store in Bend and deliver it and linger. Now and then he would show up with a duck, and she would make a special dinner that he particularly loved. She missed him with a deep, painful ache that continued to grow instead of recede as the days passed.

★ ★ ★

She was still at the table when Daisy and Mae both lifted their heads, came wide awake, and started to bark. Then she heard it, too. A car had pulled up to the house. She went to the door and opened it, and expecting police officers and perhaps Abby, she was surprised to see instead a young woman with frizzy brown hair. She was alone.

'I'm Detective Ellen Varney,' her visitor said. 'Mrs. Shaeffer?'

'You're a detective?'

'Yes, ma'am.' She pulled out identification,

and Felicia opened the door wider and motioned for her to enter.

'You drove down the mountain alone?'

Detective Varney nodded, but she was looking at the large studio with interest, ignoring the two poodles that were checking her out with equal interest.

'Well, that gets you a cup of tea,' Felicia said. 'I was just about to make some. Come on to the kitchen. Green tea,' she said, leading the way through the clutter of her studio. 'Good for the heart, or the liver, or something.' She glanced back when she realized her guest had stopped and was examining a group of watercolors in frames.

'You illustrated the Greta series!' Detective Varney exclaimed. 'I loved them when I was a child! The pictures are wonderful!'

'For that you can have your choice of honey or sugar with your tea,' Felicia said. 'Sagebrush honey, put up by a Klamath family over by La Pine. Rare, and very special.'

The detective hurriedly joined her in the kitchen area; she looked embarrassed, Felicia thought with amusement. 'Sit down, won't be a minute. You could start your questions while the kettle comes to a boil.'

Detective Varney pulled a notebook from her bag, sat at the table, and looked out over the lake. 'You can't see much of the upper end from here, can you?'

'No. You can see Siren Rock and a bit beyond, that's all.'

'Were you here on Friday when Judson Vickers was shot?'

'Yes. Here most of the time. And no, I didn't see or hear anything out of ordinary, not until Florence Halburtson called and told me about the shooting.'

She busied herself with scalding a little blue porcelain teapot, added leaves, then boiling water, and began to carry things to the table. She talked as she moved about. 'Jud was a dear friend, Detective Varney. I'd like to see whoever did that to him dropped out of a boat with an anchor tied to his feet in the deepest water out there. But I don't have any real information for you, I'm afraid. I don't know who did that, or why. And I don't know how anyone got over there in the middle of the night, unless he drove up the mountain in the daylight and came back down the next day. You know Coop's dogs didn't set up a clamor, I suppose. And they would have if anyone had put a boat out over there. And there just isn't any other way.'

'Could someone from the park area have put a boat out, gone up the finger, and hung out somewhere up there until dark? Then left at first light?'

Felicia said thoughtfully, 'First thing some of us thought of. I asked Pete Tolman about it. He gives kayak lessons, you know. The lake's a good place for beginners, no motorboats, no current, just quiet water. Pete's usually the last one to leave the lake, he and a student in a separate kayak. He makes them go through one break, up into the finger, then back out through the other narrower break, and he said no one was up in the finger when he left just before dark. He's the last one out and the first one back in the next morning. He lives over in Bend.'

She poured tea then and added a little honey to hers. 'Try it. Sage honey is very good.'

The detective added a spoonful of honey to her own tea and nodded after she sipped it. 'Very good, indeed,' she said. 'You were a close friend of Jud Vickers'?'

'A good friend, yes. I knew him when he was a little boy, and he used to come over here and play with my kids. Later, he came over to talk, to hang out now and then.'

'Do you know anyone who might have wanted to harm him? To kill him?'

'I never heard anyone talk that way about him. He was liked around here. A good listener, willing to go out of his way to shop for someone in Bend, do little favors.'

'Someone didn't like him,' Detective Varney said slowly.

Felicia shook her head. 'I know what you've been hearing about him, and probably most of it's true enough. He was a chaser, but he never caught anyone who didn't want catching. They knew what they were getting into with him. You know the story about Coyote and the pretty girl?'

Detective Varney shook her head.

'From one of the books I illustrated,' Felicia said. 'They cleaned up the original tale for the kids. It goes like this: Coyote was made up like a hurt little bird, but if you looked hard, you could see it was Coyote, all right. And this pretty girl comes by and sees the bird limping along. She says, 'You can't fool me. My grandmother told me about you. Go on about your business.' Coyote looks at her with a pitiful expression. 'I'll die out here in the cold if you don't warm me under your blanket.' He shivered and shook, and she took pity on him and picked him up and put him under her blanket. And soon, he had his way with her. She screamed and cried, and Coyote laughed and said, 'You knew what I was when you picked me up.'' Felicia smiled gently at the detective. 'They all knew what he was, you see, and I don't think he ever deliberately hurt a person in his life.'

'If some of the women he caught were married, maybe their husbands weren't happy about his romances,' Varney said.

'Maybe, but no one ever came here saying anything like that to my face.' She considered this for a moment, then said, 'I assume that a crime of passion, which would include vengeance and jealousy, I suppose, would be committed during the height of the emotional turmoil, not years afterward. And he'd been seeing Willa Ashford for over two years. A long time to wait when you're feeling an uncontrollable desire to get revenge.'

'You know her? Willa Ashford?'

'I introduced them,' Felicia said. 'Willa was putting together a retrospective of art by local artists, and she was out here several times to discuss it and select pictures to include. He dropped in one day when she was here, and they hit it off just fine. I don't believe he had eyes for anyone else after that.'

'We've heard that he wrote about the people he knew, the residents around the lake. Did anyone mind that he did?'

'Have you read his books?'

Detective Varney shook her head.

'You should. You really should. He used the lake here as the setting, you know. He changed it around, put in a resort instead of these cottages, and added a village down the road aways, but it was this lake, and some of these people he wrote about. And truthfully, I don't know if any of them realize it to this day, or if they do, they don't recognize themselves. You see, he wrote fiction, but fiction is always derived from experience if it's any good at all. And his was very good. You really should read his novels.'

'I will,' Varney said. 'What other residents were here that weekend?' she asked then.

'Well, I know Doris and Joe Manning were. They're in the last cottage. And the Beardwells were. He's a veterinarian in Bend, and they come every other weekend, when his partner is on call.' She named two others and dismissed them. 'Summer people. That leaves Gary Evans, and I haven't seen him for months. He's separated from his wife, Virginia, and she comes now and then, but he's moved up to Washington State, I think. I doubt that she was here. She would have dropped in, I think. I imagine they're planning to sell the cottage to the state; at least, that's the rumor going around, and she's been moving stuff out each time she comes. The deal is that we can stay here as long as we want, but if we sell, we have to sell to the state. It's like a little pocket of

80

individually owned property in the middle of a state park, but that's the deal we made when the state began buying up all the surrounding area.'

'I noticed that the first cottage is boarded up, empty. Is that what happens when the state acquires the property?'

'Not always. There were nine cottages at one time. One burned to the ground in the sixties and wasn't rebuilt. The state bought one back around the middle of the seventies and tore it down. It was a shack to start with, in terrible condition. The old Frazier place that you mentioned is a good building, so I guess they'll keep it in repair and someday use it for something or other. Teri Frazier drowned in the lake years ago, and Lawrence sold the place a few months later. The rest of us are hanging on.'

'Is the Vickers cabin part of that deal?'

Felicia shook her head. 'His place isn't in the park area. Neither is the Halburtsons'. In fact, Jud said he wanted to buy Halburtson's place if he ever decided to sell, which he might do. He's getting too old to be out there on the lake all the time. Eighty! That's too old to pretend otherwise.'

She caught a glimpse of a fleeting smile that crossed the detective's face, and she grinned. 'Takes one old coot to recognize another one,' she said cheerfully. 'I haven't been out on the lake in ten years. I don't need to be on the water, just close by. That's plenty for me.'

'Do you have a boat?'

'No. Sold it after Herbert died.'

The detective's questions became more and more pointless, Felicia thought. But she answered each one, and yet later, alone again with her dogs, she felt dissatisfied, as if there had been something left out altogether. She nodded to herself. The two overriding motives for murder, as far as she was aware of from a lifetime of reading mysteries and newspaper accounts of crimes, were passion and money. And even if Jud had dumped Doris Manning abruptly, and even if Joe Manning had learned of their affair, that had been several years ago, too long a time for passion still to be a factor.

She didn't even consider Willa Ashford. Jud had fallen in love with her, and she with him. Of course, Felicia reflected, things could change, but if they had changed, it had to have been within days of his death. The last time Felicia had seen Jud, the Wednesday before he was killed, all he had talked about was Willa, and still with the sense of wonder that had turned him, a middle-aged man, into a boy, with all the world's marvels spread out at his feet. Felicia had seen Willa's devastation when her husband died years before, and she had seen her come back to life finally, and then fall in love once more, and she had rejoiced for both her and Jud. Willa was out of the question.

But if he had been killed because of money, then Abby was the first person who came to the fore for motive, and that was ridiculous. She felt about Abby the way she had yearned to feel toward her own children, for whom she could never summon the same kind of unquestioning love.

None of her children had been willing, or able, to sit quietly and watch her shape dragons or monsters or elves out of clay. None of her own children had ever spontaneously hugged and kissed her, for nothing, just because. Or said she had magic hands. Felicia shook her head in annoyance: if she wasn't careful, she would become another foolish old woman who lived only in the past, one whose life existed in memories. She brought herself back to the here and now, the reality of a murderer.

Even if Abby had the motive, which she didn't, since she cared little about money, she had been at the coast, far out of reach. Not even the police could seriously consider her a suspect. And Brice, according to Florence

Halburtson, had been in Portland, so he was ruled out. Lynne, long divorced from Jud, didn't stand to profit, and she certainly had felt nothing for him for many years, although there had been a time when sheer frustration and misery might have driven her to kill.

Felicia washed the teacups and pot, and then poured herself a drink of scotch and water. It was after five; she could have a drink now. Herbert had never wanted liquor around the house, never used it himself in any form, and had been disapproving of her occasional drink. She sat at the table in the gathering darkness and watched the last of the boats come ashore, watched as lakeside fires were put out, until only darkness remained. Bits of conversations she and Jud had had over the years flowed through her mind. When she remonstrated him for putting Joe Beardwell in his first novel, he had laughed, had gone to her worktable, a card table in those days, and had picked up her model of the Iceman. The story was about an old man who froze everything he got near, who kept acquiring more and more property where the sun never shone, the frost never melted. Holding up the figure, Jud had scoffed. 'And where did this come from?' It was a caricature of Herbert, but of course

Herbert would never have recognized himself in the grotesque little figure.

'An artist,' Jud had said once, 'is a person who looks into things, not just at them.'

He had looked into many things, through them, and had written about them. And his words were true. Joe Beardwell had not recognized himself in the novel, and in fact might never have really read it, just skimmed the surface enough to say he had read and enjoyed it.

By the time she realized that Herbert was the Iceman, she had been trapped in a marriage with four children, and later she had been trapped by his need for her. People had believed her to be the dependent one, but that had never been true; he had depended on her for everything, and toward the end, the last six years, as his mind had slipped, his dependency had turned him into a son of a bitch. She thought that Jud was the only person who had ever suspected the truth about her long marriage, described again and again as the ideal, the standard for other couples to strive for. She drained her glass and set it down hard.

Jud had written her and Herbert into his second novel, *The Black Shore*, and Felicia had recognized them. She had wept when she read it, felt anger, embarrassment, humiliation, and finally acceptance of the truth, and even a deeper love and respect for the one person who had seen through the façade of a contented couple and had been honest enough to tell the truth. But did others come to that point?

Then she was thinking of the new work, the novel he had been finishing when she last saw him. If his death had not been the result of an uncontrollable passion or simple greed or even an overwhelming need for money, there was a third possibility, she thought. Fear of exposure. He had seen into and through so many things and had written about them truthfully. Was there a truth in the new novel that had driven someone to kill him in order to keep secret?

She stood up shakily and groped for the light switch. If the key to his death was in the manuscript, the police would never find it, she thought bleakly. Herbert had looked at the little clay Iceman and said only, 'Ugly little critter, isn't he?' She never knew if Lawrence Frazier had recognized his wife's death when it appeared in fiction. People saw what they expected to see, what they needed to see, no more than that.

Then she wondered: Was the manuscript still in the cabin? Was it intact?

6

For more than an hour neither Abby nor Lieutenant Caldwell said a word as he drove back toward Eugene. It had grown dark and there was much less traffic now than there had been earlier, but it was still a dangerous road that required attention.

Abby was thinking hard of the implications of someone's entering Jud's cabin during the night without being challenged by Spook. And obviously someone had done that. But how? She kept coming back to the same questions: How had he managed a boat in the dark? Where had he launched it, landed it afterward? Or she. Abby huddled in her jacket, freezing.

'I understand you work in the museum,' Caldwell said finally. 'Full-time?'

'No. Three mornings a week, usually until noon, occasionally a little later.'

'You going to keep working now?'

She had not even considered what she would do now. 'I don't know.' It was, practically speaking, a nonpaying job; she had had a choice, be a T.A., a teaching assistant, or work in the museum; neither paid even minimum, but it was part of the postgrad program she was in. That and her dissertation. Now she didn't know why she wanted the doctorate, if she wanted it, what she would do with it afterward.

'Is Willa Ashford your adviser?'

'Yes.'

'Tell me something about her, will you? We haven't been able to talk to her yet. Someone at the museum said you probably know where she hangs out when she's not home. Where is she?'

'I don't know. I haven't seen her all this week. Except at the service.'

'But she's your friend, as well as your adviser, isn't she?'

'Yes,' she said in a low voice.

'Did you and your father have a falling-out because of her?'

She jerked up straighter and shook her head. 'I don't know what you're talking about.'

'Just another rumor? Someone mentioned that maybe you and your father had a fight a couple of years ago, about the time he started seeing a lot of Willa Ashford. That things hadn't been patched up yet. Anything to that?'

'No! He was busy, traveling, book signings, and writing. And I was busy with my schoolwork, and we just weren't as close as we used to be. It happens that way when your lives take you on different tracks.' She fought to keep her voice even. 'Who told you that?'

'Did you usually wait for an invitation to go visit him?' he asked, ignoring her question.

'No. I used to drive out and call him on the cell phone when I got to Coop's place, and he'd come over and pick me up. Or sometimes I'd call first to make sure he'd be there. Sometimes he wasn't, and I used the boat and went over anyway. We didn't need appointments,' she said coldly.

'But since you both got so busy, did you usually wait for an invitation?'

She stared at approaching headlights, then more headlights, more. 'I just didn't have the time like I used to,' she said. 'He asked me out now and then if there was a special reason, like when he got an advance copy of his novel, something like that.'

'Has anything come to mind about what he called you for the last time? It must have been something special.'

'I don't know why he asked me out,' she said in a low voice.

'You were going to tell me a little something about Willa Ashford,' he said.

She shook her head slightly. 'No, I wasn't. There's nothing to tell. She was my instructor, then she was appointed the director of the museum, but she continued to be my adviser. I work for her.'

'Was she your father's lover?'

'Ask her.'

'First I have to find her,' he said reasonably. 'Okay, okay. Will you be keeping the dog now?'

'Of course,' she said, surprised.

'I thought maybe Halburtson would take her back.'

'They go down to Southern California for the winters,' she said. 'It was hard enough to get two dogs admitted to the community where they stay. It would be impossible to bring in another one. Anyway, she's part of the family; she's mine.'

'Mr. Connors likes dogs, too?'

'Sure. He grew up on a farm with livestock and a lot of dogs and cats. He's always been around animals.'

'I wondered,' he said. 'Halburtson said his dogs wouldn't let anyone but you and your father near the boat ramp. Did he mean they wouldn't let your husband in without raising a rumpus?'

She had to think about it. Every time she and Brice had gone, she had had to order the dogs to stop barking; they didn't accept Brice as family, but they hadn't known him all their lives, either. She had a flashing memory of the one time she had gone with him to visit his folks in Idaho. The dogs there had not accepted him, either. He had been gone too long, he had said; his mother had added, 'Eight years. It's a whole new generation of cats and dogs.' The visit had been awkward, the weather too hot and dry; the dust-laden air smelled of chemicals and fertilizer. After an inane discussion of the new crops, the weather, a new irrigation system, there had been nothing for anyone to say. The farm was several miles from the nearest town, nearly that far from the nearest neighbor. Driving away after their short visit, Brice had said bitterly, 'See why I had to leave? If I never come back here, it'll be time enough.' The dogs had barked as they left the property; all the way to the county road, the dogs had kept barking.

Lieutenant Caldwell cleared his throat, a gentle nudge that a question was still in the air. Abby said, 'I doubt they'd let him through without barking a lot.'

'How about Willa Ashford?'

He had been leading back to her all along, she realized. Wearily she said, 'Ask her. I don't know.'

By the time they reached Eugene and he pulled into the parking lot of a motel on

Franklin Boulevard, she had a pounding headache. 'Home,' he said. 'You can take over the driving now. I appreciate the time you've given us today, how hard it must have been for you. Thanks. I'll be in touch.'

They both got out and she walked around the van to get behind the wheel. 'Good night, Mrs. Connors,' he said, then strode away.

She drove home.

★　★　★

Coop always maintained that dogs, at least the dogs he trained, understood a limited number of words, and the first thing to do with one of them was to lead it around the property and say repeatedly, 'Home.'

'Then it will know where it can go and can't,' he had said.

When Jud got Spook from Coop Halburtson, she had been a puppy, not quite eight weeks old, still a ball of gray fluff; Abby had carried her as Jud rowed across the finger.

'Have you named her yet?'

He said no. 'How about Dust Ball?'

'Oh, Dad!' She studied the little dog. 'She looks like Casper. You know, the Friendly Ghost?'

'Thank God, Casper isn't a girl's name,' he

said. 'I can't see myself living with a dog named Casper.'

'Casperella?' They both laughed. She considered Ghost, but shook her head. You didn't really want to walk around calling ghosts. If not simultaneously, then no more than a half beat apart, they both said, 'Spook.' And Spook she was. Later Jud had reported wryly that Coop was putting both him and Spook through some schooling.

After they both graduated, when Coop said it was time, Abby had trailed along with Jud when he led Spook around the cabin and the surrounding area that was her territory, and as far as Abby knew, Spook had never strayed off the property, nor had she allowed any stranger to enter it without a challenge.

Now Abby proceeded to introduce Spook to another new home. She snapped on the leash and led the dog around the backyard, all along a high fence, past the attached garage, to the front yard, around the house, and back inside through the rear patio door. Although the yard was small and well lit, it was a slow process; Spook had to squat again and again, marking her territory, and she had to smell just about everything. 'Home,' Abby said over and over. Spook wagged her tail in apparent understanding.

Inside the house Abby took her through

each room. She would repeat the whole process the next day, just to be sure, she thought then, in the kitchen making a pot of coffee. It was after six, but Brice had said he would work late all this week, catch-up time. She took two aspirin tablets and sat down to wait for the coffee to drip. Spook lay at her feet; her ears twitched now and then as she registered unfamiliar noises — a car on the street, a neighbor's door closing, something Abby couldn't even hear. That was how Spook had been at the cabin; she knew whenever a boat was in the finger, and she never let out a sound unless and until it landed at Jud's property.

'If only you could talk,' Abby murmured. 'If only you could.' She was trying to construct a scene that had her father up in the aerie, and Spook anywhere except near him. Then she must have heard someone dock and started barking at an intruder in the middle of the night. Jud could have admitted someone, put Spook out, then gone back upstairs. She shook her head. In the middle of the night? How? She kept coming back to it. How had anyone crossed without launching a boat from Coop's ramp? And his dogs had not barked.

'Someone must have been there already, all evening,' she whispered. Had Spook barked because she wanted in, not because an intruder had come? She stared at the shaggy gray dog whose ears kept twitching. That was the only scenario that made any sense. Someone must have gone to the cabin early, before dark, and stayed overnight, left as soon as there was enough light to get through the narrow passage back to the park ramps. Or to one of the cottages.

She was still at the table, sipping coffee, when suddenly Spook jumped up and began to bark, and now Abby heard it, too. A car in the driveway, then the garage door opening.

'Quiet, Spook,' she said. 'It's Brice.' The dog stopped barking, still on full alert but quiet. Abby hurried to the front door before Brice reached it, and opened it to await him.

'Hi,' she said when he entered. 'Hi.' She stretched out both arms to him, and he grabbed her and held her so hard that it hurt.

'Oh, God!' he whispered into her hair. 'God, I've been so scared. Abby, you're okay? You're okay!'

She nodded against his chest. 'I'm okay.'

Spook sat down and watched them; her tail swept back and forth, back and forth.

★ ★ ★

A little later, sitting on the couch with her head on his shoulder, Abby began to tell Brice about her day, why the murderer couldn't have been a stranger, a camper or anyone like that. She stopped talking when he drew away in order to watch her face, as if he didn't yet believe she had come out of the stupor that had benumbed her all week.

'You don't know how it made me feel,' she said, 'knowing that I could have been there, might have prevented it somehow. But it had to be someone Spook knows, not a stranger. If I'd been there when she came in, she would have stayed for a while probably, then left, the way they do up there. She could have gone back the next day, or any other day, when I wasn't there.'

Brice nodded. 'I think you're right, honey. You realize you kept saying *she?*'

'I know,' she said. 'But a man wouldn't have been invited to spend the night. Dad would have taken him across the finger and driven him home, to the cottage or wherever. Dr. Beardwell stayed too late a couple of times, and that's what happened.'

Brice took her hand. 'Abby, don't breathe a word of what you think about this. Oh, you can tell the cop your theory, but no one else. Okay? Will you keep mum about what you think happened?'

Surprised, she said, 'Who would I tell?'

'I don't know. The Halburtsons. That old gossip, Felicia Shaeffer. Someone. I just don't think you should let it be known that you might have seen something, noticed something, or even suspect something.' He tightened the pressure on her hand.

'I'd have no reason to mention anything to them,' she said. Then very slowly she added, 'You really mean Willa, don't you?'

'I'd include her in the people you shouldn't say much to,' he admitted.

'She had nothing to do with it,' Abby said. 'You don't know how much she loved him. She would never have done anything to hurt him.' She pulled her hand away. 'You just don't realize how she felt about him.'

'I think I do,' he said soberly. 'Today I had a talk with Harvey Durham about the cashier's checks. He should know something,' Brice said, 'but he claims he doesn't have a clue about them. Who they were for, anything. But, Abby, it smacks of blackmail, extortion, something like that. Why the secret otherwise? Why not just regular checks? But what if there's a woman out there somewhere, maybe with a child, someone Jud had to pay off over the years? What if Willa found out about her, about a son or daughter he never acknowledged but had to support?

What if he was married to her? You don't know, and neither do I. But someone was raking in a lot of money. And if it was anything like that, and Willa realized she was going to be dumped the way all the others were over the years . . . '

Aghast, she stared at him. She had forgotten about the cashier's checks, more than a hundred thousand dollars unaccounted for. Could Jud have been paying off a woman, supporting another family? She remembered the two bottles of champagne. A celebration. To introduce her to her stepmother? Maybe that was who was with him that night. And he told her it was over? Why champagne if that was the case? They were being reconciled? Her headache had come back.

'Honey,' Brice said, 'I didn't mean to upset you all over again. And that might be way off base, but the fact is, we don't know what those checks were for, and I think you should let the police do their own work, and just not be talking about it with anyone.'

She nodded. 'I'll tell the lieutenant that in the past a woman did go over and spend the night and leave the following day. It happened, and could have happened again. Someone could have stayed and left at daybreak.'

'Good. And now, let's talk about food. Out, or order something in? I choose ordering in. Sound okay to you?'

'Okay,' she said.

She felt as if days and days had passed with her in a drugged state, unable to keep anything in conscious memory long enough to consider what it meant. Next week, she thought, she might sign a contract that would eventually bring in more than a million dollars, and she had not given it a single thought. Of course, she wouldn't see a penny of it until six months had passed, but even so, a million dollars! And then she thought about the two codicils her father had added to his will, another datum she had not wondered about, had simply accepted as given. Why had he done that? Why, why, why . . . ? All the things she had ignored seemed to be surfacing in waves, and they all ended with the same question: why?

7

The trouble with their neighborhood, Abby said on Sunday, was that there was no good place to walk a dog. It was a neighborhood for rising young professionals: doctors and dentists who, like Brice, were still paying off their school loans, lawyers who had not yet been made partners in prestigious firms, financial advisers on the way up. Landscaping was meticulous everywhere, with gardeners who came in regularly to maintain it, houses modestly upscale, SUVs in abundance, soccer moms the norm, a good neighborhood. Although Abby had blanched when she first saw the size of their mortgage payments, Brice had insisted that this was the place to be, and they managed to keep up payments, to keep up with all the Joneses, but if Jud had not footed her education expenses with checks twice as big as her school costs, she would be working full-time, she knew.

Cars were not that numerous, and bikes not too bad, but there were no sidewalks, and Spook flinched when anything on wheels got near. She was a forest dog, a cabin dog, a recluse of a dog, not a city dog. Spook did not like this neighborhood.

'I'll take her to the Arboretum,' Abby said, picking at a sandwich at the kitchen table with Brice. He had been working all weekend, still catching up, he said, but since she had little real knowledge of what he actually did at work, she couldn't imagine how he could catch up at home. The stock market had to be open and running for him to buy and sell, that much she knew. He often talked about his clients, but aside from buying, selling, or advising them about investments, trusts, annuities, what else was there for him to do? Record-keeping, for one thing, he had said tiredly, research investment possibilities in a constantly changing market. Review various portfolios so he would have some notion of what to tell old man Donaldson, or Mrs. Meyers . . . He was way behind after a week of doing little or nothing.

'You want to take a long walk, climb one of the trails up Mount Pisgah?' she asked.

He shook his head. 'Can't. But you should go soon if you decide to hike up a mountain. It's going to rain later on, according to the Weather Channel. Tonight, let's go out for dinner. Deal?'

She nodded. 'Deal.' She knew she needed exercise as much as Spook did; the little bit of rowing she had done had made her back and arms sore, not a good sign. Since Brice went to the gym three days a week, he probably didn't feel the need for movement the way she did, but also, she had to admit to herself, she couldn't face any more of the sympathy cards and notes, the condolences that had poured in from all over the country. Jud had touched the lives of many people, and many of them had reacted to his death emotionally. Now she was working through the box of cards and letters, responding briefly to each one.

Brice returned upstairs to his study and work, and she cleared the table, put things in the dishwasher, and got ready to leave. The phone rang and she paused to listen to the incoming call, then snatched up the phone.

'Willa? I'm here.'

'Abby, I'm glad you picked up. Are you all right? How are you?'

'Okay. I'm okay. Willa, the police are looking for you, state police.'

'I know. They've left messages on my machine. I'll give them a call, but, Abby, I have to see you before I talk to them. Can we meet somewhere?'

Involuntarily Abby glanced up the stairs, then lowered her voice. 'Yes. I'll come over to your place.'

'No. I'm not home. I don't want the police

to know I'm back until after we talk, and they might come to the house. I suspect one of the neighbors was asked to call them when I turned up.'

'Where are you now?'

'Safeway, at Eighteenth and Oak. I'll wait out front.'

* * *

Willa Ashford was forty-one and didn't try to pretend otherwise. Her chestnut-colored hair had streaks of white already, and she seldom wore any makeup and was careless about how she dressed, usually in jeans and sweatshirts or sweaters, and running shoes. Abby thought she was beautiful.

She had had a crush on Willa her freshman year, when Willa had been her instructor. At the time, Abby and Matthew Petrie were together, fighting most of the time, and with so little money that, although they both worked while they were attending school, they often didn't know if they would be able to pay the rent or buy groceries. The threat of being put out on the street had been ever present. Willa had appeared so serene, so self-assured and composed, so beautiful and intelligent, everything that Abby knew she herself wasn't, she had set up Willa as an ideal that no other woman could even approach. She had loved her, with reverence and adoration, the way she imagined good Catholics felt toward Mary.

In the spring of her freshman year, Abby had dropped out of school; there would be time later for her to go back, she and Matthew had said, and he had only one more semester to go; he would graduate, then work while she got her degree. The only thing she missed, she had confided to her friend Jonelle, was Willa. And Jonelle had said wisely, 'Honey, you're looking for the perfect mother, someone whose shoulder you can cry on. Your life is the pits, and she would make the fairy-tale mother for you to run to; that's what you miss.'

She and Matthew maxed out their credit cards, borrowed heavily, skimped on everything; she worked at a restaurant and often took food home with her, hidden in her backpack. Then she learned that Matthew was into video poker, and although he graduated and got a job, money was scarcer than ever. Seventeen months after they were married, they separated, with the divorce following swiftly, financed by Jud.

During Abby's year of absence from college, Willa's husband died of pancreatic cancer. Then, when Abby registered to return to school, she had needed permission from Willa to be readmitted to her class; she had gone to her office without an appointment, unannounced, and found Willa drawn and pale.

'Will you take me back?' Abby asked at the door, reluctant to intrude on such obvious grief. 'I'm sorry I dropped out. I'm single again, and I want to work toward my degree.'

'You got a divorce?'

Abby nodded. 'I'm sorry about your husband.'

Willa had been at her desk; she came around it and motioned Abby to come in all the way and sit down. 'I'm sorry about your marriage,' she said, closing the door. 'I know how hard that can be.'

There were tears in her eyes, and she turned away quickly; then without knowing how it happened, Abby found herself holding Willa, and Willa weeping on her shoulder. That day they became friends, more than friends; Abby found a sister that day.

The bond deepened and strengthened over the next few years; Abby changed her major to art history and, later, began to work at the museum, where Willa had been appointed director when the former director retired.

When Abby realized that Willa was seeing Jud, seeing a lot of him, sleeping with him, she had been outraged, furious: 'Leave him alone! Back off now while you can. You don't know what he's like!'

'I know him,' Willa had said calmly. 'Maybe better than you do.'

'You don't! He'll use you. He'll take and take, and when he's done, he'll be off with someone else. I know exactly what he's like. He'll kill you. You're not like the others.'

'Abby, for heaven's sake! You're talking about your father!'

'And I love him more than I can say, but I'm not blind. I've watched him all these years, using women, then putting them in his novels as if they had been objects to be examined under a microscope, dissected, spread out for the world to see, and finally discarded.' She drew in a long breath, fighting to control her fury, her anguish. 'Willa, please, you must know about some of the others, how he's treated them. You're too good for that. You deserve someone who will really love you, not just for a fling, but forever. And he can't. He just can't be that way. He isn't mean or vicious, he's just . . .' She spread her hands helplessly. 'He's what he is. He'll hurt you. Kill you.'

They were in the back courtyard at the museum, where several statues gazed endlessly into a reflecting pond. When a few people came out to stroll, Willa started to walk away; Abby caught her arm.

'You're acting like a jealous child,' Willa said in a low voice. 'I'm an adult, and so is Jud. I believe we can both take care of ourselves.'

Abby dropped her hand and watched Willa return to the museum and pass out of sight. Since that day, two years ago, they had been distant, polite, no longer sisters.

*   *   *

She spotted Willa instantly, standing outside the supermarket, her back to the parking lot; she was wearing jeans, a long shapeless jacket, and hiking boots. Abby drove through the lot and stopped, pushed the button to roll down the passenger window, and called her name. When Willa turned, all color drained from her face as she stared at the van. Abby had driven it in order to give Spook a little more room than the small Supra afforded; she had not considered what effect seeing the van and the dog would have on Willa.

'It's me,' she called. 'Get in.'

There was an awkward moment after Willa got in, before Abby started to drive. 'I phoned,' Willa said, 'but then I realized you had relatives around, so I didn't expect you to call back.'

'I didn't know you called,' Abby said. It was entirely possible that Brice had told her, but she had no memory of it. There had been so many calls, the answering machine had not been able to record them all. 'I was going to take Spook out to the Arboretum, let her run. Is that okay with you?'

'You don't have to spend time with me,' Willa said quickly. 'I mean . . . If we could just park somewhere . . . '

'Do you want to go for a walk with us?'

'Yes.'

'Okay, the Arboretum.'

Spook was standing on the floor of the backseat, her forepaws on the back of the passenger seat, whining softly. Willa turned to pet her, and Spook licked her hand.

★   ★   ★

The Arboretum, a few miles south, was a sprawling park reverting to a natural state with a minimum of human interference, enough to keep trails cleared, and to control the exuberant growth of brambles and poplars and poison oak. On the lower side was a river and a large pond with nutria burrows on the banks and ducks in the water.

The southern edge of the park extended up Mount Pisgah, where trails varied in difficulty from acceptable for strollers to trails so steep and rough that it took experienced climbers to follow them. Abby intended to take one midway between the extremes.

'I'll have to keep you on the leash until we get up the trail,' Abby said to Spook, snapping on the leash at the parking lot. Half a dozen other cars were in the lot, but it was a large area; not a person was in sight. They walked past the administration building, with its information leaflets and a large anteroom where schoolchildren assembled before starting nature walks. Beyond that building was a big barn used for an annual plant exchange, or to put on demonstrations of various kinds, to display mushrooms, with experts who would identify whatever fungus, mushroom, or toadstool the patrons brought to them, or horticulturists who identified sprigs of plants, flowers . . . Behind the barn the trail led up the mountain.

As soon as they had followed a curve or two and were out of sight of the buildings, Abby took the leash off Spook. It was against the rules, but Spook was too well behaved to cause a problem, and watching her bound off between trees, Abby smiled faintly. Creature of the forests and mountains.

Almost as if unleashing the dog had been her cue, Willa began to talk. 'A few months ago Jud told me about the fight you two had. All that time, and he never mentioned it until last summer. He told me some of the things you both said, and how ashamed and sorry he was.'

Abby watched the trail ahead of them. It was hardly wide enough for two people; now and again their shoulders brushed each other, or their arms did.

Phrases from that fight had taken up dwelling in her head, noisy tenants who would not be hushed. They clamored now.

'If you do it to Willa, I'll never speak to you again. I'll write you off completely!'

'What I do is none of your business. Willa's a big girl, which is more than I can say about you. You didn't learn a damn thing the first time out, did you?'

'This has nothing to do with me. At least I didn't hang in there and hope for better tomorrows for years the way my mother did. With some people there aren't any better tomorrows. All tomorrows are just like all yesterdays.'

'This has everything to do with you! You stepped in it with Petrie, and turned around and did it again with Brice, and didn't learn a thing.'

'Don't you dare bring Brice into it!'

'I'm watching you turn into your mother, do you realize that? You're becoming more like her every day, crying for a security blanket, and it's not there, kid. Believe me, it's not there. You provide it, or no one does.'

'I'm not talking about my mother, or Brice and me. I'm talking about you! Don't you ever consider what you're doing, one woman after another, used, tossed out? How you make them feel? Like trash! And now Willa.'

'You ever see a woman tied to a bedpost here? See me force my way in where I wasn't invited?'

'I saw my own mother cry herself to sleep night after night!'

'I was never unfaithful to her, and you know it! So does she. You're mixing apples and oranges.'

'Oh, what's the use! I should go now. Take me across so I can go.'

'Not yet. Let's finish what you started.'

'Take me, or I'll swim across. Now!'

'You're too mad to be allowed to get near a car. You'd kill someone on the road.'

She was so angry, she couldn't stop shaking.

Jud came across the cabin to her and put his arm around her shoulders. 'Just calm down, and I'll row you over.'

She shrugged him off. 'I'll get my stuff together. Let's not talk about any of this again. Never. I'll never mention Willa's name to you again. But I mean it, if you hurt her, I'll never see you again.'

The scene, two years old now, was in her head as if it had happened yesterday, and there was nothing she could do to get it out. She felt outraged and confused that he had told Willa about it. Abby had never mentioned it to Brice. He knew something had happened, but she had not said a word about it to him.

Spook came running out of the woods, gave Abby and Willa a good-natured lick, and raced off in the other direction.

'I wish I had known a lot sooner,' Willa said. 'He hated it that a fight like that had come between you, but he didn't know how to fix it.'

'We sort of patched it up again,' Abby said.

'Not talking about it isn't exactly patching up anything.'

Abby knew that and had kept trying over the past two years to pretend that being polite and dutiful was gradually healing the wounds. They had both kept up the pretense. Neither had mentioned Willa's name again.

'He called me after he talked to you last week,' Willa said, her voice almost too low to hear. 'He told me you couldn't make it out that weekend. We had planned . . . He wanted to talk to you alone; that's why he said Friday, when Brice would be at work, and that evening I was planning to join you. Then he said you couldn't make it. Abby, he wanted to tell you that we were going to get married. He . . . we both agreed not to tell a soul until he had talked to you. He wasn't sure how you would take it. He didn't want you to hear it from anyone else before he talked to you.'

Abby stopped moving. Married? She clutched Willa's arm and pulled her around to see her face. Willa had tears on her cheeks. 'He asked you to marry him?'

Willa nodded. 'Last month. We were planning to be married in November. But he had to talk to you before we could announce anything.' She wiped her cheeks with the back of her hands, then put her hands in her pockets and, hunched as if with a chill, started to walk again.

Abby stood paralyzed, too surprised — even shocked — to move as Willa went up the trail. She looked like an old woman. Then Abby ran to catch up; she grabbed Willa and embraced her and held her as hard as she could. Champagne, a celebration, how happy he had sounded. And she had said no, she couldn't make it. After a moment Willa drew back. Then, hand in hand, they continued to follow the trail upward, not speaking now.

★ ★ ★

A little later they found a log to sit on, and they talked quietly. Now and then Spook checked in, gave them a kiss, and left to explore again.

Basically Jud had finished the book, Willa said, but he had a little cleanup work to do; he had to shuffle the pieces around and get them in order, then make a final printout, and he would be done. About two weeks, he had said. He had planned to move in with her, and they would have spent weekends at the cabin.

'I couldn't get away until April,' Willa said, 'and then we were going to go to Italy, spend three months . . . A delayed honeymoon. He said he wanted me to teach him how to see art.'

Willa glanced at Abby. 'You remember that day we had an argument over him?'

'God, yes!'

'You really shook me,' Willa said. 'You were giving voice to all the problems and uncertainties I was wrestling with. I couldn't reconcile the three images of one man. He

114

came to a show at the museum once, long before I met him, and someone pointed him out to me and said who he was, the world-famous writer, hermit, and reincarnation of Don Juan, all in one pretty package. He was handsome, and with a woman, of course. Then there was the father you talked about a lot, loving, warm, funny, capable of anything and everything, a perfect godlike father. And the man I grew to know and to love. I wouldn't say naive exactly, but tentative, shy, sort of hesitant. Afraid of me. That was it, he was afraid of me in a curious way, and so careful with me, as if one wrong word, one wrong act would send me flying away. I was having a lot of trouble trying to sort things out the day you spoke your mind. I knew I loved him, and I had accepted that I might be dumped, as you so elegantly put it, and I had decided I would risk that. I had to risk that. But then I realized that he was just as afraid as I was. In spite of what we had been through, both of us, we were like two kids trying out being in love for the first time.'

When she became silent, and the silence stretched out to where it would have been awkward to refer back to that time, Abby told her about the lieutenant and the detective, about going to the cabin with them, everything. 'Did he ever mention the cashier's checks to you?'

Willa shook her head. 'One hundred forty-five thousand! He told me he had mortgaged the cabin years ago and had given Matthew Petrie fifteen thousand dollars, but that much money! No. Could he have been giving Matthew money all these years?'

'What for?'

'I don't know.'

'Friday night, it had to have been someone he knew well,' Abby said after a moment. 'That's the only way I can see someone being in the cabin in the middle of the night. Someone got stranded there, or planned to stay until dark, something like that.' She looked at the ground. 'I thought it was a woman,' she mumbled.

'I would have thought the same thing a few years ago.'

After a moment, Abby asked, 'Did he say why he gave Matthew that money, fifteen thousand dollars?'

'To pay off debts. Your ex-husband was going to skip and leave you with a mountain of debts, creditors. Jud said you were so determined not to be a burden, so independent, that he didn't think you would let him pay them off if you knew he had mortgaged the cabin to raise the money. He made your

116

ex go with him and pay people in person, with him watching. He wanted you to be free to go back to school, not feel obligated to work as a waitress and pay Matthew's bills.'

'He never told me,' Abby whispered. The money for the divorce lawyer must have come from the mortgage, too, she realized. As recently as eight years ago, Jud had still been poverty-stricken, just as she had been.

Spook ran back to them, and this time lay at their feet panting, her tongue hanging out, sides heaving. She looked very happy.

Clouds had moved in and the air was degrees colder and smelled of approaching rain. Above them the fir trees rustled in a rising wind, as if in anticipation.

'We should start back,' Abby said.

They began to retrace their way down the mountain, this time with the dog staying close by, as if she had had enough exploring for one outing.

Close to the valley floor, Abby put the leash back on Spook, and during the brief stop, Willa said, 'You know no one's going to believe he actually proposed, that we were going to be married.'

Abby looked at her, startled, then slowly nodded. It was true. Who would believe it? They hadn't told anyone.

'It's made me feel awkward,' Willa said

quietly. 'That's why I didn't want to come around when your relatives were there. They would have looked on me as the new conquest, something like that, not as his fiancée.' She ducked her head and started to walk.

'How did you find out?' Abby asked. 'Who told you?'

'The police called me, looking for you. Jud said you were going to the coast with Jonelle and a couple of other friends, and that's what I told them. Then . . . I just got in my car and began to drive, and I ended up in Bandon and checked into a motel. There didn't seem to be anyone I could talk to. Or maybe I had to be alone. I came back for the service, then took off again. Now they'll have to question me, I guess. I'll tell them why Jud called you, about our engagement, but I had to tell you first.'

'I'm glad you did.' He had sounded so happy, and she had said no, she couldn't make it.

Silently they walked past the barn, past the administration building. Other people were leaving now before the rain moved in, the first people they had seen. Their silence continued as they drove back into town.

At the Safeway lot Willa motioned toward the side. 'I left my car over there. I imagine the police will want to talk to me first thing in the morning. Will you come back to work yet?'

'Yes. I'll be there tomorrow. After . . . after they ask you questions, let's go out for coffee or something.' She reached for Willa's hand, and for another moment they sat there holding hands. Abby was thinking that of all the people Jud had known, loved, and left, they were probably the only two people who had really loved him; knowing exactly what he was like, they had loved him.

8

It was no use, Abby thought on Monday at the museum. She and two other graduate students were supposed to be packing up statues that had been on loan, but she kept forgetting what she was doing and became as immobile as one of the figures being crated. When Willa finally appeared at the door of the workroom, Abby fled with her. Willa had been in her office for hours with the lieutenant and his detective assistant.

Abby didn't ask a thing, and Willa didn't volunteer anything as they left the museum, threaded their way through a vast parking lot crammed full, crossed the street, and entered a café. At the table, with coffee before them, Willa finally spoke.

'There must be a hundred different ways to ask the same question, and they used them all.' She was wan and listless, withdrawn. 'Didn't we tell anyone at all we planned to be married? Not even my mother?' She grimaced. 'That would be like hiring a television spot or a float to go up and down every street in town broadcasting the news.' She took a deep breath and looked out the window.

120

'How can you prove you were home by yourself if you didn't see anyone, or if no one saw you? I don't know.' When she lifted her coffee cup, her hand was shaking.

'It doesn't mean anything,' Abby said quickly. 'They're asking everyone questions like that, not just you.'

Willa looked at her sadly and didn't respond. After a moment she said, 'You might as well go back home. You must have a lot of things to attend to.'

'The condolence notes,' Abby said. 'Walk the dog. Wait for the agent to call. Then I'll have to go to the cabin for a few days.' But it was true, she was useless at work; she might as well be home.

★   ★   ★

She found she could read only a few of the condolences before she had to stop, get up, and walk away, and she kept listening for the doorbell, for the telephone, for a call to say they had found him, they had the killer, it was over. The day and night seemed without end.

Christina Maas called on Tuesday; she would take a late flight to Eugene, and could they go to the cabin the following day, Wednesday? Maybe Abby, she suggested, could buy a few things for them to eat, breakfast stuff, snacks, lunch, and they could eat dinner out. Her suggestion sounded like an order, but Abby was grateful for anything that forced her to act.

'The movie contract is a done deal,' Christina said before she hung up. 'I'll tell you about it when I see you.'

★ ★ ★

Abby picked her up at her motel on Wednesday morning. Christina was wearing fawn-colored wool slacks, a long furlined raincoat, fancy boots — her 'roughing it' clothes, no doubt, Abby thought derisively.

Christina eyed Spook. 'He won't come leaping over the seat or anything, will he?'

'That's Spook, and she's well mannered,' Abby said curtly, then she started the long drive to the lake.

On the way, Christina filled her in with more details about the movie contract than she could grasp, and she stopped listening after a while. But she was awed; Christina had been negotiating this one contract for five months. Abby couldn't imagine how one agreement could take such a long time.

Already, in just a few days, the landscape had changed: the scarlets and golds were gone, many of the deciduous trees were bare;

from now until spring the dark firs would reign on this side of the high pass, then pines, and finally junipers. The front that had brought rain to the valley had been harsher in the mountains; there was snow at the higher elevations.

At the lake, after parking the van and carrying their supplies to the ramp, Abby started to pull the rowboat from the shed, and Christina stopped moving.

'I'm not getting in that little boat,' she said. 'It's too small. Where is the cabin?'

Abby pointed. 'We go by boat, or we don't go at all.' She worked the boat down to the water and tied it to a tree stump, then got the backpack and their groceries from the van. She tossed the backpack into the boat, added the bags of supplies, and took Christina's suitcase from her.

Christina was staring at the boat in horror. After a wild look all around, she moaned, and fearfully climbed in. Abby motioned to Spook, who leaped in and sat down, and then she released the rope and pushed off, rocking the boat more than she needed to. She stepped in at the last second, sat down, and took up the oars.

Christina clutched both sides of the rowboat desperately all the way across the finger, and by the time they pulled up at the ledge, she looked as if she might become seasick, she was so gray. Abby held the boat steady while Christina gingerly stepped out. Spook jumped out and raced around the cabin.

'My God!' Christina said then. 'I thought it was just a cabin on a shore somewhere.'

Exactly, Abby thought. She tied up, and they walked around the cabin to the front, where Spook was standing, wagging her tail furiously; Abby unlocked the door and pushed it open. Spook darted in, whining. 'I'll turn up the heat and then bring in our stuff,' Abby said. 'This is it.' She knew Spook would be tearing around inside, upstairs, down, searching for Jud. And she knew she couldn't bear to watch.

She tended to the thermostat, unlatched the dog door, and went back out; Christina didn't offer to help, but stood huddled in her coat as her color gradually returned.

Then, everything unloaded, they both went up the stairs. 'His study, the aerie,' Abby said.

'Good God! How many boxes are there?' Christina said inside the doorway. She walked to the desk and put her hand on the stack of manuscript. 'Is this the novel?'

'Yes.'

Christina gazed about the room, frowning. 'He must have kept every scrap of paper for his whole life. What's in the file cabinets?'

'More papers, manuscripts, correspondence. I don't know what all.'

'Well, we'll have to have a division of labor, won't we?' Christina crossed the room, pulled open a file drawer, and glanced inside some of the folders. 'Warranties, things like that. And computer stuff.' She opened a carton and looked at the top sheets of paper. 'More of the same, it looks like. And what's this?' She pulled out a few pages paper-clipped together. 'A story? Could be.' With a sigh she dropped the papers back into the carton.

'Why don't you take the novel manuscript downstairs, and I'll start going through things up here,' Abby said, trying to keep her hostility buried. She could admire Christina's cool efficiency, she thought, but not in close quarters. Watching her drop Jud's papers like that had sent a cold blast through her, and she realized she did not want that woman to handle Jud's private papers at all.

'My idea, too,' Christina said. 'The dog won't be darting in and out a lot, will it?'

'I doubt it,' Abby said in a tight, strained voice. 'She'll probably come up here and hang out with me after she's had a good look around.'

'Well, let's get started. If you can separate out the stories, essays, things like that, and make a stack, I'll start with the novel. Oh, and the advertising copy he wrote, that might prove useful, too. But no warranties or computer programs.' She picked up the manuscript, then paused. 'Correspondence should be in a separate stack.'

Silently Abby agreed. That was exactly what she intended to do, separate out everything personal and private. Christina carried the novel manuscript downstairs, and Abby sat on the floor; after a minute or two, time needed to loosen the knot inside, she opened a carton of papers.

Presently Spook came up the stairs and, after sniffing everything in the aerie, lay down with her head on Abby's leg. The only sounds were papers rustling, the wind outside the windows, and occasionally Christina's cell phone. When her voice intruded, Abby got up and closed the door.

She had emptied one box and had piles of like papers in a semicircle around her — fanfold computer stuff in one pile, advertising copy in one, papers clipped together in another, some miscellaneous things she hadn't decided about . . . The papers clipped together were on fanfold paper, too, but they had been torn apart, many of them edited in pencil, bits of stories, sketches, ideas, even complete stories, she thought, but she had read little so far. Now she stopped moving altogether as she looked over the next paper-clipped set.

Jud's first novel had been a coming-of-age story about a boy named Lincoln Colby, called Link. In it Link came to understand the adults around him, their affairs, betrayals, heartbreaks, and their generosity. Link had a dog, Sport, that got mauled so badly by a bear, he couldn't be saved; Link had shot him to end his agony, then carried the body up into the forest and buried him. When she first read the novel, Abby had realized that he had written her into it, it was her reaction to Mindy's death and burial that he had written about, and it had confounded her that he had been able to get inside her head so completely, that he had understood so thoroughly.

She sat back on her heels, stunned again, after skimming through a few pages he had written about that day, about Mindy's death and burial, from his viewpoint and from Abby's. No names were given, but the details were all there: her feelings, a description of the deepened bond between father and daughter their shared grief had brought about, all there.

She closed her eyes, recalling the scene from the novel. After burying the dog, Link had taken his rifle out into the forest to track the bear and kill it, but when he scanned the surrounding area with binoculars, he saw a woman on the jetty at the resort. Temple, that was her name. Temple something. Temple had been Link's first love, an older woman who had seduced the fourteen-year-old boy and taught him about sex, taught him about betrayal when she laughed at him later and sent him away. A man joined her on the jetty, and they struggled; she fell into the water, and the man turned and ran back to the resort. She didn't resurface. When Link was able to move again, he came across the tracks of the bear and realized it was just ahead, a certain shot, but he simply stood and watched it amble off into the woods; he went back to the resort, where boats were out and people were in the water searching for Temple's body. They said she lost her footing and fell, she must have hit her head. Link stood with his rifle and gazed at the man he had seen struggling with her, then he turned and walked away without saying a word.

The final image of the novel was of the adolescent boy walking away with his rifle, but in the background the war drums were beating in Vietnam.

Abby had been so shaken by finding herself, in the guise of a teenage boy, exposed, open to the gaze of the world, that she had paid little attention to the last few pages, but now she recalled them vividly. She stared at the many boxes around her. Had her father written scene after scene from real life, later to be fictionalized, disguised only to those unaware of the reality he had written about?

'Oh, my God,' she said under her breath. She remembered how disturbed Jud had been about the drowning death of a woman out by Siren Rock. When? She had still been in high school. It had happened in the fall; she had stayed in town that weekend, and he had come out alone for a few days, then returned haggard and more upset, and curiously more energized? driven? excited? than Abby had ever seen him. She had not understood then and she didn't now, but he had been different, fervid and absent. That was it; he had withdrawn, lost in a way she could not comprehend. He had said only that someone had drowned. Temple? She shook her head. Teri. Teri Frazier.

Had he seen that, too? Had he witnessed what happened that day? Had he written about it in the same way he had written about Mindy's death?

She began sweeping the office with a searching gaze, looking for a place to hide the papers she was holding. They were not for Christina's eyes, or anyone else's. He had published what he had chosen to tell; this was personal and private. She found herself regarding the pile of other papers clipped together, and she realized she had to read every bit in that stack before she turned it over to Christina.

Deliberately she upended the box she had been going through, and put the Mindy papers back in it, topped them with pages of computer code, and leaned back. What else had he written about in that graphic omniscient style? Reluctantly she pulled the stack of paper-clipped pages closer, picked up the top one, and started to read.

Soon after that Christina called up the stairs. 'Let's have lunch now. Take a break.'

★ ★ ★

Neither spoke as they ate sandwiches in the living room. Christina had spread out the novel chapters on the kitchen table. She looked drawn and pinched.

'It's hard, isn't it?' Christina said after finishing her coffee.

Abby nodded.

'Is there any way we could have food sent in for dinner?' Christina asked then. 'Abby, I confess I'm terrified of that little boat, and we'd be coming back in the dark, wouldn't we?'

'For heaven's sake, there's no take-out place around here,' Abby said, sharper than she had intended. More moderately she added, 'Let's make a list, and I'll run over to Bend and shop. We can cook in for the next few days.'

'Thanks,' Christina said. 'Nothing elaborate — frozen entrées, TV dinners, I don't care what we have. I'll do the cooking,' she added, surprising Abby very much.

This would work out better than breaking and heading for Bend for dinner, Abby decided. There was no way she could get through all of Jud's papers by Sunday morning unless she stuck with them every waking hour. She didn't understand how Christina was accomplishing anything at all, since she seemed to be on the phone most of the time.

She went back upstairs while Christina started making her list, and she gathered all the papers she did not want anyone else to read yet and hid them under computer stuff in the carton she had started to fill. Then she went down and looked over the list. Dinner for two, four nights, bagels and cream cheese . . . Vodka and wine. Orange juice. They debated briefly whether she should take Spook or leave her, and although it was clear that Christina did not care for dogs, it was also clear that she was afraid to stay in the cabin alone. Afraid of the lake, the boat, afraid of the silence, Abby thought darkly; what had Jud seen in this woman? She left Spook to guard the house and shoved off in the rowboat. Christina's cell phone was ringing again.

★ ★ ★

It was dark when she returned. She had been stopped many times in town by people who wanted to express their sympathy, their grief, try to give her comfort. Jud had been well known, admired, liked; he had been one of them. Then, on the black water with the light shining on the other side, she found herself blinking back tears.

Other times when she had come in after dark, looking over her shoulder at the emerging cabin, at the welcoming light, she would see Jud standing, waiting for her, to give her a hand with the boat, a big hug and kiss, with Spook at his side, wagging her tail furiously. That night the cabin looked small and lonesome. The aerie was dark, invisible against the black trees. When she got closer,

132

she whistled, and Spook appeared on the lowest ledge, her welcoming committee.

Carrying the bags inside, she saw that Christina was pale, fearful. 'I kept hearing things,' Christina said. 'I kept thinking of bears or wildcats or something. Or someone creeping in from the woods. Let's not leave me here after dark, okay?'

'Sorry,' Abby said. She really was. Lynne had always been afraid up here alone at night, too, or alone with only Abby. 'I kept running into people.'

Christina began to take things out of the bags, stashing them away in the refrigerator, on the counter. 'I know you think I'm a terrible coward, and I guess I am. I think you're frighteningly brave.'

Abby laughed and shook her head. 'We're all afraid of something,' she said, repeating what Jud had told her a long time ago. 'I'd be terrified alone at night in New York,' she added.

She turned away to take off her jacket and gloves; it was a very cold night, and the warmth of the cabin felt good. 'What are you afraid of?' she had asked Jud, and he had grinned and said, 'Of being found out. Passing myself off as a writer. They'll find out what a fraud I am and boot me out the door.' She was fighting tears again.

'I intend to have a drink, and then I'll put together some dinner,' Christina said. 'Can I make one for you?'

'Thanks. But not now. I'll get back to that stuff upstairs.' She fled.

★ ★ ★

Late that night, listening to the noisy forest, the wind in the trees, an occasional owl scream, she kept thinking of the bits and pieces of her own life she had glimpsed through her father's eyes, bits and pieces of his life with Lynne, a scene from Lynne's viewpoint where she had been so sympathetically treated that Abby had gritted her teeth and stopped midway through. But he had been able to do that, get inside the other's head and see it from both sides. He had understood both sides, and had become the villain again and again.

He had blamed himself, she thought bleakly, for all the hurts and the poverty, the quarrels, the bitterness, the divorce, all of it. He had blamed himself, had suffered such guilt, and had not spared himself when he fictionalized the incidents. In the second novel, the boy Link had returned home after a ten-year absence, and it was understood that he had been to Vietnam, had gone to school somewhere, and had married a young woman. Abby knew where the second novel title had come from. She had asked what he would do if there was a power outage and he had to row across the finger to get home.

'Well,' Jud had said, 'first thing, always carry a flashlight. Always have one in your pocket or somewhere handy. When you cast off, turn left, keep close to the shoreline, check with the flashlight as you go. It's the long way home, but you'll make it that way. Just follow the shore all around the finger until you bump into the ledge out back.'

'Follow the black shore,' she had said in perfect understanding. Lynne had looked terrified at the very thought. He had called his second novel *The Black Shore*, and the novel was about the boy grown into a man now, groping his way through the blackness of memories, a bad marriage, broken promises, with no welcoming light visible anywhere.

Abby had read another fragment, a description of her when Lynne remarried and became pregnant, and Abby had asked Jud if she could come live with him. He had used that piece, too, but in a way she had not recognized until now. Link's mother died, and in the second novel he had expressed Abby's emotions perfectly. She had not thought of her mother as dying, but perhaps she had felt abandoned as her mother withdrew into another life, leaving Abby motherless. Jud had known even if she hadn't, and he had used that in his novel.

Restlessly she turned over, then over again. What else? She had to reread the novels. She felt as if she had read them with the understanding of a child, with eyes that didn't quite focus, skimming over passages that were obscure, emotions that hit too close to home, even if she had not understood why that was so at the time. She had seen only the surface, and the surface was the least important part, after all. She had to reread them.

★　★　★

She sorted, read, and hid papers all day Thursday, on into the night after a hasty dinner with Christina. The stack she was hiding was growing very large, but there was another growing stack of stories and essays for Christina. Whenever she had any doubt where a particular piece should go, she put it with her own hidden papers.

On Friday afternoon she came to several sheets clipped together, with the heading *Teri*. Her hands were shaking when she started to read them. Again, from his point of view and hers, sometimes separately, sometimes merging, running together, starting with one, then without warning switching to the other in mid-sentence. Some of it was incomprehensible. She turned the paper over, but the one that followed simply had block letters: SIREN ROCK.

Once Jud had come to speak to her lit class, and in answer to a question he had said, 'It's like being in a ground blizzard with snow blowing every which way, no form, no shape at all, just all the individual snowflakes in motion. That describes how a novel begins in my head, bits of stuff, characters, incidents, scenes all whizzing around, but all at once they begin to coalesce, and I can see a shape forming out of chaos. A snowman, by golly. The novel is born when that happens.'

No one had understood a word of it, including her.

She started to read the few pages again and found she was not seeing the words, as if her mind refused to deal with them now. Slowly she put the paper clip back on, folded the papers and tucked them under the waistband of her jeans, and pulled her sweatshirt over them. Moving as if in a trance, she stood up and left the aerie, went downstairs to the closet, and pulled out her jacket, a wool hat, and gloves.

'I need to get some air,' she said dully.

Christina hardly even looked up. She had said she would finish reading the novel chapters that morning and then start the impossible job of putting them in order. Now she stood with papers in both hands, the table covered with other papers, and Abby walked out with Spook at her side.

She climbed the driveway to the forest service road and started to walk. The road was no more than a track through the forest, never maintained very much, and in the past half a dozen years not at all. Jud had said the state foresters decided to let it revert to wilderness. It wouldn't take long for it to become indistinguishable from the woods pressing in on both sides. She had paid no attention before, driving here with Caldwell and the detective; she paid little more attention now, automatically sidestepping rocks or roots, the occasional broken seedling tree, the more frequent brambles that were filling all available space. A flotilla of tanks couldn't kill them. Spook dashed ahead, out of sight, came tearing back to take off in a different direction through the woods, back again. Happy, Abby thought bleakly. This was the world Spook knew and loved; she was happy here.

At the bridge over the north finger, Spook was waiting for her, tongue out, panting, waiting for a signal. Ahead, down to the water, back?

Abby turned to her right and clambered over the rocky ground to a mammoth boulder, where she sat down and gazed at the creek. It was shallow, with many riffles, a series of little falls all the way down to the lake nearly a hundred feet below. Moss covered the boulders and blowdowns; the air was misty and cold. Spook went to the water for a drink, and stood sniffing the air. If Abby threw a stick into the water, across the creek, anywhere, Spook would be after it like a streak of lightning, she knew, but she didn't want the dog to get in the frigid water.

Now she pulled the papers out from under her jacket and shirt, opened them, and started to read. She skipped over the first part, a vivid description of the hot spring pool.

'We have to leave, or I'll be stuck on the wrong side of the lake all night,' he said. 'Would that be so bad? You can stay with us.' She was playing with him again, the hot smell of sulfur water in his nose, her body smell, his own body, and the resinous scent of pine all mingled, intoxicating. She

139

smiled languorously, and sank under the water, where she fondled his penis . . . He pulled her up furiously. 'He's here, isn't he? If you want him to know, why don't you just tell him?' 'And spoil half the fun? Forbidden fruits. You know.' I will be like a cat, smiling, lazy, languid, and he will stamp around and want to hit me, but of course he never would. He climbed out of the hot pool and toweled himself roughly, jerked on his clothes. 'We're through. Show's over.' 'Don't be an idiot. It's fun with you, and you have fun, too. Admit it.' I shut my eyes and she was there, like a gardenia bud cool and pale in the late heat. 'I have to get back. It's a long walk.' 'Not yet, my love. I will take you a short way.' She is so beautiful, so beautiful. 'My love,' I murmur again and again. Again the tears want to fall and again I must not, must not. 'Be whole, my love, go home and be whole, unhurt and free, and in time I will be like a dream you once had, a lovely dream that must vanish like the ghosts when you awaken.' Her hand in his, guiding him through the forest. She stops and pulls her long hair up in a swirl, puts on her cap, and now she is a shapeless figure in black pants, black shirt, black cap. 'Good-bye, my love.' Then she is gone, vanished in the dense

140

forest, and he stumbles after her. 'For God's sake, stop acting like a schoolboy! He knows. He always knows.' 'You've used me to taunt him. You really are a bitch.' He goes down the rocky trail too fast for her to keep up; she is the furious one now. 'You can't do this to me, you bastard. I decide, not you.' I throw a rock and catch him on the shoulder; I want to hurt him, to see him fall down, bloodied. He just moves faster, out of sight, and I run to catch up. He is nearing the break before he sees her in the canoe coming after him, and behind her at the back of the cottage, Lawrence with a can of paint, brush in his hand. The canoe is faster than the rowboat, Lawrence sees us, he knows where I'm going, why. It isn't too dark yet, but I won't be able to come back. He'll have to bring me back. He turns toward Coop's ramp. He'll wait for her and put her in the car, take her back to the cottage and push her out. No confrontation, not on her terms, not this way. She's paddling too fast, on her knees, her face ghost-white in the gathering dusk. Lawrence raises his hand with the paintbrush, opens his mouth, going to call her back, warn her? He lets his hand fall to his side and I realize she turned too soon. I yell something, I don't even know what, then she crashes and the jolt throws her onto the black rocks, into the water. Lawrence turns around and starts to paint again.

It didn't come to the bottom of the page, just stopped there, and on the next page in block capitals were the words SIREN ROCK.

9

Later that Friday afternoon the cabin phone rang, but since the many incoming calls had all been for Christina, Abby didn't even glance at the receiver on Jud's desk. She assumed that Christina had given out the cabin number as well as her cell phone's. Abby had called Brice a couple of times and did not expect anyone to call her; today, however, Christina yelled up the stairs, 'It's for you.' Abby stood up and lifted the receiver. Her legs had started to cramp from sitting for too many hours on the floor; she stretched one, then the other before she spoke.

'Abby? It's Felicia Shaeffer. I heard you were at the cabin.' She sounded faint and distant, and Abby realized that she had not heard the click of the downstairs phone being hung up.

'How are you, Felicia?' she asked, listening for the click.

'Oh, I'm fine, but there's something — '

'Felicia, hang on a minute, will you? I can't hear you on this phone. I'll go down and use the other one.'

The downstairs phone was off the receiver, on the end table near the couch. Christina was at the table, her back to the couch.

'Let's try this one,' Abby said to Felicia.

'Someone's with you?'

'Yes. I brought Dad's agent up to look at his new novel.'

Felicia hesitated, then said softly, 'Is she going to take things to New York with her?'

'That was the idea,' Abby said, her gaze on Christina's back. She appeared unnaturally stiff and still.

Felicia's voice dropped even lower. 'Don't let her take the only copy of anything, Abby. I think — Abby, would it be possible for you to drop in for a few minutes? I'd really like to talk to you for just a few minutes.'

Felicia had been one of Jud's closest friends, and she had always treated Abby like a granddaughter, but a conspiratorial tone in her voice made Abby suspect that she was not proposing a social call. She said, 'We're only here for a couple of days. We have to leave early Sunday.'

'Anytime tomorrow. I'll be here,' Felicia said swiftly.

'I'm glad you called,' Abby said. 'Thanks. I'll do that.'

When she hung up, she eyed Christina thoughtfully. Was she a snoop, or had she

144

really left the phone off without thinking of it again? Now Christina moved; she put down papers she had been holding and picked others up, to all appearances engrossed in them.

Silently Abby left the room and returned to the aerie, and this time she sat at Jud's desk drumming her fingers, thinking, gazing out the window. The aerie, with windows on every wall, was enclosed in greenery on three sides, green pine boughs, green alders with their red bark, green mosses . . . The fourth wall had taller windows framing the lake. A hawk sailed past that window without a wing motion, in a long sweeping glide. She brought her gaze back to the cartons she had not gone through yet; there were three remaining, and one half-finished. Then she looked at the stacks she had set aside to hand over to Christina. Advertising copy, stories, essays, sketches, anecdotes . . . There were hundreds of pages of printouts, five, six hundred . . . And the stack she had hidden away had about that much material. She decided to change her tactics, take out everything remaining that was not obviously computer- or advertising-related, and keep all of it; she knew she would have too little time now to go through everything carefully, the way she had been doing. She went back to work.

Dinner that night was more strained than usual. Their relationship had not been an easy one, and the time spent together at meals or just in passing had done nothing to relax it. Carefully Abby said, 'I think I'll take all the stuff you want to carry back to New York to a copy shop in Bend and get Xeroxes made first.'

'You don't know what you're proposing,' Christina said sharply. 'There are several drafts of chapter after chapter in that pile.'

'It doesn't matter,' Abby said. 'High-speed copy machines, an hour or so. Some of the stories I've put aside for you are the only copies. I don't think the only copy of anything should be taken away.'

'Normally that's a wise thing to do,' Christina said coolly, 'but this is not a normal situation. If I'm going to act as agent for his material, you have to trust me.'

Abby shrugged. 'But it's my decision,' she said. 'Things get lost traveling, misplaced, the plane can crash. Besides, I want to compare the various drafts with his disks, with what's on the hard drive. That's going to take a lot of time. I'll go early, get back well before dark tomorrow.'

'What am I supposed to do if you take all this stuff away for hours?'

'Start with the advertising copy, see if you

146

really want to keep any of it. I'll leave that here.'

Christina's eyes took on a glassy appearance. 'As you say, it's your decision. You've found things about yourself up there, haven't you?'

'Of course. We always knew he wrote about the people in his life. Are you in the new novel?'

Christina shook her head. Watching her, Abby realized that the past few days had taken a terrible toll; now she would guess her age closer to fifty than forty, and she looked as if her eyes were troubling her. With a start of surprise Abby thought, She's been crying. Impulsively she said, 'You really did care for him, didn't you?'

Christina poked at the food on her plate, a prepared manicotti, frozen, ready to be popped into the oven. It was leathery, the cheese tough, with a tomato sauce unnaturally red. She put her fork down, picked up her glass of wine, and drank it all. 'It's complicated,' she said slowly then. 'Neither of us was looking for a commitment, nothing permanent. We both knew and accepted that from the beginning. But I cared for him as a writer in a way I don't think you would understand.'

Abby felt her cheeks grow hot, and she

ducked her head to keep from saying anything that might lead to a fight.

'I'm sorry,' Christina said. 'That wasn't meant as a put-down. You loved him as the man, your father, and I imagine he was a wonderful father, and no doubt you appreciated him as a writer, respected him, all that. I found him attractive as a man, but I've known and been attracted to many men, maybe too many, but I loved him as a writer, revered him as a writer. That's the difference. That's all I meant.' She refilled both their wineglasses and sipped hers, then said in a low, fierce voice, 'I could kill the one who did that to him. I would like to kill him myself, with my hands.'

'Me, too,' Abby said in a near whisper. Abruptly she stood up. 'You're not going to finish that, are you?' She pointed to the food on Christina's plate.

'No. I'm done.'

'Tomorrow I'll get some steaks, potatoes, veggies, real food,' Abby said, clearing the table. She paused. 'Can you tell much about the novel yet? Have you put it in the proper order?'

'No. Some chapters have several drafts, and I'm beginning to think that some pieces aren't there, not written yet maybe.'

Abby sat down again. 'The police said a

disk is missing. Someone turned off the computer without saving the last things he worked on, and he took the disk. He must have taken part of the manuscript, too.'

'Why?'

'I don't know.'

They both looked at the untidy stacks of papers, and Christina shook her head. 'How could anyone have found a particular section? How long did he spend searching?'

'I don't know,' Abby said again, more harshly. She closed her eyes hard. Someone up there searching, Jud's body on the stairs, blood soaking into the carpet runner, Spook outside barking . . . The images would not go away. Such a burning hatred flared for the killer that she became rigid.

Christina's fingers on her wrist made her jerk her eyes open. The fingers felt hot, as if Christina were feverish.

'You're shivering,' Christina said. 'Are you all right?'

She was freezing and shivering, and burning up with hatred. 'All right,' she said. 'Leave all this stuff. I'll clean it up later. I'm going to copy everything from his hard drive to disks. It will take a while.' The police had made copies, she remembered, but that didn't count. She needed to have her own, compare files, compare everything.

★ ★ ★

She was at Jud's desk working on the computer files later when Christina came upstairs, bringing coffee.

'I was thinking, if what he was working on wasn't saved, what good is this going to do?' Christina asked, setting down a mug. 'I thought you might need this. It's been hours. It's after one.'

Abby leaned back and picked up the coffee gratefully. Her neck was stiff and hurting. Too tense, concentrating too hard. 'Unless it was written over, it's in there,' she said. 'You can delete, but it's still there until you write over it. The trick is to find it. He had his automatic backup set for seven minutes, that part's easy. And the rest that wasn't saved automatically is still there, too.' In fact, she had learned that Jud had written a separate backup program that saved every single keystroke as he worked. Power outages were too common here in the mountains; he had prepared for them. 'Tomorrow I'll have to buy more disks when I go to town.'

'If you find the missing pieces, will you send them to me?' Christina asked.

She no longer was demanding anything, pleading rather, fearful of Abby in a new way, as if she had seen something change, someone unknown emerge, and she was not sure how to talk to her now.

'Yes,' Abby said.

★ ★ ★

The next morning Christina helped carry boxes of papers to the ledge, where she watched Abby stow them in the rowboat. Today Abby had brought out a folded tarp and her rain gear. It was going to rain before she got back. 'Are you okay?' she asked Christina before she pushed off.

'Yes, of course. I'll start reading advertising copy. I'll be fine.' She looked frightened at being left again, as if Abby might strand her, or might have an accident and be taken to a hospital or something. But whatever she feared, she feared the boat and the water more, and she had not even suggested that she go with Abby. She would keep Spook with her, she had agreed. Spook clearly wanted to get into the boat with Abby.

It was very cold, perhaps snow weather instead of rain, Abby thought, sniffing the air. There were no studded tires at the cabin; she would check the carport, and if there weren't any there, she would buy some and have them put on while she did the Xeroxing. And there was Felicia waiting for her. She would

151

be gone quite a while, she thought gloomily, thinking of Christina going through Jud's files, reading correspondence, old bills, notices of discontinuance of service from utility companies. Abby had hurriedly looked into many file folders and decided to leave them alone. Let Christina get a glimpse of the man Lynne had known, loved, and left. Abby had copied all the correspondence files to disks, and Jud had never kept paper copies of his own letters. Let Christina see the many fan letters, the reviews . . .

There were no studded tires in the carport. She carried the boxes to the van, got in, and started it up, but when she came to the turn to the county road, she headed toward Felicia's cottage. No one was out on the lake; it was too cold and threatening.

Abby loved Felicia's workroom with its smells of paint, varnish, old paper, wax, cinnamon. The cottage had always smelled of cinnamon, she remembered from years past. Today Felicia drew her inside with both hands, embraced her and kissed her cheek. 'My dear child,' she murmured. 'Come in, get warm.'

'I can't stay,' Abby said, stooping to pet the poodles. Daisy and Mae were excited, happy to see her, their stubby tails wagging their entire bodies. 'That agent is alone in the

152

cabin, and I have to go to Bend. Can you come with me? We can talk in the café at the copy shop.'

Felicia nodded. 'Who is she?' She went to the bedroom for her jacket. She was dressed in a heavy sweater and wool pants, boots. The clothes should have looked incongruous with her face so pink and wrinkly, her hair as snow white and curly as the dogs', but she looked entirely natural to Abby. She was putting on a thick plaid jacket when she came back.

'His New York agent. She wants to take his novel back with her, and the short stories, anything I'm willing to let her have.'

'Let me just check the stove. I was going to make us some tea.' Felicia looked inside the kitchen area, shook her finger at the dogs, and said, 'You girls behave yourselves. I won't be long.'

* ★ ★

Abby drove to the copy shop, unloaded the boxes, gave directions about copying, and left Felicia at a table with a carton on another chair, the material Abby had put aside not to be copied, not to be shown to anyone. She took the van to a service station for tires and walked back, and now she sat down next to Felicia and drew in a breath.

153

The building was long and low, three businesses sharing the space, the copy shop with one attendant, several self-service copy machines, and two high-speed, high-volume copiers, both in service with Abby's material. Separated from that section by a counter with office supplies in a display case was the café, four tables, coffeemakers, doughnuts and pastries and sandwiches in cases. Two teenage girls sat talking at one of the tables. Farther on there were more display cases with knick-knacks, a few pieces of handmade jewelry, some local pottery, and other odds and ends. Maxine Rutherford ran the gift shop and the café, and as far back as Abby could remember, she had been there on duty, day after day, year after year.

'Abby,' Maxine said, approaching, 'I'm so sorry about Jud. Are they making any progress yet on the case?'

'I don't know,' Abby said. 'Thanks. Just coffee, please.'

Maxine withdrew, and in a moment brought a mug of coffee, glanced at Felicia questioningly, and left them alone again. Felicia already had a small pot of tea.

Now Felicia leaned forward after a quick glance at the two girls, who were deeply into confidences apparently and paying no attention to anyone else. 'Dear, unless there's an

154

eyewitness, and there isn't, or unless they find someone's fingerprints that shouldn't be at the cabin, the police won't come close to learning who killed Jud.'

Abby stared at the old woman, surprised by the vehemence of her voice, the way she had plunged directly to the point she wanted to make. On the way to Bend, Felicia had asked about Willa Ashford, asked about Lynne, how Abby was holding up, things of little consequence, and Abby had assumed that she just wanted to talk, after all.

'This is all I've been thinking of,' Felicia said. 'It's all I can think of. The police will look for a mysterious stranger, someone like that, and they'll get further and further away from the truth. You're holding the clues, Abby, in that box' — she pointed to the carton on the third chair at their table — 'or in that pile of stuff you're getting copied. That's where the truth is, but the police won't recognize it even if they see it.'

'Willa thinks they suspect her,' Abby said slowly. How much did Felicia know about the way Jud wrote, that he had used real incidents, real people heavily disguised?

'Oh, good Lord!' Felicia said. 'Willa! That's what I mean. They won't get near the truth by themselves. Jud and Willa . . . I think for the first time he was really in love, and she was, too. Willa!'

'She said they were going to be married,' Abby said.

'I believe that,' Felicia said, nodding vigorously. 'He was floating on air for months. But let me tell you what I've been considering. Someone might have suspected that Jud would be writing the truth about him. That implies it was someone very familiar with the way Jud worked, his raw material, and it means that someone had time to look for whatever it was he was afraid of at some point. That narrows it down.'

'Parts of the novel seem to be missing,' Abby said faintly. 'And a disk is missing.'

Felicia nodded again, as if in satisfaction this time. 'But you can see the problem. If you're in one of his novels, you might recognize yourself, some aspect of yourself anyway, but who else would relate that particular incident to you? I saw myself and Herbert clearly, but I don't believe anyone else did. And I saw Joe Beardwell and Joyce after I learned how to read the novels.'

'Did you recognize Teri and Lawrence Frazier?' Abby asked, nearly whispering now.

Felicia drank her tea and refilled her cup, keeping her gaze on the little pot. It took her a long time to answer. 'I saw them,' she said finally. 'Changed, circumstances different, the witness different. Lawrence knows; he always knew that Jud saw whatever happened that day. Even before the novel was published, he had to sell out, move away.'

They became silent when the girls stood up, put on jackets and hats, and left. A blast of cold air swept through the building when they opened the door. Maxine moved down to the gift shop section and busied herself there, and they were alone in the café.

Abby was considering what Felicia had said: someone who had had time to learn whatever it was that Jud was writing. Someone who had access to the cabin when Jud was absent, who knew what he was looking for, not just engaging in a blind search that night. Someone who had known about the handgun in the drawer. Who knew about Spook and the dog door.

'But there's still the problem of how anyone got there and out again,' she said after the long silence.

Felicia waved that away. 'If we can find out who, then we will find out how,' she said firmly.

'What do you mean?'

'Abby, I want to help find out who did that. And I can. I know how to read his novels, I know the people involved. Jud was smart. He built a resort at the lake and brought in a lot of people from all over the world, with their intrigues and schemes, their wounds, their ambitions, but the people he really wrote about were people he knew well. He saw things, heard things, and didn't forget. You've been away for a long time, ten years now, busy making your own life, you might not even know some of the people he used in his work. And the way he went back and forth in time, things that happened when you were a child, before you were born even, turn up in new scenarios. I want to read the novel. I want to find out who did that to him.'

Abby stared at her, this old woman with her curly white hair, whose fingers could turn a lump of clay into a dragon or a bird or a person so effortlessly that it looked like magic, and she realized that although she had known Felicia Shaeffer all her life, she did not know her at all. Her eyes were bright blue, and so piercing, Abby felt as if her brain cells were being examined, her blood vessels visible, her thoughts tangible. Felicia had said that she and her dead husband were in one of Jud's novels, but Abby had not known that; she had not recognized them as a couple in the cast of characters, the parade of scenes, the play of incidents.

'He was more than just a friend,' Felicia said. 'He was sometimes a brother, sometimes a son, a confessor, a confidant. More than just a friend. I want to find his murderer and see him die for doing that to Jud.'

Slowly Abby nodded. 'So do I,' she said. 'But I can't leave the novel out here. I have to compare it with disks, try to find the missing sections.'

'Not here. I'll come to town and stay at the condo. I can come to your house every day.'

'No,' Abby said quickly. She remembered Brice's words, urging her not to confide in Willa or Felicia, and she had talked to both of them. And now she would join forces with Felicia. They would work together on the novel, on the fragments. 'Where is your condo?'

They were still talking, planning, when the attendant from the copy shop came to the table to say he was done. 'It's a great big stack of boxes,' he said. 'Help you carry them to your car.'

'I have to go get it,' Abby said. She added a box of floppy disks to the finished work, paid the man with a credit card, and didn't even blink at the size of the bill. She left to retrieve the van, with the new tires in place, then collected Felicia and the boxes, and headed for the supermarket, and finally back to the lake. Rain mixed with snow began to fall as she drove. At Felicia's cottage, they clasped hands briefly and Abby said, 'I'll call you on Monday. Be careful driving in.'

10

By the time Abby reached the cabin, rain was coming down hard, driven by a cutting wind. She was wrapped in a water-proof hooded poncho, and the boxes and bag of groceries were all protected by the tarp, but the wind was very cold and the rain stung her face; she was chilled when she pulled up to the ledge. Christina was there with Jud's oversize umbrella. Although there wasn't enough wind to create real waves, the dark water had a chop, and now and then it sloshed up over the ledge, over Christina's feet. Spook didn't seem to notice that it was raining; she stood near the boat, wagging her tail wildly, spraying water all about.

They got everything inside the cabin. 'I left the originals in the van,' Abby said. 'Not much point in lugging them across, then back in the morning.' She had also left the private papers locked up in the van.

'Never mind that,' Christina said as Abby took off the dripping poncho, then hung it up on a peg in the kitchen. 'You're freezing. Sit down.' She hurried across the cabin and pulled a throw off the couch, came back and draped it over Abby's shoulders, drew it in close around her, and nearly pushed her down into a chair. 'I made coffee. It's hot, in the carafe. Just sit still and get warm.'

Another side of the woman, Abby thought, one she had not glimpsed before. Christina brought coffee and then knelt down to take off Abby's wet boots. Her own feet were still wet, but she was paying no attention to that. 'I'll do it,' Abby said in protest, and pulled off her own boots. Christina picked them up and placed them on a mat by the door. She hurried out to the bedroom, came back with Abby's fuzzy slippers, and put them on her.

'You should dry your own feet,' Abby said.

Christina looked down in surprise, then hurried out again, this time to return with her own slippers on, holding her wet boots. They were very handsome — snakeskin? alligator? Something decorative, and impractical for this part of the world.

'I just want to make sure nothing happens to you before you get us back to dry land,' Christina said lightly. She put her boots next to Abby's, then got herself a cup of coffee and sat down at the table.

Abby smiled at her, and Christina shrugged.

'When Jud came to New York the first time, right after he sold *Siren Rock*,' Christina said meditatively, 'his editor suggested he should get an agent and gave him my name. He called, we met, and it was like finding an adolescent boy in my charge suddenly. He was so eager to see everything, understand everything. He wanted to take the tourist boat around Manhattan, something I'd never even done before, and I'd lived there most of my life. I showed him around for a week, every afternoon somewhere different, museums, the Statue of Liberty, library, my favorite deli . . . bookstores. He was insatiable for books.'

She was gazing past Abby with a distant look. 'He made me see my own city through his eyes. I still don't know how he did that. Then he left. I felt like a mother must feel when her only child goes off to college.' She was not drinking the coffee, just holding a mug with both hands, as if to warm them.

'He came back with the next novel, and he insisted that I read it while he waited. I said I couldn't read it in the office with the phone ringing, people coming by, so much distraction. I said I would read it overnight and call him, but he insisted that I had to read it immediately. We went to my apartment, and he read the newspaper, magazines, manuscripts, whatever he picked up, while I read his novel. He made dinner while I read. I

163

started to cry. The first novel was good. More than that, it was very good, but the second one, *The Black Shore*, it made me cry. And I fell in love with the writer. Before, he had been a companion, a pal, like a ward almost, shy and tentative; suddenly he was Jud the writer. He knew what he had; he was exultant. His excitement couldn't be contained, and neither could mine.'

She became silent, gazing at the black lake beyond the cabin.

'Yesterday, you cried again,' Abby said softly.

Christina nodded. 'Yes. The new novel is the best thing he ever wrote. Even if it's never finished, just as it stands, it's beautiful, powerful, his best work yet.'

'It's finished,' Abby said fiercely. 'He told Willa it was finished, he just had to arrange the pieces, discard early drafts, put it in final shape. Whoever stole the disk, and the pages, whoever turned off his computer didn't touch the hard drive. It's there, and I'll find it. We'll get it together and get it published. I promise you.'

* * *

The next morning they left the cabin early, in a driving rain. It was a nightmare boat ride across the water for Christina, but she helped with the boxes, held an umbrella over Abby as much as possible as she loaded the van, helped her drag the boat into the shelter of the shed. She didn't complain when Spook shook water on them both.

Abby had warned her that there might be snow on the pass over the mountains, and there was, not a threatening snow, not this early, just messy enough to slow traffic to a crawl and turn the world into a surreal black and gray landscape with startling patches of white in unexpected places. On the west side of the pass, the snow gave way to rain again, the world became green again; it was still raining when they came to a stop in the driveway at Abby's house.

'If there's someplace where I can change, repack my bags,' Christina said hesitantly. 'I want to put the manuscript, all that other stuff in the carry-on. I'll put clothes in the cartons and check them through.'

'Upstairs, a spare bedroom,' Abby said, and led the way into the house, where Brice met them with an anxious expression.

'They kept saying snow in the mountains,' he said, holding Abby close. 'It scares me when you're up there in the snow.'

'Just in the pass,' she said. 'And not much.

We have a lot to bring in. Volunteers accepted.'

★ ★ ★

Later, at the airport in Eugene, Abby helped Christina unload her baggage and get it into a cart. There was an awkward pause as they regarded each other. Christina was once again the stylish New Yorker, her makeup perfect, her hair perfect; Abby felt like a bum in her old jeans and boots, her poncho. Christina held out her hand and they shook hands solemnly. 'He said you were always the most terrific kid in the world,' Christina said. 'I think you're still a terrific kid. Thanks.'

Abby drove home through the driving rain and let herself in; Spook greeted her as if she had been gone for months. Brice came down the stairs as she was getting her poncho off.

'You really look exhausted,' he said, studying her face. 'You're trying to do too much, too soon. Sit down and we'll have a quiet drink and talk.'

He had a fire going in the living room; she sank down gratefully on the couch and leaned her head back. Brice went to the kitchen and returned with a tray that held cheese, crackers, and Irish coffee.

'She's the most brittle woman I've ever

seen,' he said, sitting next to Abby on the couch. He put one of the cups in her hand. 'What all did she take back with her?'

'A copy of the novel manuscript, and a lot of short stories and essays. Some go back nearly thirty years.' The coffee was very good, not too strong with Irish, heavy whipped cream on top, sweet. Just what she needed. They were quiet for a time, sipping the coffee, eating cheese.

'Is the novel finished, publishable?' he asked when she put her cup down, empty.

'She said it's very good. He told Willa it was finished, so it just needs piecing together, we think. She's going to work on it in New York, and I'll work on it here. Between us, we'll get it in shape.'

Brice reached for a piece of cheese and then said slowly, 'You've talked to Willa? I thought . . . Never mind. The police are asking a lot of questions about her. She told them that Jud proposed. They asked me if I believed her story. I had to say no. I don't believe it. And if she's lying about that . . . '

She felt very tired. The warmth of the house, the fire, the Irish in the coffee, had relaxed her; she wanted to go to sleep. She had forgotten that she had not yet told him about her walk with Willa. Sunday night, when she arrived home, Brice had been

167

furious at the office secretary, who had put a memo in his in-box that a client was due Monday morning and had not included his file for Brice to review. He had gone back to the office to find it himself. All they had talked about on Monday night was Jud's contract; Brice had been stunned by the amount of the option, fifty thousand dollars, and the purchase price if they made the movie: one and a half million. Tuesday? She could no longer remember why she had not brought up her conversations with Willa, only that she hadn't. Then she recalled his anger because the police had gone to the office that day and asked his associates questions. That had not been a good time to bring up Willa, either. Well, she thought, now it was out in the open. 'Willa doesn't lie,' she said. 'Why can't you accept her word?'

'She wasn't his type,' Brice said after a moment. 'Honey, you love people so much, you're blinded. Your father wasn't the type to settle down with one woman. And Willa wouldn't accept less than that finally, no more than I would, or you would. But you can't see that affair the way the rest of the world sees it.'

'You hardly even know her,' Abby said. 'What makes you so sure what she would settle for?'

'I know her well enough to know that she's steady, responsible, that she has a lot of self-respect. Like your mother. Like you.'

'Like you,' Abby said, trying to keep her anger in check.

'Yes, like me. Darling, face it, Jud wasn't like us. I'm not saying bad or evil or anything like that, just different.'

'And you think that this steady, stable, responsible woman went out there and shot him dead,' Abby said harshly.

Brice flushed slightly. 'Yes, I do. I think Willa killed your father because he told her he was going away as soon as the novel was wrapped up. He hinted as much last summer, remember?'

She shook her head. 'No, I don't remember anything like that.'

'He said there was a lot of world he hadn't seen yet, he had a lot of catching up to do, starting with southern France and Italy, that he needed a rest from words, from books, and a lot of looking to do.'

'He and Willa planned to go to Italy in April,' she said, remembering the conversation he was talking about. They had been on the back ledge; her feet had been in the water, they had all been swimming. The basalt had absorbed a lot of heat, hot under them, the water cold on her feet.

169

'He didn't say that,' Brice said.

'She did.'

Later that day she and Jud had gone to visit Felicia. Brice had begged off; he had said he wanted to nap, but she had thought that he simply didn't want to spend any time with Felicia, who, he had said once, was a terrific bore. Jud had warned her that she would get sunburned if she didn't put a shirt on, and she had worn one of his over her bathing suit. She blinked hard, trying to erase the memory of rowing her father across the lake to Felicia's cottage. He had laughed and said she had lost the touch, she was getting soft.

'What else did the police have to say?'

'That lieutenant wants to see you tomorrow. He brought a list of people who had signed in at the campsites, to see if I recognized any names. I didn't. And he had a picture, a drawing of a guy who flew into Bend that night. I never saw him before. He wants you to give him a call first thing in the morning.'

'Now they think someone might have flown to Bend, walked to the lake, swum across and shot my father,' she said scornfully, thinking of Felicia's mysterious stranger.

'I don't know what in hell they think,' Brice said. 'But not that; it's just another one of the lieutenant's loose ends. They're more interested in Willa.' He looked at the fire then. 'What they're suggesting is that she could have driven up Friday afternoon, all the way up to the cabin. During the night they had a quarrel, he signed off, and she shot him and then searched for whatever he had written about her, and the next morning she drove back down and out.'

Abby's mouth had gone dry as he spoke. Willa had been questioned for more than two hours on Monday; she had been badly shaken afterward and had said practically nothing about the session. Abby shook her head. 'I don't believe it! I'll never believe it!'

Brice turned to her, his face stiff in a frown, his expression remote. 'The point is, you don't know,' he said intensely. 'They don't, either. But it could have been like that. I think you shouldn't be working at the museum for the next few weeks, not until this thing is settled, done with, until they come up with answers. And, for the love of God, don't spend time with her, tell her anything you suspect, confide in any way. Not yet.'

Abby stood up, her arms folded tightly against her body. Before she could say anything, Brice shook his head and motioned her back down. She remained standing.

'Honey, listen, if they clear her, if that guy

171

who flew into Bend did it, they'll nab him eventually, and I'll apologize. Maybe he was an extortionist, a blackmailer. Maybe he's still hanging around. No one knows. But, Abby, you have to take the suspicion of Willa's involvement seriously, consider it a possibility, and be careful. That lieutenant, Caldwell, he's taking it seriously, and he's no fool.'

He leaned back on the couch and closed his eyes for a moment; he looked bone tired and very young, and frightened. 'Lieutenant Caldwell suggested that you should be very careful. Honey, you should keep away from all of this, don't speculate, don't voice your suspicions, just get on with those sympathy notes, see if you can put the novel together, do whatever else you have piled up. Start thinking about what you want to do with a lot of money. Make plans. Next week you'll get the Hollywood contract, and that's going to take time to read, to study. You don't need the museum job on top of everything else. If you decide to go back to it in a year or two, or just a month or two, it'll be there. But keep away from Willa for now. Please.'

'Put it out of mind, get on with life, let the police handle everything,' she said bitterly. 'That's what you're really saying, isn't it? You think I give a shit about the money, the contract, plans for next year? I haven't given any of that shit a single thought. All I can think of is that someone shot and killed my father! Can't you grasp that? Someone killed him, and if there's anything I can do to help find out who that was, I'll do it. If I need to talk to Willa, or Felicia, or anyone else to try to sort it out for myself, I'll talk to her. If I get an idea — *speculate* — and if that speculation seems valid, I'll tell the police. I'm not going to back off and wait and see what happens. I can't!'

'Goddamn it, Abby! That's all you can do! You start prying, meddling, and you put yourself in danger! That's what you can accomplish.' He jumped up and went to the hearth, poked at the fire viciously, then swung around to face her. He was very pale. 'Let me tell you what I've been seeing happen to you. First a kind of deep shock that I was afraid you might not snap out of, might need medical care for, even an institution. And now some kind of obsessive behavior that's even scarier. You're becoming obsessed, even delusional if you believe you can do the police work. They come up with a likely theory, and you simply dismiss it without a second thought. For more than two years you and Willa were distant, hardly even friends, and now suddenly you believe every word she utters! That's irrational, Abby, and it's scary.'

She turned her back and started to walk away stiffly.

'Damn it, Abby, this needs saying, and you need to listen! You had a rift with your father; everyone does sooner or later. You had to cut that string, if not over one thing, then something else would have come along. Kids have to cut the strings! I did. You did. We all have to. You couldn't keep jumping into the car and running out there every time he snapped his fingers. You know that and you're denying it, and you're letting your guilt drive you into some kind of paranoid thinking.'

'Who the fuck appointed you to be my shrink?' she cried furiously, jerking around to face him again. 'Just back off! You're not my keeper.'

'You need a keeper!' Suddenly he stiffened, staring at her. Slowly he replaced the poker he was still holding. 'Christ!' he whispered. 'He's doing it now, after his death. He couldn't do it alive, and now he's doing it, coming between us, separating us.'

'He never tried to come between us!'

'He did, in a thousand little ways. You were blind to his manipulations, his little digs. He never liked me; from the day we first met, he had it in for me, and you were blind to that. I never said a word, I couldn't. Your fixation was too deep, and it didn't matter, not really;

as long as we were together, you were happy with me, our life, the rest didn't matter. Let him dig and poke, I thought. You were my wife, we loved each other, and you would come to see him one day, see the truth about him.'

Abby shook her head. 'It wasn't like that,' she said angrily. 'He was willing to accept you; you were the one who was judgmental, too disapproving of him, of his lifestyle, living out alone like that. Before you knew anything about his past, the women, any of it, you were disapproving. The first time I took you out to the cabin, you said, He's strange, isn't he, not quite all there. I said he was reclusive, people who lived out like that tended to be reclusive, but so what? And the time we went up to the hot spring and you were so shocked because people took off all their clothes. Shocked that he had allowed me to go there ever. He thought that was funny. For you to be that shocked. He said with a body like yours you should strip to the buff most of the time. You acted like a preacher warding off an unrepentant sinner, and he thought that was funny.'

'Everything I take seriously, he thought was funny,' Brice said. 'He mocked everything I did and said.'

'Well, you really never said much to him,

175

did you?' She heard her voice become sharper and drew in a breath, then said in a more conciliatory tone, 'I can't remember a real conversation between you two ever. He didn't give a rat's ass about money, finances, and you turned mute when it came to books or art. I wasn't blind to what was happening. There it was, and it was okay. I could love you both, different as you were; I could and did love you both. I never expected or wanted you to be more like him, or for him to be like you. All right, you disapproved of my father, so did I a lot of times. I could accept that. But he never did or said a thing to try to come between us, never. He was generous to us, and he left us strictly alone. No gratuitous advice, or questions, or interference of any sort.'

'If I was out of line, I'm sorry,' Brice said, his face wooden, his voice almost toneless.

'Not *if*,' she snapped.

He hesitated, then nodded. 'I'm sorry. Let's just say we saw the same things and interpreted them different ways. Leave it at that. And, Abby, we're having the first quarrel we've ever had, and it's about him. At least you can agree to that, can't you?'

'I'm not sure it's about him,' she said slowly. 'I don't know what it's about.' She started to walk toward the foyer. 'But let's leave it alone. Is there anything in the house for dinner? I don't want to go out. I'm too grubby and in no mood to get dolled up. I'd rather have a pizza or something later on. Right now I'm going to start hauling that stuff upstairs.'

Brice closed the fire screen. 'Pizza's okay. I'm going up, too. I'll carry those boxes.'

★ ★ ★

Her room had become a cluttered mess, she thought disgustedly after Brice set down the third carton and withdrew in silence. Novel, short stories, the bits and pieces of Jud's life, her life, everyone's life in another box. The box of notes she had already written and not mailed yet, and the other box with the sympathy notes she had not answered . . . And now a stack of computer disks, and she knew there wasn't space on her computer to hold the contents. She was still too angry, and too tired, to start sorting, organizing, putting away . . . She sat down at her desk and closed her eyes.

No one ever mentioned how exhausted the survivors would be, she thought. In novels and movies they simply picked up the pieces and got on with things. How would Jud have handled that fight downstairs? she wondered then. And her eyes jerked open. Had he written about their fight over Willa? Had he seen her point of view? Had he written himself as villain? Her gaze fixed on the box that held his unpublished and unpublishable scraps, scenes, his camcorder reports. Their fight had been about Willa. Had he already been in love with her two years ago? What had he written about Willa?

Suddenly it occurred to her that her fight with Brice had started out with Willa; that was the root of it. Willa. Twice now. The only really bitter fight she'd ever had with her father, about Willa. The only fight at all she had ever had with Brice, about Willa.

She wondered again how Jud would have written about her fight with Brice. He would have seen both sides, she told herself, and tried to make her mind work the way Jud's mind had. Brice's side: worried about her, frightened that she had been more than a little crazy for a week, more frightened that she seemed oblivious to what he believed was the truth, that she could be in danger if she meddled in police matters, that Willa was a prime suspect and could be dangerous. As aware as she was that if anyone fell into the lake, that person could die; the water was so cold now that hypothermia would be swift following the shock of a plunge into ice water.

Worried about her driving in the snow; she had not told him about the studded tires, but that wouldn't have alleviated his worry all that much. He always said it was the other guy you had to be afraid of when it snowed, a maniac losing control, going into a skid, hitting you.

And, of course, he was a survivor, too, probably almost as tired as she was. And the stress of having the police suspect him, as, of course, they did. Motive: money. What else? Her money, but his, too, as far as the police were concerned. Having the police check his alibi, question his associates, check the motel he had stayed in, everything.

Then, his work. This was always a bad time of year, starting to prepare the annual reports for the clients, on top of the day-to-day routine. Preparing for the annual audit, making sure everything was in order. And this year was particularly bad, as he had said, with the market doing insane gyrations and clients who were anxious and demanding.

From his point of view, she was the one being unsympathetic and unyielding, unreasonable at a time when they both were under such tremendous stress that they needed each other's support, not withdrawal and contention. She bit her lip as the realization hit her that this was probably how Jud had worked through so many things, by seeing both sides clearly.

She sat thinking, unmoving for a long time, and finally decided that it didn't really matter if they believed different things; it had never mattered in the past, and it didn't now. They were different in almost all ways, but neither of them had cared. She could never believe Willa had killed Jud, and he did believe it was a possibility. Since neither of them knew anything concrete about Jud's death, there was no reason to talk about it. All they could do was speculate, and then quarrel. So, leave it alone. He wanted her to stop working at the museum, and gazing at the many boxes of papers scattered about the room, she agreed, she should quit for now. Attend to matters at hand. And he would have to accept that she was seeing Felicia now and then. No reason to say every day, she told herself, but neither would she pretend she wasn't seeing her. Compromise, she told herself. Take the first step, or the anger that had arisen would deepen and become too ugly to deal with later. What she would not do was let it simmer just below the surface the way her fight with Jud had simmered for two years. She nodded at her own reasonableness and left the study.

It was after six-thirty when she tapped on

his door, then opened it. 'Pizza? Anchovies?'

He looked startled, almost disbelieving. It was a standing joke: he had said once that anchovies on pizza made him want to throw up. She always suggested them. She grinned at him, and he got up from his desk, crossed to her, and put his arm around her shoulder, and together they went downstairs to discuss pizzas.

11

Waiting for Lieutenant Caldwell to arrive the next morning, Abby went over the list of errands she had to do that day: drop by the museum and pick up the few things she had left there. She had called Willa and told her she wouldn't be able to keep working for a while. She had to buy a laptop computer. Knowing she couldn't afford it, she had decided to use a credit card, and by the time the charge appeared, she would have something ready to tell Brice. In six months she might become a rich bitch, she thought darkly, but today she was broke. On reflection, it seemed this had been her life as long as she could remember, always something coming in tomorrow, seldom enough today. She returned to her mental list. She had called Felicia and planned to go there from the computer store. Then grocery shop. It was time to start cooking again.

Lieutenant Caldwell arrived promptly at ten, as he had said he would. He looked different, she thought, admitting him, and realized it was because he was wearing a very nice business suit, dark gray wool, even a necktie, and he was carrying a well-worn briefcase. He looked like an attorney.

He petted Spook, who had come to sniff him, renewing acquaintances. 'How are you?' he asked Abby. 'Feeling a little better, I hope.'

'I am,' she said. 'Can I get you coffee?'

'Thanks,' he said. 'I'd love some. I hate that drive from Salem. I hate I-Five,' he added. 'Is the mutt adapting to city life okay?'

'She's fine,' Abby said coldly, and turned to go to the kitchen. The lieutenant followed.

'Maybe we could sit in here and talk,' he said, gazing about the kitchen, the dinette table. 'I'm a kitchen kind of person at heart.'

She shrugged and started to make coffee. He sat down at the table, opened his briefcase and pulled out a folder, then put the briefcase on the floor.

'Just a few things I'd like to show you, talk over with you,' he said. 'I don't want to take up too much of your time, and I'm due in court right after the lunch break.'

She looked at him in surprise. An attorney going to court; she had been right. 'This case, my father's murder?'

'No, no, nothing to do with it. In my work, things sort of pile up, old cases, new ones. This is an old one.'

She came to the table as the coffee dripped

through the machine. 'It takes a couple of minutes.'

'Yeah, I know. Okay, first, this drawing. It's an artist's drawing from a description we got. Familiar to you?'

She studied the drawing he placed on the table before her. Male, long blond hair, two gold studs in one ear . . . the man Brice had told her about. She shook her head. 'He flew into Bend that night?' she asked. 'Didn't he have to give his name or something? I didn't know there were flights to Bend at night.'

'No commercial flights. This was a private delivery company. You know, steaks from New York, orchids from Hawaii. Special wedding dress from Chicago. Things like that. Pay enough, and you can get delivery on the same day of almost anything from almost anywhere. Sometimes the pilots make a few extra bucks hauling a passenger. Against company policy, but the pilots are underpaid and the company turns a blind eye to anything they can't afford to see. So anyway, this guy knew about the regular Friday-night delivery to Bend, and he offered the pilot two hundred bucks for a ride. No name asked for, none given.' He sighed and moved the picture aside.

Abby went to pour the coffee and brought the filled mugs to the table. He took his

184

black, he said, and thanked her. 'But you should add some cream and sugar to yours,' he added. 'And eat a doughnut or something.'

She felt her cheeks grow hot. 'What else do you have?' she asked crossly.

'A list of people who reserved campsites for that Friday. Fourteen sites in use Friday, more folks drifted in on Saturday, but we passed on them.' He handed the list to her.

She scanned the names, then started over and considered each one. Finally she shook her head. 'But what about the others in the groups? This one says a party of four, or six in this one.'

'Another list,' he said. 'We got all their names.'

The second list was longer, but as fruitless as the first had been.

'Okay,' he said, putting the lists aside with the picture. 'It's a wash. We thought it might be. Pete Tolman, you know him, the kayak guy?' She nodded. 'He swears he was the last one to leave the finger, to leave the lake just when it was turning dark, and he and his gang were at the shore loading up to go back to Bend until after dark.'

'Why are you bothering with all this if you know it's pointless?'

'Making sure it's pointless,' he said mildly.

'Tying up loose ends when and where we can.'

'You checked my friends, I suppose, made sure I was at the coast?'

'Sure, and the manager of the place where you stayed,' he said. 'They verify you were up until nearly two. Couldn't make it work,' he said with a slight grin. 'And we checked your husband's associates, and the motel where he stayed. Again, a long drive, three and a half hours at a minimum, and only if you hit the gas hard and never let up. You guys were the first two we checked out. Usually it's a family matter,' he added, rummaging in the file folder. 'Next, moving on, the cashier's checks. Take a look, will you? See, the first column is what he was paid and when for his novels. The second column is when he withdrew the cashier's checks and the amount. And the last column is a list of trips that followed immediately after he got the checks.'

She felt her brain go numb as she stared at the figures. Then at the trips. Each time he got a cashier's check, he had gone to San Francisco.

'See,' the lieutenant said, as if aware that she was not really tracking the numbers, 'his first novel, published in 1989, only made him twenty-six thousand, minus the agent's ten percent. So roughly twenty-three thousand, spread over two years. Not much to live on for two years. But he managed to get four thousand in a cashier's check in 'ninety-one, and take off.

'The next time, he did a lot better financially, but again, not as great as the numbers make it look. His agent explained that; although the figure adds up to over three hundred thousand, he got about half that after taxes and commission. And that was over a three-year period. Say one hundred seventy-five thousand. And over that period three checks that came to forty-one thousand, and ten grand to you for a wedding present.'

He stood up, holding his coffee mug. 'You mind if I help myself? You want some more?'

She shook her head, staring at the figures before her. Over the past three years her father had drawn four more cashier's checks. Each time he had then gone to San Francisco.

Caldwell returned to the table and regarded her soberly. 'Mrs. Connors, who did he know in San Francisco?'

'I don't know. He never traveled until recently; there wasn't any money for traveling until recently. When he got out of the army, he went to Santa Rosa to stay with his parents for a few weeks, and then up to San Francisco, where he met my mother. They were married and came back here together. He was only twenty when they married. That's the only time I know of that he was even in San Francisco until a few years ago when he went on a book promotion tour.'

'He was in Vietnam, wasn't he? A nineteen-year-old kid in Vietnam. Could he have met a girl then, had a child with her?'

Brice's theory, she thought bitterly. Another family somewhere, a child he had to support. She shook her head hard. 'He wouldn't have kept it a secret,' she said. 'He wasn't like that. He acknowledged everything, accepted responsibility for everything he did, even things he wasn't really responsible for. He didn't try to hide anything.'

'Everyone has secrets,' Caldwell said. 'I've learned that over the years. Everyone has something lurking in the background. And he used that money for something. Not into offshore wells, heavy drugs, or racehorses, was he?'

'No! I don't know what those checks were for!'

He took the paper back and gazed at it for a moment, then with a sigh placed it on top of the other papers he had put aside. 'Let's pretend for a moment that he did have another family somewhere, just for the sake of a theory. Okay?'

'It's not okay! He didn't.'

'Well, I'll pretend. How would that have affected Ms. Ashford, if she found out?'

Brice again, she thought angrily. 'I won't speculate on that because it's not true, or even close to the truth. They were going to get married.'

'Can you give me the name of a single person who knew that before she mentioned it herself?'

'No, I can't. Felicia Shaeffer knows it's true, even if no one told her. He intended to tell me that day. That's what his call was about. He wouldn't have told anyone else before he told me.' She jumped up and went to the patio door and stood with her back to him, seeing nothing outside. 'You can't place her in the cabin that night, you can't get her in and then back out, and you know it.' She swung around. 'When you drove up there, were there little trees on the roadway? Did you see any knocked over?'

'Good,' he said. 'Good thinking. The answer is no trees knocked down until I got there. One of the reasons I wanted to drive up was to see the condition of the road. Afraid we did a lot of damage, set back the reversion to wilderness quite a bit that day.'

'But Brice . . . ' She stopped. 'You encouraged him to speculate that someone might have gotten in by car. Even when you knew it couldn't have been like that, you let him think it.'

'I encourage everyone to speculate,' he said apologetically. 'Never know when someone will come up with an idea you might not have thought of yourself. Why don't you speculate just a little?'

'Dr. Beardwell,' she said after a moment. 'He knows the dogs, he treats them, gives them shots; they wouldn't bark at him. He could have gone over and back.'

'You know better,' he chided. 'Apparently everyone knows his gang goes out there to play cards and get smashed. Every other weekend, regular as tides, that's what he does. And what he did that night.'

She did know that. He never drank even a glass of wine between his bouts with the bottle, but when he was off, when his partner was on call, he got flat-on-his-face drunk.

'All right. Try this. Someone called Dad, and he picked him up and rowed him to the cabin. After he shot my father, he swam back to the other side, not to Coop's ramp, up where you were looking at the tree roots.'

'Better,' he said. 'Of course, the water temperature was down below fifty, maybe too cold for a middle-of-the-night swim?'

'He took a wet suit with him, like scuba divers use.'

'Better yet. And carried his clothes in his backpack?'

'You didn't find any trace of a boat being dragged through the woods, did you?' she asked then.

He shook his head. 'Nope, not a sign.'

She returned to sit at the table, then said slowly, 'In the past, before Dad got serious with Willa Ashford, now and then a woman would go to the cabin in the daytime, stay overnight, and leave the next morning. In her own boat. It could have happened that night, and when he said no, he wasn't interested, she shot him, then rowed out as soon as there was enough light.'

'Names?' he asked mildly.

She shook her head. 'I don't know who. But I could tell that a woman had stayed overnight a few times when I went up there.' She remembered a cruel joke she had overheard years ago. If you had a missing wife, check under Jud's loft to see if she had parked a rowboat or a canoe there before you called the sheriff. Her fairy cave, she had thought miserably; she never had gone into it again after hearing that. 'She could have put a canoe under the loft.'

'That space goes back a ways, doesn't it? Ten, twelve feet?'

She nodded. 'And it would have been deeply shadowed, impossible to see if anything was there unless you got close and really looked.' She was seeing the fairy cave again, the ledges that made up the floor, stair steps to the farthest end, sometimes a dungeon, or a tower, where she had placed a foam mattress on the highest shelf, with just enough space to lie down and reach up to touch the planking over her head and pretend she was aboard a spaceship, or a sailing vessel going to an exotic land, a stowaway in hiding, Rapunzel waiting for her prince . . .

'Well,' he said after a moment, 'I asked you to speculate. You sure opened the door to a lot more possibilities, didn't you?' He grinned and said, 'I thought you might have mentioned Halburtson.'

'You're out of your mind!'

'Probably.' He did not sound happy as his gaze came to rest on the list of camping parties. 'But someone in one of these groups . . .'

Abby watched him suspiciously, afraid he was simply lulling her into believing she had given him a valid idea, the way he had lulled Brice into believing Willa could have driven up the mountain road.

He shook himself, then asked, 'Did you and Ms. Maas read the novel manuscript? Is it all there?'

'I haven't read it yet. She said parts seem to be missing, but she can't be sure until she tries to put it in order and then reads it again.'

'That's what our guy is finding. We're beginning to think that no one in the department is going to be able to put the novel pieces together right. We're barely literate up there, much less literary experts. Our guy keeps complaining that a writer should have an outline, notes, something like that. But if he did, we haven't found them.'

'He didn't. He never outlined or made notes.' He just had a huge stack of raw material, camcorder records, to sift through, she added silently.

'Well, I guess that's all I was after now,' he said. 'I'll leave the picture and those names with you. Look through that stuff now and then, let it sink into the back of your head, and maybe you'll recall something. Try to imagine that man with slightly different hair, shorter, darker, longer. Like that. And without the ear studs. He doesn't look anything like Matthew Petrie, does he?'

'Good heavens! No! I never saw that face before, I'm sure of it. But, Lieutenant, it doesn't make sense that a stranger flew into town just to kill my father! If no one in Bend recognized him, he must be a stranger to the area.'

He stood up and said reflectively, 'Well, not many people hang out at the airport that time of night. You know, we were talking about speculations. Here's another one. Someone could have hired him to go there, could have told him about the dog, the dog door, the gun, everything.'

She stared at him, aghast. 'You're talking about a . . . a hit man? A paid assassin?'

'Speculating, Mrs. Connors. Just speculating. But remember, there's a lot of money unaccounted for, a hundred forty-five thousand to be exact.' His look now was sympathetic. 'You know what the title of the new novel was?'

She shook her head.

'The file is labeled GUILT.'

'That doesn't mean anything. He hardly ever started with a title. It was the last thing he did most of the time. That probably was just the working title.'

He shrugged. 'If you come across anything in his papers or the manuscript that you think is relevant, I hope you'll let us in on it.' He started toward the hall to the front door. 'I can let myself out.' Then he paused and turned to her. 'If you recognize any of those names, or that face, or find anything in the papers, Mrs. Connors, I think you'd better not mention it to anyone. Or if anyone approaches you for a large sum of money, the next payment, maybe, just give me a call. Anytime, day or night. A message will get to me.'

★ ★ ★

She continued to sit at the table for a long time after he left; he had been warning her to be careful, exactly as Brice had warned her. Don't talk, don't tell anyone if she found anything incriminating in the novel. She felt benumbed, unable to move, to think. A hit man! Next payment! All that money! GUILT.

12

When Abby went to the museum later, she met Willa in her office and told her that she and Felicia were going to spend time together and find the missing pieces of the novel, put it all in order, see if they could find a clue about who had shot Jud.

'Let me help,' Willa said desperately. 'Please, Abby, let me help.'

Abby hesitated a moment. Slowly she said, 'You know he wrote about all of us, the people he knew. You might find yourself . . .'

'Don't you think I know that? My God, Abby, the police think I did it! Maybe there's something in there to show them, to prove I'm not lying.' Her voice dropped to a whisper. 'Maybe there's something that no one except me will see, something that only I will understand . . .'

Abby nodded. That was how it worked much of the time. No one on the outside could see what he had really been saying, only the one person who had been there, had heard the words, seen the expressions, could read the hidden text. Willa looked ill, she realized, haggard, as if she had not slept enough for weeks. She had lost her father, Abby thought then, but Willa had lost her future. She embraced the older woman, and it was settled. Willa would help with the novel.

Abby bought the laptop computer, made another copy of the novel manuscript, and took it to Felicia's town house; they planned for her to be there daily after Brice went to the office. Willa would go after work, and Felicia would work at it off and on during the day and evening. Abby hadn't told Brice about the computer yet, or about the other things Jud had written that she was not willing to share with anyone else, and she would not tell him that Willa was involved in any way. His fear for her, Abby, was too real, too immediate for her to add to it in any way.

She began making dinners again, hastily prepared meals that did not require much thought. Brice never complained about meals; he said he had been a bachelor for so long, any home-cooked food was like ambrosia.

After dinner each night she went to her study to work on the notes of condolence, she told him, and to sort more of the papers. He took that without complaint also; he had seen the boxes of papers and knew they had to be sorted, but as the days passed, he began to show an irritability that manifested itself in unexpected ways. He complained about Spook, always wanting in or out. He complained about Christina Maas: Where was the goddamn movie contract? What was she doing? And what were the cops doing? Nothing! They must have enough to make an arrest, to move forward. He complained about people she had never heard of, clients, she assumed, and about his workload with year-end reports coming up, and the annual audit, and did she remember to take his gray suit to the cleaners, and the house was starting to look like a teenage hangout.

Well, that was true, she admitted to herself; she was not as neat as he was and tended to leave a sweater on a chair, or her shoes in the living room, and for weeks she had not dusted, or vacuumed, or done anything else about housework. Tomorrow, she promised herself, she would clean things up a bit. Then she forgot when she got involved once more in comparing the disks with the hard drive. She found the missing pieces of the novel and read them, then reread them, making no sense at all of the contents. There was one entire chapter and a piece of another. Out of context, she decided, they appeared completely harmless to anyone, but in context, read by the right person, maybe they were dangerous. She put them aside to take to Felicia's house, to be added to the manuscript.

'What's really bugging you?' she asked one night when Brice said he had no clean shirts. He had several shirts ready to wear, she knew. He had put them through the washer and dryer himself when she had forgotten to do them. She was clearing the table, taking plates to the dishwasher, and had both hands full.

'You,' he said bluntly. 'You've become so obsessed with what you're doing, you don't have time for me, for us. You were like a zombie one week, then gone for a week, and now, here in this house, every day you're farther away, more distant. You're never here when I call, or else you just don't even bother to pick up the phone — I don't know which is worse. Abby, come back. That's what's bugging me. I want you back.'

She put the plates down and went to him, and they held each other fiercely, her face against his chest. 'I'm sorry,' she said. 'Brice, I'm sorry. I just feel like I have to get through with all that stuff before things can start getting back to normal. I can't help it. I have to finish things. It won't take much longer.'

'Christ,' he said into her hair, 'I've done it again. Come on like a spoiled kid. I'm the one who's sorry, who has something to be sorry about. I just miss you so damn much. I love you so much, it's killing me to see you so hurt, so possessed. Let's go upstairs,' he said huskily.

She nodded.

'Wait a minute,' he said, releasing her; he set a plate of scraps on the floor. 'So she won't whine outside the bedroom door.' They both laughed and went upstairs.

★ ★ ★

Later that night, after Brice was asleep, she got up again, finished clearing the table, and then went to her own room to read some more. And on Friday morning she returned to Felicia's town house. Possessed, she thought, ringing the bell.

The condominium was on a hillside overlooking Amazon Parkway, a meticulously landscaped site that Felicia called the prison yard. She called her one-bedroom unit her jail in town. It was a handsome jail, beautifully furnished with antiques and with her artwork on the walls, no messy paints or clay in sight. Abby was surprised to see Willa there; she had not noticed her car parked at the curb out front.

'I took the day off,' Willa said. 'We're so

near the end, I couldn't stand it, not finishing.'

Willa had found herself in the novel several times; one time she had blushed, and another time she had wept. The passages were lyrical, joyful, erotic, but of course no one else would know he had been writing about her. Abby could imagine the lieutenant's expression if they insisted that that was how Jud really had felt about Willa; he would be polite, she thought, and his noncommittal mask would snap right in place.

'I put the last chapters together last night,' Felicia said as Abby took off her jacket. 'And I finished reading the entire novel. What I'll do today, while you both catch up, is start making notes about the characters I recognize.' She looked at Abby with great sadness. 'It's a wonderful novel,' she said softly. She went to the living room to her rocking chair, with both white poodles at her feet, a notebook on her lap, and manuscript pages on an end table within reach.

Abby and Willa went to the dining table and started to read.

*　*　*

It was late in the afternoon; they had been working for hours when Willa dropped the chapter she was reading onto the table; her face was white and tears stood in her eyes. 'It wasn't fair,' she whispered. 'God! Sending children to fight a filthy war! It was sinful, wicked. Those men behind it all should be tried as war criminals, all of them! Execution is too good for them!'

They all knew that although Jud called his character Link, he had been writing about himself. Link's ordeal in Vietnam had been Jud's ordeal, and he had finally gotten to it in the last novel. The chapter Abby was reading had Link drafted, tested, and assigned to communications; he became a radioman for the troops. A knot had formed in her chest when she read about a beautiful young Vietnamese woman, a girl of seventeen, who was a translator for his unit. One day his sergeant, a Texan of gargantuan proportions, yelled, 'What the fuck does this fucking shit mean?' Link had said, 'I think it says they got lost, ran around in circles looking for the latrine.' He had glanced at the girl and caught a fleeting grin on her face that always before had been without expression. They had tea together, then took a walk, talked. They did it again the next day, and the next . . . She told him her grandmother warned her not to swim in the river because there was a giant ray with a tail that could reach all the way across the river and catch someone, drag her to its mouth, and eat her in one bite.

'Did you swim in the river?'

'Oh, yes. But I kept an eye out for the ray. The convent school was a kilometer from my house, and every day I took off my clothes, most of them,' she quickly added with a little smile, 'and I told my brother to carry them home for me. I swam home.'

'Why not all the clothes?' he teased.

'Because Grandmother said the leeches will crawl into a girl. You know. And she will swell up like this, and then she will die.' She held her hands out from her body to show the swelling, like the last trimester of pregnancy. Her hands were so tiny, her fingers perfect, each one perfect. Her wrists were as small as a child's. 'When you swell up and die,' she said gravely, 'the leeches come pouring out, like a black stream. So,' she said in a practical manner, 'I didn't take off all my clothes. I kept my pants, and tied them very tightly around my legs with cords, and another cord tight around my waist. To keep the leeches out.' They both laughed.

They made love that day.

Willa stood up and went to the sink, and Abby returned to the chapter she was reading. The knot of dread grew until she felt filled with it as page after page described the love affair between Link and the Vietnamese translator he called Sammy.

They met behind the camp, in the mess tent between meals, in the communications tent. She took him to a hut in the forest where they could pretend the rest of the world had vanished. He told her about Rabbit Lake, the village he had grown up in, and she told him about her family, her village. They made elaborate, incredible plans to run away together, away from war. She wept with fear when he went out on missions, and with relief when he returned, and he promised he would never kill any of her countrymen. It was a lie. He was the one who transmitted the orders for air strikes, for helicopter firepower, for reinforcements. She said she feared her brother would kill him, and how could she bear such a thing?

'Your brother? But you're . . . I mean . . . I don't know what I mean.'

'You know. Three brothers, one fighting for your cause, one against. Father against son. Brother against brother. Mother against daughter. Husband against wife. That's what this war has done to us.'

She began to fold up the sheet. She always brought a clean sheet for them to lie on. 'It's time,' she said gently. Then, kneeling, holding the sheet against her breast, she said, 'Once a year, one day a year, we can put aside the war and honor our grandmother. My brothers, my uncles, all of us can put the war aside. If for one day, why not two, then three? Why war that never ends?' She looked at him sadly and shook her head. 'You can't answer, my love, nor can I. It's time.'

He thought that his love for her would kill him; his heart could not contain such love without shattering.

Abby put down the last page of the chapter and, without looking up, put the paper clip back on it, laid it on the stack of manuscript she had finished reading. She felt as if her own heart might shatter.

Reluctantly she reached for the next chapter, the one that had brought about Willa's outburst. Willa came up behind her and rested her hand on Abby's shoulder, pressed her cheek against Abby's head for a moment, then went back to her own chair and picked up another chapter without a word.

Abby read swiftly. Sammy and Link were together every minute they were off duty. He wanted to marry her, take her home when he got out, or stay with her in Vietnam. It was all he could think of, ways to keep her forever. Then one day he was called to the captain's tent and was confronted there by his lieutenant and the Texan sergeant.

He stood at attention as the lieutenant told him what they wanted. He detested the lieutenant, blond, mid-twenties, an MBA in real life, a lieutenant in Vietnam. All they wanted, the lieutenant said, was the date of a family celebration and the location. He thought of the many ways he would like to kill the lieutenant with his icy eyes and pink cheeks.

'Yes, sir,' he said, and he knew all three men watching him were aware that he was lying. He would warn her, he thought, tell her they would use her in some way.

The sergeant began to bluster, to threaten, and the captain held up his hand. He was in his forties, experienced, a career officer who knew his men. 'Listen, son,' he said. 'We all want the same thing here, for this goddamn war to be over. That's all any of us wants, to get it over with and go home. This girl's oldest brother is a colonel in the Vietcong, and we want him. We don't want him dead, or hurt. We want him alive. The more of their officers we can turn, the sooner the war ends. He's multilingual, just like her; they all are, the whole family. He can be helpful. Not dead, he can't be, but alive, convinced that they can't win, he can help us get out of this goddamn mire we're in.' He nodded toward

206

the lieutenant. 'He'll lead the platoon. They'll walk in and take one man, then leave with him. The celebration will continue, no one hurt, no shots fired.'

'Yes, sir,' Link said, exactly as he had before. The captain flushed, and the lieutenant looked ready to spring at him.

'Meanwhile, you're restricted to camp,' the captain said. 'Communications tent, mess hall, your tent. Period. Think about it, soldier. Dismissed.' He turned to the sergeant and said, 'Tell Sammy I want her in my office ASAP.'

He thought all that day, that night. They had planned this, all of it. They had allowed him to be alone with her for hours at a time, given him time off when she was off, looked the other way when he went into the forest with her. No one else had been able to get close to her, but he had, and they had seen it and planned to use his love for her, hers for him. He thought, They had bugged the hut, heard what she said about honoring her grandmother one day a year, heard everything both of them had said. He felt nothing but hatred for them, all of them. He realized he could say nothing, someone might be listening; if he warned her and they overheard, they might seize her and treat her like a spy, force her to talk. The thought filled

207

him with terror. He tried to avoid her, but it was useless; they worked at the same time in the same place. She looked at him longingly, and reached out for his hand one day when they were alone. He drew away and turned his back.

'What have I done, my love?' she whispered.

'I have work to do,' he said brusquely.

'My love, please, look at me. What has happened? The captain said I cannot leave the camp, you cannot leave. What has happened?'

'I don't know. I think they're afraid spies have come in or something.'

From the corner of his eye he could see her shake her head, could see the glint of tears in her eyes. She faced the wall and gazed at the map there. He doubted she was seeing it.

'I must leave for a short time,' she said. 'What will they do to me if I leave without permission?'

'They'll decide you're a spy and deal with you the way they deal with all spies.' He saw a shudder ripple through her.

'Always before they let me go home to my village for a day, for two days. Now they say I must stay here. But I must go home, just for one day. On Sunday I must go. My grandmother . . . She needs me for just one day.'

He dashed across the tent, to clamp his hand over her mouth, to make her unsay the words. The lieutenant entered the small communications tent then and looked at them both coldly. 'It doesn't appear that either of you is interested in the work you've been assigned,' he said. 'The captain wants you right now,' he said to Sammy.

Abby was reading faster and faster, her hands sweating, her heart racing. This was the woman he had written about; in the incident about Teri Frazier's death, he had combined Teri and this Vietnamese woman, his lover.

For the next two days Link could not find her; the captain was keeping her busy, under lock and key — translating a classified document of some sort, someone told him. Sunday morning the lieutenant and sergeant took a platoon out; Link had not been assigned as radioman for this mission. An hour after they left, Sammy appeared at the communications tent, and he felt his knees give as relief swept through him. 'Walk with me,' she said. The captain, at his desk reading something, barely glanced up. He said, 'Take a walk, soldier.'

They walked without touching or speaking. Then she took his hand and pressed it to her cheek. She led him to a place he had not seen before. There was a tiny stream. They bathed, made love, and then walked some more.

Abby had come to the part she had read before. 'Be whole, my love . . . ' Sammy left him in the forest, and he followed her. He heard music and realized she had gone to her village. He stumbled through the forest toward the music and reached the clearing of the village at almost the same time the platoon appeared at the far side of it, tiny figures emerging from the jungle, their rifles ready, spreading out to encircle the small houses. Someone was running from house to house, and the Americans began shooting.

Then the real shooting started, and the Vietcong swarmed over the platoon, firing from all directions. The platoon had walked into an ambush.

Link sank to the ground. He was there when the first two helicopters appeared and were shot down. He was there when other helicopters came in and firebombed the village. When the rescue squad appeared and scoured the area for the wounded and the dead, he was the only survivor they found; they carried him out.

Abby was trembling when she put down the last page.

'You need a drink,' Felicia said, and handed her a glass that was mostly scotch. 'And you both need to stop for today,' she added. She started to put the novel chapters back in the box.

Abby took a drink and choked; the scotch burned her mouth, her throat, all the way down. 'I have to go home,' she said faintly.

'Yes, you do. I figure that tomorrow Willa will finish the last chapter, and over the weekend I'll get my notes pretty much done.'

Abby had told them that she wouldn't be able to come over during the weekend. She had to spend some time with Brice, or he would flip out totally. She would finish reading the other copy of the novel at home.

'On Monday we can talk about it,' Felicia said. 'Willa, stay for dinner?'

Willa shook her head. 'Thanks. I . . . I have to go home, too.'

'Yes, I expect you do,' Felicia said.

Abby was grateful for Felicia's matter-of-factness, her steadiness; she had read the entire novel, she knew exactly what Willa and Abby were going through now, and she was the calm storm center that was holding them both together, keeping them from dissolving into tears. Hesitantly Abby asked, 'Did the girl, Sammy, did she die that day?'

'I don't know,' Felicia said. 'For Link the war ended that day; he never referred to her again. I just don't know.' She looked at Abby sharply. 'Pull yourself together, child. No one outside this house realizes how autobiographical his novels are. And we don't know what really happened that day, or to whom.'

Dully Abby nodded, thinking, Brice was right all along. Someone knew something terrible, had extorted money, had blackmailed Jud, who had believed he had lured his own comrades into a deadly trap. That girl, Sammy, had used him; his own officers had used him. She had come back to haunt him. Maybe she had been watching him for years, and as soon as she thought there was any money to be had, she demanded it. Abby thought of the working title of his novel, and she knew it was his real title, the final title, the end of the four-volume novel: *Guilt*.

13

After Abby finished the last page of the novel on Saturday afternoon, she sat at her desk gazing out the window for a long time. Finally she nodded and drew in a breath; the best thing he had ever written. The ending had left her reluctant to reenter the world of the concrete, the real world. She wanted to stay with the novel longer, think about it, feel whatever it was she was feeling for a very long time. Peace, she thought in wonder; she was filled with a sense of peace she had not felt in many months.

Almost reverently she reached across the desk and rested her hand on the mahogany box; she knew she was thanking him, thanking God or fate or whatever it was that had granted him enough time to finish his work, finally to find the peace he had looked for.

She did not stir until Spook made a low noise in her throat and lifted her head, her ears twitching, her signal that Brice had come home. At lunch Abby had told him that she was finally through responding to the sympathy notes, and he had breathed a sigh of relief. And, she had added, she would finish the novel and have it ready to send to Christina on Monday. He had gone out on some mysterious errands of his own.

She went down to greet him.

'Done?' he asked, hanging up his jacket.

'Done.'

'Great. Happy ending?'

She hesitated. 'I think so.'

'Oh, God, more ambiguity. Never mind. I'll wait for the movie.'

They had argued once about one of Jud's novels, which Brice said was such a mixture of fact and fantasy that he couldn't follow what was really happening, couldn't tell what was real.

'It's all real,' she had said, amused. 'Sometimes you use metaphors to express what can't be said outright, but that doesn't mean the metaphors aren't real. You bypass the rational mind and go straight to the symbolic.'

He had clamped his hands over his ears in mock horror. 'English lit lecture time. Spare me. I damn near flunked it.'

'And you should have flunked it, you illiterate hulk.'

Now he reached in the pocket of his jacket and drew out an envelope. 'Guess what?'

'I give.'

'Tonight we're going out on the town. Dinner reservations at Willie's, show at the Hult Center. David Copperfield, magic show. They had seven seats left. I snagged a couple.'

It was a fun night, an excellent dinner followed by laughter and marvels. Brice looked so smug, he made her think of a doctor who, after many vain attempts, finally found the right medication for a difficult patient. And she had needed desperately to laugh, to relax.

Her dreams that night were filled with illusions, with magic. She reached for Felicia's hand, and Felicia turned into a stranger. She was in a house of mirrors where she could see Brice but could not get to him; she bumped into herself again and again. She was swimming to the cabin that kept receding farther and farther out of reach, and there was something in the water with her, something dreadful, fearful, invisible. She was drawn to a flower, a gardenia just opening. She picked it, and it turned into a lovely naked girl, and then she was the girl holding a tiger in the palm of her hand. It began to grow, and she knew it was devouring her, she was turning into the tiger. It was neither painful nor frightening, just interesting to know she was becoming a tiger.

Brice had already eaten breakfast and was reading the newspaper when she went down the next morning. No matter what time he went to bed, he was awake before seven the next morning; her internal clock didn't keep time that way. It was after nine.

'Good morning,' they said in unison. Laughing, she blew him a kiss and went on to make toast and pour coffee. They were out of juice. Today she would make a shopping list, she promised herself.

'I kept dreaming of magic tricks,' she said at the table with her coffee and toast.

'He's good, isn't he? There's a show that comes on now and then on TV, they explain how some of those tricks are done. We should watch it sometime.'

She shook her head. 'And spoil the fun? I'd rather think it's magic.' She began to read the comics section as she ate, and he went back to the section he had been reading. Neither spoke again until she got up to pour another cup of coffee.

'Abby,' he said then, 'I can take the notes and the manuscript to the office and mail them there. You won't have to bother with the post office. But what next? When will you finish the rest of the stuff you brought home?'

'I don't want my notes put through a postage machine,' she said, thinking of the many handwritten notes she had read, the ones she had written in response. 'That seems so institutional. I'll do them.' More slowly she said, 'It's going to take some time to finish the short stories and story notes, all this week maybe. I don't know. And I'll have to go back to the cabin and sort through the rest of the files. As literary executor, that's my job now. I just don't know how long it's all going to take.'

He stood and crossed the kitchen, got more coffee for himself, and brought it back. 'Next weekend,' he said, 'let's go together, early Saturday, box up everything you think you have to look over and bring it all home. Close up the place for the winter. Bury your father's ashes. It's time, Abby,' he said gently. 'It's past time.'

She felt herself stiffen with his words, and she couldn't help it. 'Not yet,' she said through tight lips. 'I'm not ready yet.'

'You asked me a few days ago what's bugging me, and I told you part of it. There's another part. Those ashes in our house, in the same room with you day after day. Maybe I'm superstitious and never knew it before, but it's bugging me to the point where I dream of them. And if it's doing that to me, I can't

217

imagine how it's affecting you. It's like he's haunting us, a presence here all the time.'

'Oh, God, Brice — '

He held up his hand and said, 'Hold it a minute. You know that the Halburtsons will take off by the end of the month and no one will be anywhere near you, not for miles. You can't go up there alone, and next weekend is the last weekend I'll have free until after the first of the year. We have to do it then, Abby.'

He was being reasonable, she knew, but this had nothing to do with reason. 'I just can't right now,' she said.

'Can you tell me why not?'

Miserably she shook her head. 'I'm just not ready. Give me a few days to think about it. Don't push me right now. Maybe I have to wait for the police to come up with something. I don't know why. Just not yet.'

He regarded her for a moment with a bewildered expression, then his mouth tightened and he turned away. 'I told you how I feel about having his ashes in my house. It's more than grotesque, it's obscene, like you're becoming a member of the cult of the dead. How I feel apparently doesn't mean anything to you. Think about it then. But next weekend I want it to end, Abby. I want our life back.' He left the room, taking his coffee with him.

218

A few minutes later, up in her room, moving mechanically, she began to put her notes in a box, to be stamped, mailed. Three rolls of stamps, she thought distantly, and remembered how touched she had been when she first started to read the letters and cards that had poured in. How grateful for those that had no return address. And grateful for those that implored her not to respond, those that acknowledged her grief and the burden of responding. Grateful for the illegible ones that she couldn't respond to.

Gradually the room would be cleared of all these things, she thought, gazing at the box of cards and letters that had come in, the box of his private papers she had not yet read, the early drafts she had extracted from his novel, and the finished manuscript ... Her gaze came to rest on the mahogany box; she shook her head violently. Not yet! First she had to know who killed him and why, and who had blackmailed him and why, who he had known in San Francisco ...

The novel had not given her any clue. But of course he wouldn't have written about a blackmailer, or a possible murderer. There had been no mention of San Francisco.

Suddenly she shifted her gaze to the box of

cards and letters she had answered. Some of them had come from San Francisco. She had stopped reading every word; again and again the message had been the same, how much his books had meant, how important they had been to the writer . . .

Frantically she began to go through the box, searching for a San Francisco return address. She found one, another . . . Fourteen in all. Seven from Oakland. Nine from Berkeley. She sat at her desk and opened the top one: 'Dear Mrs. Connors, I feel I have to express my sorrow over the loss of your father. His books were so important to me personally that I felt he was my friend, someone who understood me as no one else could . . . ' The next one was very like that, and the next. Most of them had been like that. She opened another one. 'My Dear Mrs. Connors, Please accept my deepest most heartfelt sympathy for you in this time of grief. The world has lost a very fine writer. I have lost a dear friend.' The handwriting was old-world, spidery, difficult to read, with words that she could not decipher at all. There was something, something, ' . . . such hope as they never dreamed of. He will be sorely missed, but never forgotten.' There was something else that she couldn't make out. Then the spidery signature: Fr. Jean Auguste.

She read it again, then studied the envelope. A different hand had addressed it in clear, bold script, and the return address didn't include a name, merely a street number and city.

Father, she thought. She had addressed her response *Fr.* but it meant Father. A priest. A dear friend. She examined the spidery writing again; the writing of someone very old, maybe sick. Hastily she scanned the other notes from the San Francisco area, but she knew this was the one she had been looking for. Father Jean Auguste. A dear friend. Her hand was shaking, she realized with surprise, and put the letter down, rubbed her hands together as if they were chilled. She had to go see him. He would know about the money, or tell her who to talk to, tell her something. He would know something.

★ ★ ★

'What on earth are you talking about?' Brice demanded. 'You can't just take off and go see someone you never heard of. Tell that lieutenant his name, let him investigate it. That's his job.' She had opened his study door without knocking; he was at his desk before his computer, which was scrolling lists of numbers. He blanked the screen and

221

jumped up, crossed to her and grabbed her arm, nearly shoving her out of the room, into the hall.

'I'm going,' she said, jerking away from him. 'I have my reservation, sevenish in the morning. I'll come home on the eleven o'clock flight tomorrow night.'

'For God's sake, Abby! This is craziness! Who is he? Call him on the phone. You don't have to go down there.'

'I do have to.' She hadn't told Brice the priest's name, and now she was glad. Brice might decide to tell the police, but she might learn something that could never be told to anyone, not the police, or Brice, or anyone else. Jud had kept his secret until he died, and she would do the same thing if necessary.

'Let's sit down and talk about this,' Brice said, his face flushed with anger.

'I'll sit down, but there's nothing to talk about. I'm going to see that priest tomorrow. My father met someone in San Francisco, and this is the only hint so far of who it might have been.'

She walked downstairs and he followed; they went to the living room, where she sat on the couch and he walked back and forth jerkily.

'You don't know a thing about him. He might not even be there now. Wasted effort, and expensive. You scare me, Abby. You really scare me acting like this. He could be a loony-bin candidate, a cult leader or something. I just won't let you do this!'

'Do you really think you can stop me?'

He stopped pacing and stared at her. 'This is what I mean,' he said hoarsely. 'I can see you changing day by day, changing into someone I don't know anymore. You're having a breakdown or something.'

She jumped up from the couch. 'Oh, for heaven's sake! Shut up, just shut up! And stop telling me what I can or can't do. I'm going to take Spook for a walk.'

She had Father Jean Auguste's letter in her purse, and her response to it; she took her purse with her when she left the house. Tomorrow, she thought. Tomorrow.

14

Abby stood outside a Victorian house on Geary Street and checked the address once more against the note she had received. There appeared to be two entrances to the house, one up a flight of steps, the other at a lower level, with a winding ramp leading to it. Slowly she climbed the steps, drew in a long breath at the top, then rang the bell. She thrust the note into her pocket.

The door was opened by a plump, middle-aged woman in a gray long-sleeved dress with a white apron. Her gray hair was pulled back in a bun, but a few tendrils had escaped to curl over one ear. She could have been typecast as a servant in a play set at the turn of the century. 'Yes?' she said.

'I'm looking for someone,' Abby said hesitantly. 'Father Jean Auguste. Is he here?'

'Father Jean? Yes. Please, come in. He'll be happy to receive a guest.'

The smell hit Abby then, medicinal, mixed with floor wax, antiseptics, cleaning fluids ... Hospital smells, she realized, gazing about the foyer she entered. Many flowers on low tables, a few easy chairs arranged in conversation groups, a highly polished, wide-plank floor, broad carpeted stairs, and a hall partly visible with closed doors on both sides.

'What is this place?' she asked in a low voice.

'You don't know?' The woman had started walking toward the stairs; she turned to look at Abby. 'It's a hospice,' she said. 'I'm Sister Monique. Father Jean Auguste is upstairs. Are you a friend of his?'

'No. I've never met him. My father was a friend. Father Jean Auguste wrote me a note a few weeks ago when my father . . . when he passed away.'

A doubtful look crossed the sister's face, and she came back the few steps she had taken. 'He wrote to you recently?'

Abby pulled out the note and handed it to her. Sister Monique read it and handed it back. 'I'm very sorry,' she said. 'I was surprised that Father Jean had written to anyone these past few months. He's very ill, my dear, and very weak. His mind is lucid, but his medication causes him to lapse into sleep frequently. If that happens, you must leave. Now, come along. I'll take you to his room, and if he's awake, I imagine he'll be glad to see you.'

As they went up the stairs, Abby's dread

225

grew. They reached a hallway with many doors, a few of them open to reveal small rooms, hospital beds, flowers on windowsills, people who had come here to die. A nurse with a tray entered a room and closed the door.

Sister Monique stopped walking. She glanced at Abby, then said, 'If you're going to be ill, or start crying or anything, it would be better not to pay a call. For his sake,' she added crisply.

'I'm all right,' Abby said.

After a searching look, the sister tapped lightly on the door and opened it a crack to peer within. 'Ah, Father, you're awake. How fortunate! You have a visitor!' Her voice had become cheerful, and she had a wide smile on her face as she entered the room, motioning Abby to follow. 'Mrs. Connors has come to see you, Father.'

He was so shrunken, his body barely raised the comforter over his frame. Music played softly, Berlioz. He had been facing the window; slowly he turned his head to gaze at Abby. His skin was so thin and translucent that his bones showed, his veins. His sparse hair blended into the white of the pillow. One skeletal hand rested on top of the comforter. It appeared that he was trying to raise it, but he succeeded only in moving his fingers slightly.

Sister Monique moved a straight chair close to the bed, glanced around the room, then said, 'Ring if you want anything, Father.' A call button was pinned to the comforter near his hand.

'Mrs. Connors? Jud's daughter?' the old man asked in a whispery voice.

'Yes, I'm Abby Connors,' she said, and sat in the chair close enough to touch him. The room was claustrophobic; it contained a bureau, the chair she was in, a bedside stand. Potted orchids in bloom filled the windowsill, gay yellow, a deep rosy red, white. A crucifix hung on the wall opposite his bed. A CD player on the bedside stand played the Berlioz.

She shouldn't have come here, Abby thought despairingly. She didn't know what to say to him, what to ask him. 'I'm sorry to bother you,' she said finally. 'You wrote me, and I — '

'Did he find peace?' the old man asked, his voice almost inaudible.

She nodded. 'Yes. He found love and peace before he died.'

He closed his eyes and mumbled something, and she wanted to touch him, not let him fall asleep yet, but she didn't dare. He was praying, she realized. In Latin.

'Thank you, child,' he whispered after a moment. 'I prayed that he would find peace. In the bureau, top . . . ' A spasm shook him; the comforter rippled with his movement. 'Papers,' he said. 'They'll tell you.' He sighed deeply and closed his eyes.

This time he did not open his eyes again, and for a moment she was afraid he was dead, but his fingers twitched on the comforter, as if feeling the texture of it. Silently she stood up, put the chair back against the wall, then went to the bureau and opened the top drawer.

There was a sweater, bed socks, a few sheets of letterhead stationery and some envelopes. She looked in the other two drawers: empty. Slowly she returned to the bedside stand and opened the single drawer there. Hospital items, lotion, powder, a small basin . . . There was nothing else in the room. There was no closet, nowhere else to look. She went back to the bureau, picked up a sheet of stationery, and drew in a sharp breath: Xuan Bui Institute. Vietnamese. They would tell her something. That was what he had meant. She folded a sheet of the stationery and put it in her purse, then gazed at the dying man for a moment, wishing she knew how to pray, wishing she believed it would do him any good for her to try. Quietly she slipped out.

★ ★ ★

It was nearly noon when she left a taxicab on Tenth Street and looked about apprehensively. A warehouse district? Massive buildings lined both sides of the busy, wide street, warehouses that had been converted to other uses. Some upper windows were curtained, Venetian blinds hung at some of them, and small business establishments were housed on the street level. She started to walk, passed a Korean restaurant that advertised hot pepper ribs, a Brazilian restaurant with FEIJADA in fading letters on the window. A used-furniture store with sad-looking beds and dressers on display. And then windows with drapes, and a door that had a neat little sign: XUAN BUI INSTITUTE.

It also had an OPEN sign. A bell announced her presence when she opened the door and walked inside to a room out-fitted as an office with file cabinets, a desk, telephone, a computer, another door that opened as she entered. A beautiful Vietnamese woman came into the office and smiled at her. 'Can I help you?'

Staring at her, Abby said, 'I was looking for

an institute, a school or something like that.'

'Xuan Bui Institute,' the other woman said, her smile broadening. 'This is the office; the school, I'm afraid, is in Vietnam. What can I do for you?'

She was dressed in black jeans and a T-shirt with silk-screened water lilies on it, Adidas shoes, no jewelry. Her hair was short and straight, gleaming; she was very lovely, her face ivory-toned like an antique cameo, with fine bones.

'I don't know,' Abby said almost helplessly. This woman was too young to tell her anything she needed to know, she thought. And Americanized, not really Vietnamese. Her diction was flawless, without a trace of accent. 'Father Jean Auguste said someone here could tell me something. Is there anyone else?' A nameplate on the desk had the words THANH BUI. A name? Abby didn't know.

'Father Jean? He sent you?' The woman's eyes widened, and her smile vanished. 'You're Judson Vickers's daughter?'

Abby nodded.

Swiftly the woman crossed the office space and turned the OPEN sign around. 'I was going to close up and have lunch,' she said. 'I'm Thanh Bui. I can answer your questions. I addressed the note to you, but Father Jean wrote it himself. Please, have lunch with me.'

Abby hesitated only a second, then nodded again, and they walked from the office out to the street. Neither spoke as Thanh led the way to the corner, past a few businesses, then into a restaurant. 'Vietnamese,' Thanh said. 'We'll have *pho*, my daily lunch.' She smiled slightly, spoke in Vietnamese to a counterman, and went straight to a booth. There were a dozen or more other customers in the restaurant, most of them Vietnamese. Some of them spoke to Thanh as she passed, in Vietnamese, English, even in French. She responded to each in kind. 'What do you want to drink?' she asked when they were both seated. 'I already ordered soup for us. I'll have jasmine tea; it's very good here.'

Abby shrugged slightly. 'That's fine.' She didn't care what she ate or drank, and doubted that she could eat anything. 'You knew my father?'

'Just a second,' Thanh said as the counterman approached, bringing them water. She spoke briefly to him, and he left. She studied Abby for a moment before she said, 'I never met him, but I know much about him.'

Abby's disappointment must have shown, she thought, leaning back, exhaling. Another dead end. Pointless.

Thanh regarded her with sympathy. 'I'm very sorry about your loss,' she said. 'I didn't know him personally, as I said, but I share your grief. Many people share your grief.'

Abby's hands were folded on the table, and for a moment she feared that Thanh was going to reach across, take her hand, touch her; she put her hands in her lap.

'Here's our tea,' Thanh said as the counterman returned to place the pot and cups on the table. When he left again, she poured for them both. 'I'll tell you what I know, and afterward you ask your questions.'

She did not wait for a response. 'We lived in Saigon when I was very young, no more than a baby,' she said. 'My father was an engineer and my mother worked for the French embassy as a translator. She speaks six languages fluently,' she added. 'When the French left, Father Jean told my parents that others would come, the Americans would come, and they should return to the countryside, where they might be safer. He got her a job teaching at a convent school not far from our grandmother's village, and that's where we moved. My parents, three brothers, and my sister. We had been relatively wealthy — middle class, I suppose you would say — and suddenly we were peasants.'

She sipped her tea and drew back as the counterman placed large soup bowls and a number of small condiment bowls on the table. Thanh named the various additions to the soup as she added them to her own bowl: cilantro, flakes of red pepper, rice noodles, other things that Abby had never heard of.

'Try it,' Thanh urged her gently. 'I imagine you haven't recognized your own hunger.'

Following Thanh's example, Abby added some of the condiments, and the soup was delicious. She really had not recognized her hunger pangs.

'So,' Thanh said, continuing her story as she ate, 'it happened as Father Jean had predicted; the Americans came, the war became a ravenous monster. My father was conscripted, and we never saw him again. Then my oldest brother vanished into the forest one night when he was sixteen. The next year another brother went into the forest. No one told me anything: I was too young. Later I knew that they had both joined the forces from the north. When my sister, Xuan, was sixteen, she began to work for the Americans as a translator. My mother had taught us all well; Xuan was a good translator.'

She put down her spoon and gazed over Abby's shoulder, her expression remote now. 'One day Father Jean came to tell us good-bye. The school would be closed, the nuns recalled, and he would be sent to the

233

United States, to work with the Vietnamese refugees. He had come from a town in France, in the Burgundy region; it was his dream to return to his own village one day, but he never did. Then the Americans burned the school; they said the Vietcong were using it as a meeting place.'

She drew her gaze back to Abby. 'This was all a very long time ago,' she said softly. 'Before you were born even. And I was a child. For us it's no more than history.'

For Thanh it was more, Abby knew; pain of the memories was clearly written on her face.

'By the time I was eight,' Thanh went on briskly, 'I was seeing what I had not seen before, although it had been there to see. Xuan was meeting with our brothers in secret. A few miles away from our village was the American camp where she worked, and from it missions were sent out daily. The soldiers from that particular camp were greatly feared; the captain who ordered the missions was considered one of the best soldiers, very smart and cunning, and without mercy. My brothers and sister, and others, of course, were plotting to entrap the best unit from that camp, the best soldiers, the most hated lieutenant, and destroy them.'

She lifted her teacup, then set it down without a sip. 'My sister was a very important part of the trap,' she said slowly. 'Her job was to seduce a soldier, to make him fall in love with her, and pretend love for him, and to confide in him, tell him about an important family meeting that would take place on a certain day. A meeting that would bring in officers from the Vietcong to participate in a celebration. She knew that what she had to say must be reported to the soldier's superiors, or at least be overheard by them. I don't know how they managed the details, but that is what happened. She used the young soldier; his own officers used him and learned of the celebration, and they planned to raid it, to capture and kill important officers, destroy their rendezvous site. Everyone used the innocent young soldier,' she said faintly. 'He was your father.'

For a time neither spoke; Abby couldn't have spoken, her mouth was too dry, her lips too stiff. The same story her father had told in the novel, a few details changed, but the same story. The Vietnamese translator had seduced him, used him, discarded him, just as he had written about Sammy, who had seduced the boy Link and discarded him.

Thanh seemed lost in the past. She broke the silence. 'Most of this I learned from my brothers later,' she said. 'Over a period of several days the villagers quietly left the village; my mother took my youngest brother and me and our grandmother to my uncle's house. The Cong moved into the village to keep up the appearance of normalcy, to light cooking fires, tend the vegetable gardens . . . Then they left also, but the fires were burning, cooking smells in the air, a few animals wandering about. Normal village life. The Americans moved in, and someone began to run from house to house warning the people that they were coming, or so it appeared. The Americans began to shoot. And the Cong sprang the trap. They annihilated the American unit that day. No American in it survived, and only one of our people was killed. My sister. She was the person they saw running from house to house.'

Abby remembered what Jud had written; the beautiful girl, his lover, had taken him into the forest and left him. She knew what was coming; she wouldn't have gone back to the village.

Thanh said very quietly, 'The plans went awry. She was not supposed to fall in love with the big American, but she did. And she betrayed him. She made our brothers promise not to hurt him, to ensure his safety, and she took her part in the final scene, her act of atonement. He saw her get shot, and he saw the helicopters come in later and firebomb the village. He knew. He collapsed, and my brothers stood guard over him until the American rescue team arrived. They did not harm him, but they believed he would also die. They said he became a ghost that day.'

Abby wanted to cry out, No! He hadn't written it that way. Up until now she had believed every word, but not this. It was Teri Frazier he felt guilty about, not the Vietnamese girl. She couldn't speak, couldn't move. Thanh reached across the table and touched her hand.

'Let's walk back to the office,' Thanh said. 'I told them I'd pay the bill later. I think we're finished here.'

On the sidewalk, oblivious to the busy street, the traffic, passersby, Thanh began to talk again. 'Back in 1991, Father Jean told us a man appeared on his doorstep one day, your father, who had brought with him a cashier's check for four thousand dollars. He asked Father Jean if he knew about the family of Xuan Bui, if any of them had survived the war, if the village had been rebuilt. The check was for the village, he said, and his name could not be revealed. At that time he didn't even tell Father Jean who he was. He was afraid they would reject the money if they knew the source, Father Jean said, and he said the man apologized for the meagerness of the check. Father Jean assured him that that much money in Vietnam was a fortune.

'The following year he came back, with a bigger check, and that time he began to ask questions about the school, had it been rebuilt, or a different one built. When Father Jean told him there was no school near that village, he became excited, and said he wanted to build a school there. That it would take time and patience, but he would do it.'

They had reached the office; she unlocked the door and they entered. She did not remove the CLOSED sign. Motioning for Abby to follow, she led the way through the office to the next room. 'We'll be more comfortable here,' she said. She smiled and gestured to a round table with half a dozen chairs drawn up around it. 'Not much more comfortable, but a little. This is where we plan and scheme.'

They talked for a long time. With the American's money and the priest's influence in the church, they had acquired the land and construction had begun; her mother was the school administrator, and Thanh was the American coordinator, the one who hunted down the best bargains in computers, paper, textbooks, even teachers. She brought out photographs that showed the development of the school, from a forest reclaiming the land, to a clearing, a tiny one-room building, another, then a larger building that housed three classrooms, a dormitory, and an office. She gave Abby copies of legal documents that detailed where every penny had been spent.

'As soon as he stipulated the name of the school,' she said, 'we knew the name of our benefactor. Xuan had talked about him to us, and about us to him. We knew. Father Jean has honored the promise he made to keep our benefactor anonymous; he has never mentioned his name, but there was no need. When Father Jean became ill, they set up a trust fund in a bank here in San Francisco, and the money is funneled through it anonymously. Now, some of our own people are starting to contribute, not merely with money but volunteer workers, even volunteer teachers; in time the school will grow and thrive. A memorial to your father, and to my sister.'

15

On Sunday night Felicia Shaeffer had dinner with her daughter Sara, Sara's husband, John, and their three children. Sara was an executive secretary for a group of attorneys, John worked in the city building-permit department, and they both took their positions, their responsibilities very seriously. Their children took their jobs as grandchildren seriously also, she thought, suppressing a sigh, as she listened to the youngest, eight-year-old Sylvie, play a tortured piano piece. Dinner had been exactly correct, broiled skinless chicken breasts, some weird potatoes in a casserole with fat-free sour cream, green beans that had been heated but not really cooked — and at this time of year everyone, except Sara, knew you had to cook them; God alone knew how far they had traveled, how long ago they had been picked. Everything measured, calories counted, so many grams of fiber provided, down to the salad sprinkled with lemon juice and dry-roasted sunflower seeds. All very healthful. Sara, like her father before her, did not believe alcohol was good for you, and served none, not even wine with dinner. At nine o'clock Felicia yawned widely and said old people like her belonged in bed along about now. She escaped.

Back in her own one-bedroom jail, she petted her two dogs affectionately, then went to the kitchen and poured herself a glass of wine. How on earth had she managed to bring up such . . . she groped for a word, found it . . . *puritanical* children? What had she done wrong? It was the damn pendulum effect, she thought glumly; she was of the sixties' live-and-let-live generation, they were the new pure, holier-than-thou generation. She pitied them, hoping the pendulum had found its farthest reach by now and soon would start back again.

Daisy and Mae were eyeing her anxiously, doing their dance, wanting to go out, needing to go out after hours inside. At home she could open the door and let them out when necessary, but here she had to bundle up, put them on leashes, walk with them. It wasn't as if they ever stayed out a minute longer than they had to, they were house dogs, after all, but they were used to the freedom of choosing when to go outdoors. And so was she, she thought, looking about the tidy little apartment with distaste.

'All right, girls,' she said then, and got her

heavy jacket from the closet. She pulled a stocking cap over her head, over her ears, added warm wool gloves, and they were ready. Actually, she needed some fresh air to clear her mind. A visit with her perfect children and theirs always left her feeling strange, an alien among weirdos. Tonight she had no intention of going to bed anytime soon; she had some heavy thinking to do. A brisk walk first would help.

Tomorrow Willa would come by after work, and Abby had called to say she wouldn't be there at all, not until Tuesday. That was fine, Felicia had decided; there were things she had to do before she talked again with Abby.

★ ★ ★

At the same time that Abby was leaving the room of the dying priest on Monday, Felicia was opening her door to admit Lieutenant Caldwell. 'Come in, come in,' she said. 'Back off, girls, down.' Both poodles were sniffing his legs with great interest; they retreated and sat down, keeping their eyes on him. 'I'm glad you could come yourself. Detective Varney is very pretty, but she certainly is young, isn't she?'

He smiled and nodded. 'Young and pretty, and a very good detective. But your message said you wanted to see me, so here I am. You have something for me?'

'Let me hang up your jacket,' she said. 'Do you want coffee?'

'I'll keep the jacket, and coffee would be good. Never turn down coffee, that's my motto.' He was wearing jeans with boots, and a windbreaker over a sweatshirt. He looked as if he planned to go undercover on the Eugene mall or, more likely, infiltrate a lumbermen association meeting.

'That's a long drive from Salem,' she said, motioning for him to follow her to the kitchen.

'One hour twenty minutes.'

She nodded, suspecting that few details escaped his notice. The coffee was made; she poured two cups and pointed to the sugar and cream on the counter, but he used neither. They returned to the living room, where she sat in her rocking chair, and he on the couch; in the small room he was almost close enough to touch.

'So tell me what you have,' he said.

'Last week Willa Ashford, Abby, and I worked at putting Jud's novel in order. Abby found the missing pieces, and we included them. Have your people found those parts?'

'We recovered everything on his hard drive,' the lieutenant said.

'And they didn't help your cause,' she murmured. 'Have you made any headway at all, Lieutenant?'

'We're tying up loose ends, running down leads, the usual thing.'

He was being cautious, giving nothing, and being very patient. She had noticed how people divided themselves: those who were patient with an old woman in a rocking chair, and those who began fidgeting, eager to get away, on to other things. She was glad he was a patient man; what she had to say couldn't be rushed.

'Are you a reader?' she asked. 'Have you read Jud's other novels?'

'I don't do much fiction,' he said. 'Biography, history, that's my speed. I haven't read him except for the new novel, and I admit that we're not at all certain we have it in the proper order.'

She nodded regretfully. 'Then there must be parts that don't make much sense, continuing motifs that appear in all the works, characters and subplots he comes back to now and then. I suspect that you're more oriented to the concrete, to details, and his work is very nuanced, things hinted at, shapes lurking in the background, the kind that if you turn to examine them, they're gone, but you know they're there again as soon as you

244

stop trying to focus on them.'

He nodded. 'It's a puzzling book.'

'Take that blond man, for instance,' she said then. 'What the pilot saw was long blond hair, ear studs, and cash in hand. If you had seen that man, I imagine your description of him would have included his height, weight, the color of his eyes, whether he had moles, good or bad teeth. Most people don't collect real details at all; a general impression is all they retain.'

He was watching her closely over the rim of his coffee cup. He set it down and leaned back. 'You recognized him finally?'

'No, no. I didn't mean to give you that idea. I think that when you find him, you'll learn that he was going home to a family crisis, a wife in labor, something of that sort. Out on the desert somewhere, or up in the mountains. I tried to turn him into someone I might know,' she added. 'That's what I do, start with someone real, and begin making changes, a longer nose, or shorter, hairier, prettier or uglier. But I couldn't make him into anyone. He's a stranger who was on a mission of his own that night, I'm afraid.'

'I doubt that you asked me to come around to tell me you don't know who he is,' Caldwell commented dryly.

'No, I didn't. I hoped you had read Jud's

other books by now, so that you'd have a bit of understanding about the section I want to talk about. Jud was a very complicated man, Lieutenant. Very complex, and smart. He did a smart thing when he created the resort for his background. It allowed him to bring the world to his doorstep, you see. Sometimes playfully, farcical even, sometimes very seriously. He satirized politicians mercilessly, Hollywood charlatans who channeled Indian spirits, aging stars, people of all sorts. He had fun with them. They aren't likely to recognize themselves because, like most of us, they look at the surface, or more likely they see the face they want to show the world, and that isn't how Jud painted them in his work. I think he saw people from the inside out, and then created just enough surface details to give them a sort of reality. A different way of seeing.'

'You think you recognize some of the people he was writing about?'

She nodded. 'Some. Quite a few, actually, once I caught on to what he was doing. I extracted some pages from the novel for you to read, if you will. Not a lot, just ten or fifteen pages at most. Would you do that?'

'Now?'

'Yes. Then we can talk about them.' She had the pages on the table at her elbow and picked them up to hand to him. He stood up, came and took the pages reluctantly, then sat down again, began to read. He was only skimming, she knew. He had read those pages before probably and had made no sense of them, and he didn't expect to make sense of them now. Watching him, she was not surprised when his expression changed to one that was not exactly angry, but was no longer the placid, neutral one he had worn before.

'Fill me in,' he said. 'What are you getting at? That's Matthew Petrie he's talking about? Is that it? And what's the nonsense about the mud bath?'

She shook her head. 'That's why it would have been helpful if you had read the other novels,' she said. 'I'll try to tell you as briefly as I can about the mud bath first. In the first novel Link's father owns the resort, a piss-poor sort of place that he begins to fix up, to renovate. There's a hot spring on the property, and some basalt basins with little pools of water that seep in from the big hot pool. He bulldozes the trail to the big pool, but then he has all this dirt to get rid of, and he decides to create the mud bath out of one of the smaller pools. So the customers then can take a mud bath, go up through the next several pools, and by the time they reach the largest hot pool, they've been washed clean of the mud. A good idea, but it doesn't quite work out the way he planned. The warm water combines with elements in the dirt and makes a mud bath with a terrible smell, sulfurous, not enough to be dangerous, but very unpleasant.'

She smiled faintly. 'This was one of the recurring themes that Jud had fun with,' she said. 'You see, the boy's father, in the novel, I mean, is a well-intentioned man, a bit inept, whose plans often go awry. He finds that it was much easier to dump sieved dirt into the basin than it is to get it out again, and finally he makes another trail to the big hot spring, and simply hopes that no one will come across the pool of mud. But to his surprise, stories begin to circulate about the mud bath. Some say it is rejuvenating; most say it's simply soothing, relaxing. A few try it and find that the stench of the mud clings to them no matter how hard they scrub to rid themselves of it. Over the years the mud bath becomes a draw in itself.'

She was gazing at the lieutenant fixedly; he had taken off his jacket and tossed it down on the couch, and he was going to become impatient, she knew, yet this part had to come first.

'One of the properties ascribed to the mud bath was that it had the power to wash away one's sins, restore grace or innocence. Now, Link, the protagonist of all the novels, was a child when the mud bath was created; he watched it being made, and he believed none of the stories, and of course his father was a nonbeliever, but the stories were there, and people came to put the mud to the test. A kind of dark baptism, if not blasphemous, then at the very least a perversion, I guess.'

'Mrs. Shaeffer — '

She held up her hand. 'I'm getting to those pages I asked you to read, Lieutenant. But you had to know some of the background first. In the novel Link's mother dies when he's a young boy, and his aunt Sookie takes her place in his heart. She has a son, Buster, a few years younger than Link, the man who appears again in those pages. The boys were never close, and Buster left when he was about twenty or so, and now, a middle-aged man, he's come back. But we learn his history; he is a big-time gambler who poses as a successful and respected real-estate developer. But he's really a gambler.'

'Petrie,' Caldwell said. 'Mrs. Shaeffer, before you go on, I have to tell you we located him, one of the loose ends we've tied off, and he's out of this. Accounted for. Nowhere near Oregon.'

She shook her head. 'Let me finish. See,

Matthew Petrie was the kind of gambler who might put two dollars on a horse, and then jump up and down, yell, get all excited over the outcome of the race. The character Buster is nothing like that. He could put down half a million and never twitch an eyelash outwardly, regardless of the outcome. Different breed of gambler altogether. So, anyway, he comes back, and he has a deal for Link that is irresistible, he says. He will double his money for him in thirty days; all he needs is seventy-five thousand dollars to get it off the ground. Link tells him no, and Buster begins pressuring him for the money.'

She motioned toward the pages on the couch by the lieutenant. 'Well, you read it, you know the kind of pressure he began to exert. His mother, long since impoverished, and quite old, has no money; Link is Buster's only hope.

'Finally, in real desperation, Buster confesses that he gambled and lost to a syndicate that has sent collectors after him; they'll kill him if he doesn't pay up. It would kill his dear old mother for that to happen, he says.

'Link considers his aunt Sookie, and he knows she has the will of an iron horse, and then he recalls an incident from his and Buster's childhood, when Buster took Link's marbles and lost them to the village hotshot player. He says, 'You're still playing with someone else's marbles, aren't you?'

'Soon the collectors come looking for Buster, and he runs up the trail to the mud bath and jumps in to hide. They go up the main trail to the hot spring, fail to find him, and leave. When Buster next turns up, no one can stand to be near him, the stench is so bad. And he can't rid himself of it.'

She smiled again. 'I imagine when you came to that part, it bewildered you, since you didn't know the history of the mud bath.'

'Now that I know the story,' Caldwell said slowly, 'I have to confess, Mrs. Shaeffer, I'm still bewildered. You know who he was talking about, writing about? This character he called Buster?'

'Yes. I believe Brice Connors has been playing with someone else's marbles.' She paused, regarding the lieutenant. 'When Jud first introduced Buster, he was writing about Matthew Petrie, but he's changed in the last one. Now he's Brice Connors. Once you read Brice instead of Buster in that section, there's no mistaking him. Jud was an excellent observer.'

Caldwell eyed her steadily for several seconds without speaking, his face completely blank. He picked up his cup and looked surprised to find it empty.

251

'Yours is gone, and mine is stone cold,' she said, rising from her rocking chair. 'Do you want more?'

'Thanks, but no. You've given me something to think about, but I should be on my way.'

'I have more for you to think about,' she said sharply, and walked into the kitchen to pour out the cold coffee and refill her cup. He followed.

'Think about Jud's will,' she said. 'He added that six-month waiting period years ago, when there was a possibility that Petrie might try to get money from Abby if Jud died prematurely. There really wasn't anything much to leave her at that time, but he wanted to protect her any way he could. But he added that designation with a thirty-day contingency clause just a few years ago, when he knew there would be a great deal of money. And at that time he did not change the six-month waiting period, he left it in there, still protecting her. But not from Petrie any longer.'

Abruptly Caldwell walked out, came back with his own coffee cup, and filled it. 'Go on,' he said. 'What else?'

'He intended Abby to inherit,' she said. 'But if they happened to be in an accident together and she survived him by only a few days, or weeks, then she would not have inherited. I think Jud had no intention of letting Brice ever touch a cent of that inheritance. You know the terms of the will. If she dies within thirty days following Jud's death, the executor, Jud's attorney, will dispose of Jud's estate in a manner to be disclosed at that time, and not until then. A cat and dog hospital? Various assorted people? No one knows. Years ago my late husband talked about that clause to Jud, urging him to straighten out his affairs. The clause protects the estate from inheritance taxation twice in a short period of time, that was Herbert's concern. Jud laughed and said if they taxed nothing twice, they'd still get nothing. But later when there was an estate to protect he added it. I think he had a different reason, to keep Brice from touching the money. And he bought insurance for Abby for at least thirty days with that clause.'

She sat at the small dining table in the kitchen; Caldwell sat opposite her.

'Mrs. Shaeffer,' he said soberly, 'you're making some very serious charges. You realize what you're implying?'

She waved that away. 'Just listen,' she snapped. 'Last summer Abby and Brice called Jud and said they'd be out for a few days. He was really surprised. He knew Brice didn't like him or approve of him and that he tried to keep Abby away as much as possible. Jud was hurt by it. During that visit Jud and Abby came to see me, but Brice stayed back at the cabin. Abby said he wanted a nap, he wasn't feeling well, the stock market had taken a nosedive, his clients were screaming and yelling, and he was up all night, night after night. I think he went under then. And not with just his own money. One day last week Abby mentioned that he was in a state of nerves, year-end reports coming up, the annual audit coming, clients driving him crazy. I think he's running scared, and he has to raise money before the auditors arrive. Neither he nor Abby knew about the six-month waiting period, and they didn't know about the designation with a thirty-day contingency clause. That must have sent him reeling.'

Slowly, as if selecting his words with great care, the lieutenant said, 'But he'd still have to wait six months. What you're hinting at just won't compute, Mrs. Shaeffer.'

'It does,' she said. 'I asked my attorney about the six-month period, and he said that unless there's a contingency clause attached, the way there is for the shorter period, that provision would be nullified with Abby's death. Brice would inherit immediately, no

254

waiting period, after the thirty days have passed.'

'Then why would Jud Vickers have left the six-month clause in?' Caldwell asked. 'Why not a trust fund, let her have the interest and protect the principal? It doesn't make sense.'

'That's too controlling. He didn't want to control her from the grave. He never tried to control anyone, but Jud sized up Brice Connors the day they met. Brice tried to get him to put money in his company very early, and a year or so ago, when the market rose like a skyrocket, he tried again, promising really big returns. Jud knew he was a gambler from the start. And he knew he would get in trouble. Gamblers always lose eventually, that's what he said about Matthew Petrie a long time ago, and what he said a few years ago about Brice. Then, last summer, Brice made a desperate plea for help, and Jud said no, and later wrote the scene you just read, changing the surface, keeping the core of it.' Very softly she added, 'I think he left that clause alone because he knew there would be trouble, if not soon, eventually. Six months gives Abby time to smell the stench, recognize the source.'

'When did you ask your attorney about these matters?' Caldwell asked brusquely.

'One day last week. I didn't mention names

255

or tell him why I wanted to know, just what the terms mean.'

'Right after you read that section of the novel?'

'Soon after, yes.'

Caldwell shook his head. 'Mrs. Shaeffer, you've built a case that rests on a few pages of a work of fiction. You don't like Brice Connors, and neither did Jud Vickers, and you were extremely fond of Vickers and upset by his murder. Everything you've said is based on your dislike, a story in a book, and your imagination. And what you're doing is dangerous. You can't go around accusing people of murder, of plotting murder.'

'Lieutenant, believe me, I have not called a press conference, and I'm not going around accusing anyone of anything. I called for you to come here, remember. I haven't breathed a word of this to anyone else, certainly not to Abby. She must not become suspicious of her husband, that's the last thing I want.'

'Exactly what is it you do want?'

'I want you not to be kind and patronizing. I want you to listen to what I'm telling you, and to do something about it. I want you to stop beating the bushes for a blond-haired man, and stop wasting time looking for an extortionist or blackmailer, or whatever you think about that aspect. I want you to concentrate on Brice Connors, the only one with a real motive for killing Jud. I want you to stop ignoring the rope you keep stumbling over while you're off tying up nebulous loose ends that could blow in the breeze forever as far as Jud's murder is concerned.'

Suddenly the lieutenant grinned and leaned back in his chair. 'You want a lot, Mrs. Shaeffer. I'm sorry if I appeared patronizing, no intention there. I'm not. I'm interested in anything you have to tell us. But, Mrs. Shaeffer, please believe this, we have checked him out. And Abby Connors, too,' he added. 'That's always first, you understand, the immediate family. We can account for every minute of her time, and his. We can't put him in that cabin between one and two in the morning, no matter how hard we try.'

'You mean you can't put anyone inside the cabin at that time,' she snapped. 'Not just him. I've told you who did it, and why. With a whole police force at your disposal, it seems to me that you could find out how he managed it.'

Caldwell pushed his cup back and stood up. 'We can't build a case on simple conjecture, Mrs. Shaeffer. You've given this a lot of thought, obviously, but unless you have a shred of evidence, real evidence, it's a fantasy. I appreciate your efforts. Please take this in the spirit in which it's meant,' he said earnestly. 'I know that real police work might look tedious and unproductive from the outside, but we are following up leads, interviewing people, more people than you realize, getting statements, comparing them, looking into records, and bit by bit through our own plodding, laborious methods we get things done. Not as fast as you'd like, but we're making progress.'

Then, even more soberly, he added, 'And I urge you not to repeat what you've told me. Believe me, Mrs. Shaeffer, the consequences could be severe.'

Felicia stood up also; the interview, the dialogue, conversation, whatever it might be called, was over. 'You're like the knight who gets on his horse and gallops off in all directions,' she said. 'I believe that once you know the right direction, you'll find the trail and whatever evidence it will take to convince you. And once you accept who, then you'll find out how. The trouble is,' she said, leading the way into the living room, watching him pick up his jacket and put it on, 'you'll run out of time. Or Abby will. At midnight Sunday, the thirty-day contingency period will end; she will be the legal heir to Jud's estate. And from that moment on, she will be in danger.'

16

By the time Willa showed up after work, Felicia had dinner started, the table set, and wine open. She ushered Willa into the kitchen. 'Hang your jacket over a chair,' she said. 'It's pouring again, isn't it? You must be freezing.'

'Well, it's raining,' Willa admitted, holding her jacket at arm's length. 'It's going to drip on your floor.'

'Let it drip. I'm making a Middle Eastern lamb *khoresh*, and this time you have to help me eat it. I'm having scotch and water. You want that, or wine? Help yourself to either.'

Willa was eyeing her curiously; Felicia ignored the look, uncovered a pot and sniffed, thought a moment, added a pinch of cinammon, and covered it again. 'That will hold it while we talk.'

Willa poured a glass of wine and sat at the dining table across the kitchen. 'Was Abby here today?'

'No. She said she had something she had to do. She'll be here tomorrow.' Felicia sat opposite her and studied her face. Willa was not beautiful, but striking, with good bones, lovely hair, deep-set blue eyes that were only slightly less shadowed than they had been the previous week. Her grief had left its mark on her expression, one of sadness, a remoteness that never used to be there. For a short period Felicia had feared that Willa would go into a real depression following Jud's death, a clinical depression; her remoteness had been frightening, but she was coming back, not all the way yet, but she was coming back. Basically Willa was levelheaded and very intelligent, possessed of an analytical bent that exceeded Felicia's, and that was what Felicia was counting on now, that steady, analytic intelligence. She took a drink of her scotch and set the glass down, and then without any more hesitation told Willa about Caldwell's visit, their conversation.

'He didn't believe a word of it,' she finished. She had watched Willa's expression change to incredulity, disbelief, maybe even pity.

Now the younger woman lowered her gaze and sipped wine without speaking. Felicia waited out the silence as Willa thought. Finally Willa said, 'It sounds plausible, possible, but Felicia, he was right, you can't accuse someone of murder based on a few pages of fiction, and you don't really know for sure that Jud was writing about Brice. The cousin appeared in the first novel; he wasn't just created.' Her eyes widened and she leaned forward slightly. 'Have you told Abby this?'

'No, of course not. I'm telling you because you're intelligent, and you know Brice. Do you think he's capable of it?'

'I know him,' Willa said, 'but that's all, just barely know him. He isn't interested in any of Abby's friends. And then, after Jud and I . . . I'm sure Brice didn't approve. He became even cooler. Polite and cool. I confuse him,' she said with a little shrug. 'I'm in the art world, which he doesn't trust, but I'm also in administration, which he understands. It's hard for him to decide where I belong.' She looked past Felicia, thinking.

Then she said, 'Capable of planning it, maybe. He's the type who can plan elaborate financial deals and such, with all the details that go along with them, but the execution of the plan is a problem. There's still the means of getting to the cabin, which apparently no one has been able to figure out. Felicia, you must know the police had to have suspected him first thing. Isn't that how it works, the family first, then widen the circle to include outsiders? But they would have checked him out, and his alibi must be strong enough to stand up under their investigation.'

More forcefully she said, 'Aside from that, there are too many unanswered questions — all that money in cashier's checks, the strange man who flew into Bend that night, maybe a woman from Jud's past. There's just too much no one knows.'

Felicia nodded, not at all surprised. 'What I'd like you to do is go to the living room and read that section again, and think Brice, not Buster. See what you make of it with Brice in mind. I'll finish up our dinner.'

They stood up simultaneously, Willa to go to the living room, Felicia to the stove. She lit the burner under the rice, then took the salad greens from the refrigerator, washed and ready to be tossed with vinaigrette. Spinach leaves were washed and stemmed, ready to be added to the lamb for a minute or two only. Yellow saffron and yellow split peas, a few apricots, had turned the *khoresh* a lovely golden color; the bright green of the spinach would complete it. For dessert she had chilled pear halves; she would add a scoop of vanilla ice cream and top it with caramel sauce. And that was how dinners should look, and taste, she thought with satisfaction when it was time to call Willa.

She found her on the couch, staring off into space with a thoughtful look. 'Ready or not,' Felicia said. 'You know where the bathroom is. Get yourself a towel if I forgot to put one out for you.'

She dished out the rice, carried food to the table, and by the time Willa joined her, everything was in place.

Willa picked up her wine and drank it all. 'You're right,' she said in a low voice. 'I didn't see it before, but he caught Brice, the way he talks, the way he moves, everything. And I didn't see it.'

'Of course not. You expected the little bastard Buster, and that's who you saw. It's like one of those object/ground pictures, where first you see only one image, then suddenly it flips and you see the other one and can't find the first one until it does the flip again. The point is you can see one or the other, but not both simultaneously. Now let's eat while it's hot.'

Willa praised the dinner, but with a distracted air, as if she was still considering the pages she had just read, the implications. Then she nodded, as if she had reached a conclusion, and she concentrated on the food. 'This is so wonderful! Do you do this all the time? Just for yourself?'

'Of course not,' Felicia said. 'That's why I enjoy company, to give me a chance to eat what I like.' She had a vivid memory of Herbert carefully separating peas from zucchini; he never had liked things mixed on his plate, or in the pot, she added to herself.

After they were finished, the table cleared, Willa said, 'Even if we know without a doubt that Jud was talking about Brice, it's not enough. He could be in serious trouble financially — a lot of people are — but to go from there to murder is different. There's simply no way we can connect him with it. But neither can we wait for him to try it again. We have to tell Abby what we suspect.'

'Not yet,' Felicia said quickly. 'Do you think she'd accept it? Go back home and face him knowing I believe he killed her father? She might never speak to me again.'

'We have to,' Willa repeated firmly. 'If it's true, she'll be in danger, and you know that. She has to be told.'

'I agree,' Felicia said, pleased that Willa had worked through the implications for herself. 'The question is when, and how. She'll need time to think about it, and not in his presence. And we need evidence of some sort, something to open that lieutenant's eyes. I suspect Abby can furnish something relevant, but again, when and how?'

'What do you mean, she can furnish something?'

'When you live with a person, there are a lot of things going on that you don't

264

consciously see, or that you choose to ignore, just to keep the peace. Or you put them out of mind, to think about later. I've known Abby all her life,' she added, 'and I know to what lengths she'll go to keep the peace; she's seen quite enough fighting for one person.' She thought of what she had told Lieutenant Caldwell: once you know the right direction, you can find the trail. Object/ground again. 'I think that when Abby puts her mind to Brice, seriously considers him a suspect, things will surface. But she'll need some time away from him for it to happen.'

Willa walked back and forth in the living room, thinking about it, and finally said, 'We could tell her you're planning to go to the lake this weekend, and I'm going with you. I'll ask her if I can go to the cabin. There are a few things I left there that I'd like to pick up. There really are,' she added unhappily. 'She said there's a lot more material she has to sort out, and the cabin is locked up; she'd have to give me the key, or plan to go herself. I think she'll go; I think there are things she's finding that she doesn't intend to let anyone else see. If she's willing to go back now, I imagine she'll stay for several days, and I'll take time off from work a few days.'

'That's good,' Felicia said. 'Let's drive up together on Friday. And we can all three get together Saturday, or even Sunday.'

★ ★ ★

Abby was in the San Francisco airport, sitting in an empty waiting area. She had arrived three hours before her flight time, but there had not been any place she wanted to go, anything she wanted to do after leaving Thanh. Now she sat as if in a trance, seeing in her mind that terrible day in Vietnam, watching in her imagination the figure in shapeless black peasant clothes and cap run from house to house, seeing her shot, and then shot again and again, her body tossed this way and that by the thrust of bullets, seeing Jud collapse.

He blamed himself for her death, blamed himself for the deaths of his entire platoon. The day she died, he became a ghost.

Abby realized suddenly that since his death, what had obsessed her was not his murderer, not altogether; it was the mystery of her father. And his written words, his act in creating a school, Thanh's words, had given him to her. Whatever doubts she had had were gone, erased by the sight of her father's bold signature on the official bank documents

266

that had set up the trust fund, provided for auditors, outside overseers. It was all of a piece, she realized, from Teri Frazier's death to the death of his Vietnamese lover, all the guilt, the anguish, all one.

She recalled the old priest's words; he had prayed Jud would find peace. And finally after so many years of wandering, of being lost, unable to kill himself since he was already a ghost, unable to live wholly, driven by guilt and regret, he had found peace.

There was no blackmailer. She no longer believed in a hit man, a hired assassin, if she had ever believed in one. His killer had been someone close, not a phoenix rising from dead ashes.

When a child started to cry near her, she looked around in surprise; the waiting area was filling up. Mechanically she rose and walked until she found another waiting area without people, and she sat there until it, too, began to fill with passengers waiting to board their plane.

Eventually she made her way to her own gate and found that her flight had been announced, that most passengers were already aboard. She got in line.

★   ★   ★

267

It was raining in Eugene when she left the airport terminal to retrieve her car. For a time she sat watching the rain streak down her windshield. What to tell Brice, she kept thinking. How much? Her father had worked hard to keep this part of his life confidential, secret from her, from everyone. It had been important to him to keep it secret; she could do no less. But she had to convince Brice that there was no blackmailer lurking about. Do you swear to tell the truth? she mocked herself, and answered, Some of it anyway. In evading the whole truth, she realized, she would be the one to drive the wedge that Brice was convinced her father had tried to put between them. Jud never had, but his secret would do it.

She found her parking ticket in her purse, dug out money to pay at the exit; when she put her purse back on the passenger seat, her gaze stopped at the manila envelope Thanh had given her containing the financial records and photographs of the school. Swiftly she opened the glove compartment, jammed the envelope inside, closed and locked the door; then she started the engine.

Later, in the living room at home, with Spook at her feet, a comforting fire burning in the grate, coffee on the table before her, she told Brice about the priest. 'He's so old, in his nineties, and he's dying. He slips into sleep, wakes up ... My father knew him, respected him, and through him, Dad was giving all that money to a good cause, a worthy cause. A school. That's where he went in San Francisco, who he saw, what he did with those cashier's checks.'

Sitting opposite her, Brice watched her face as she talked. He leaned forward, his eyes shining with excitement. 'Jesus Christ, Abby! You did it! Those bumbling cops falling all over themselves getting nowhere, and you just up and did it! That's it. An extortion ring of some sort, using a senile old man, getting money from who knows how many people. Jud said no more, enough's enough, and they had to kill him, keep him from talking, from exposing the whole scheme. You did it!'

'It isn't like that,' she said sharply. 'Dad wanted to give them the money, he started it all himself, found them himself. The priest is old and dying, but he's rational. No one's using him for anything.'

He was paying little attention, she realized. His eyes had narrowed, and he nodded. 'Maybe they're using the old priest without his awareness. Maybe he believes whatever you think he does, but it doesn't change anything. No one gives money away like that without a record, without declaring it on their tax return. And Jud didn't claim any such charitable contributions.'

He brought his gaze back to her and said softly, 'Honey, face it, people have sides we can't know. Your father might have had a terrible secret from his past that you know nothing about, something important for him to keep secret. Important enough to pay out a hell of a lot of money to keep buried. But there comes a time when you say, No more. He reached that point. And, Abby, whatever it was that he did, that he wanted to hide, it doesn't matter now. It can't hurt him now. Let the police shake down that extortion ring; maybe they can even get some of the money back.'

She shook her head violently. 'Stop it! I'm telling you, it's true. I . . . ' She had started to say she had talked to Thanh, had pictures, records. She drew in a breath, and more quietly said, 'I learned enough to know it's true. I won't let the police badger that old man. Let him die in peace.'

'Don't be so naive,' he said. 'A group like that, they'd have a good story, or they'd never get a penny from anyone. That's to be expected at the very least, a plausible story, documents of some sort to back it up, and a string of suckers on the line. I know you believe whatever they told you. If you didn't, they'd be out of business. That's how they work.' When she shook her head again, he added harshly, 'I thought you were burning with desire to find out who killed your father. You know something that could lead the police right to them. You have to tell them whatever you know.'

'If I have to, I'll tell them I know where the money went, and that it has nothing to do with his murder,' she said just as harshly. 'And that's all.'

'They'll never accept that.'

'That's all they'll get. If you don't tell them anything, they won't even ask questions about it. Brice, I'm asking you, keep this confidential. My father wanted it kept confidential, and so do I. There's no confidence game, no extortion, no blackmail. He did what he did because he wanted to. And if he had wanted it known, he would have talked about it! Can't you even imagine that not everyone feels the same way about money as you do? Can't you accept that it wasn't important to him?'

'Christ!' he muttered. 'I'm going to get a drink.' He stalked from the room.

As soon as he was out of sight, she opened her purse and pulled out the sympathy note Father Jean Auguste had sent her, with the return address on the envelope, her response,

271

and the letterhead from the institute. Quickly she got up and went to the hearth and thrust them all into the fire.

She watched a paper start to curl, as if flinching from the flames, then catch fire all over all at once, and fall like a black ghost of itself before shattering into ash. Suddenly she thought of all the private papers upstairs, papers meant for no one's eyes except her father's, and she bit her lip.

If Brice told the lieutenant his suspicions about an extortion plot, she started, then changed it to *when*. He would. He would phone the lieutenant, who would come to hear him out, and then come to question her. What if they demanded all of Jud's papers in their search for the extortionists? A subpoena for the papers. Those in her possession, and those still in the cabin.

She was startled by the sound of Brice's voice. He had come in with his drink. He stood very close, but he didn't touch her. Very quietly he said, 'Sweetheart, I'm sorry I upset you all over again. You've had a fierce day, up at the crack of dawn, damn airplanes, time with a dying man. Emotionally and physically, you're beat. Let's get some sleep.'

'You go on,' she said. 'I need to unwind.'

'Okay. You have a few calls on the machine. I got some roast beef and cheese if you want a sandwich or something. Don't stay up too late.' He walked out of the living room.

She listened to her calls, a couple of friends, then one from Christina Maas, who wanted Abby to call back at her first opportunity. Stiff, businesslike voice, brusque manner. Abby nodded, but she had seen another side of her, and that side was in her mind as she listened to the brief message. The last call was from Coop Halburtson, who sounded ancient on the phone, much more so than in person. 'Abby, you there? Look, Florence and I will be heading out, down to California on Saturday. Time to pack it in for the winter, I guess. We'd love to see you before we leave, if you have the time to come out. If you can't make it, I'll put the key to the boat shed in the mail for you. But we'd love to see you before we take off. Give us a call.'

She thought of the old couple, looking out over the black water at the black emptiness of Jud's cabin, knowing that this time he wasn't coming back. And poor Coop. When he looked over now, did he see again the horror he had found, Jud sprawled on the stairs, his face destroyed, the blood? She remembered that Jud had told them he wanted to buy their house when and if they ever decided to sell it.

Slowly she walked upstairs to her room and

sat at the desk. Tomorrow she had to get stamps, mail her notes, send the manuscript to Christina, and find a safe place for Jud's papers. She leaned back, but in her mind she was gazing at the mahogany box, and she reached out to touch it. It felt warm to her touch.

It was time, she thought then. Whatever she had been waiting for no longer was compelling her to delay, forcing restraint. It was time to bury her father.

17

Brice was on the phone when Abby went down to the kitchen the next morning. He blew her a kiss as he continued his conversation.

'Right, right. I understand. Look, why don't you come around to the office, say, about eleven or so, and let's hash it out there.' Listening to the caller, he looked at Abby and raised his eyebrows in an expression of helplessness. 'Okay, I'll wait for you.'

He disconnected the phone and put it on the table. 'My clients are driving me crazy,' he said. 'I think it's a conspiracy.'

'You could always go back to school and become a ... an orthodontist,' she said, waiting for toast to pop up. 'I think they keep very regular hours and never give out their home numbers.'

He laughed. 'That guy,' he said, pointing to the phone, 'against all the advice I could shovel on him, did a crazy thing. He bought into a company heavily, used his own company's money to do it, and now the stocks he's holding are good for starting fires. He'd track me down if I moved to the North

Pole and wore a polar bear suit. He wants someone to get him out of the jam he's in.' He glanced at his watch. 'While the phone's all warmed up, why don't you give the ice lady a call before I have to take off?'

She looked at him curiously, then remembered that Christina Maas wanted her to call back. And she wondered how Brice could do this. Last night he had been so upset — betrayed, furious, hurt, a whole gamut of dire emotions all acting on him at once; this morning it was as if last night had not happened, as if he had wiped the slate clean with a night's sleep. Every day a new beginning, she thought then, and could even envy that ability. Not only each day, sometimes from one hour to the next; yesterday's toothache, this morning's heartache erased, gone from memory.

It was eight, eleven in New York, as good a time as any to call Christina. She had jotted down the telephone number on the memo pad, and she saw her note there to call Coop Halburtson; she had forgotten that one, too. She called Christina, and once more was struck by her businesslike manner; apparently she simply didn't indulge in any small talk.

'Abby, I'm glad you got back to me. The movie contract came in yesterday, and it looks okay. I'll FedEx it to you. It's clearly

276

marked where you have to sign, and where you have to have it notarized. It looks good. How are you coming with the novel?'

'It's done. I'll put it in the mail today. I found the missing sections and included them with a note to tell you the pages where they belong. I think we have it in the right order.'

When Abby disconnected, Brice was watching her expectantly. 'Well?'

'The Hollywood contract arrived, she'll send it FedEx. I have to have something notarized, then send it back.'

'Wow! Another movie! Honey, that's great! I'm so glad for you.' His eyes were shining; he grabbed her and hugged her hard, then kissed her forehead. 'Now you can have your toast and coffee, and I'm off to the salt mines. See you later.' Whistling, he dashed out of the kitchen, out of the house.

That morning she went to the post office and bought stamps and a large padded envelope, the kind Jud had used to mail his manuscripts. By eleven she had everything ready to mail on the table by the front door; and by then, she thought, Brice had probably talked to Lieutenant Caldwell. Or maybe not. Even if she hadn't actually begged him not to tell the lieutenant about the checks, the school, she had asked him not to. That should be enough, she thought.

She returned to her room, where she regarded three piles of papers: one held ten or more short stories, or the starts of stories; one held private papers that she had read; one was still unread, unknown. No safety-deposit box, she knew; they could subpoena the contents. If Brice confided in the police, she added. Nowhere in the house; they might search, or Brice might, looking for a clue to the priest, the school he didn't believe in. Felicia's place, she decided. At least for now, until she found a better solution.

Hurriedly, as if Caldwell might appear any moment, she searched for her old backpack, the one she had used daily when she rode her bike to high school, and later to her university classes. There were some broken pencils in it, scraps of paper, tattered and shredded Kleenex. She stuffed it full of Jud's papers and closed the fasteners, and then, abruptly, she sat down on the side of the bed.

What was happening to her, to her marriage? She was simply assuming that Brice would tell Caldwell everything he knew, everything he suspected, in spite of her asking him not to. She had never kept secrets from him, not really; if there were things in her past they never had talked about — her life with Jud, her first marriage, even the fight with Jud — it had been more because she had known

278

he wasn't interested in her past than for any other reason. She nodded; he lived for now, right now, not yesterday or last year. Every day a new start, she thought again, every day a renewal of tomorrow's dreams, never a replay of yesterday's problems. That helped explain why they had never fought before the way they seemed to fight these days. There had never been anything left over from the day before to fight about. She had watched her parents' battles, listened to them, feared them, and swore it would never happen to her. But it had happened with Matthew. After the first excitement of love, or lust, was spent, there had been nothing but infighting, and always about what had already happened, yesterday, last week, two hours earlier. Once out of that marriage, she had sworn never again, never, never . . . For years following her divorce she had avoided the suggestion of entanglement, of commitment; at the first argument, regardless of how trivial, how meaningless, she was out of there. Gone. No more, never, never. And that's how it had been with Brice, both of them at once calm and passionate, with no arguments, no fights, no real disagreements.

No talk about the past, hers or his, or theirs. Yesterday's mistakes, misjudgments, bad decisions, gone, dismissed and forgotten.

Every day, every hour a new beginning. She remembered that she had meant to suggest that whatever had happened between him and his parents should be settled, put to rest, forgiven, and thinking of it now, she knew there was no point. He had no regrets, no second-guessing, nothing to forgive or be forgiven for. Whatever happened was over and done with. Today a new day.

Even as she thought this, her gaze was roaming about restlessly, and she realized that with the manuscript gone now, the cards boxed and in the closet and her notes gone, with the other papers stowed out of sight, the room looked barren. Brice might suspect she had taken away more than just the manuscript and notes; she jumped up to scatter the short stories around a bit, to give the room a more disordered appearance, the way it had been yesterday.

Her gaze rested on the mahogany box, and she said to herself, 'Not my secrets. His.'

She left the room and went back downstairs, this time to call Felicia, make sure she would be home. Maybe they could take all the dogs for a walk, Felicia suggested; she would wait for Abby.

Then, reluctantly, Abby called the Halburtsons. She felt guilty about not calling sooner, for avoiding them when she had been at the cabin before. Florence answered the phone, her voice hesitant and her words vague, the way they always had been, as if in mid-sentence she lost track of where she had intended to go, or lost interest in whatever she was saying.

'Dear, I'm so glad you called. It's earlier than we usually leave, but . . . Coop's been so . . . He's out doing something in the boat shed, I think . . . Maybe a change would be good. Saturday morning seems a good time.'

Abby closed her eyes, listening. 'I'm sorry I haven't gotten in touch,' she said, and was interrupted.

'Dear, we understand. But we'd hate not to see you before . . . Coop even thought we might drive in to Eugene, but . . . '

'No. Don't do that,' Abby said. 'I'm coming out there this week. On Friday. I'll come see you on Friday.'

★   ★   ★

The first time Abby had asked Felicia if it was all right to bring Spook with her, Felicia had snorted. 'Don't be silly. Bring her, bring an alligator if you want to. That's why I bought this jail cell instead of just renting an apartment, so I could do what I want in it. If I decide to drive nails in the wall, or paint my

281

floors red, no one's about to tell me to stop or kick me out.'

Abby took Spook after that. Now she carried her backpack into the condominium and set it down; the dogs all greeted one another with suspicious sniffing, front to tail, and they all passed muster. Spook looked like a roughneck country cousin next to the elegant white poodles; both of them could have passed for windup toys in her presence.

'I have some papers in there,' Abby said. 'Private things.' Wrong beginning, she thought, and stopped, started over. 'Yesterday I went to San Francisco and met someone who used to know Dad. There's no blackmailer, no extortionist, nothing like that. Dad was financing a school, it's that simple, but Brice can't believe that in this day and age anyone would do that and not claim it on his tax return, or let it be known. Their attitudes about money — Dad's and Brice's, I mean — like day and night. Brice still thinks there's extortion or something like that.'

'Accountants,' Felicia said scornfully. 'That's exactly how Jud would have done it, privately. He didn't care any more about money than those foolish dogs do.' She looked at the backpack. 'So what do you intend to do with that?'

'I thought for now, for a few days at least, maybe I could leave it here. On Friday I'm going up to the cabin. I'll take the stuff with me. I'll try not to get in your way or keep you from anything. If that's all right.'

Felicia looked at her shrewdly. 'You think Brice will tell the police about your trip, that you learned something?'

Miserably Abby nodded. 'He really believes that Dad was being blackmailed to keep some gang quiet about something, and that he finally said he wouldn't pay any more, and they killed him so he couldn't expose their extortion scheme. He's probably already called Caldwell. They might even come here to see if you know anything about it.'

Felicia nodded. How she would love to sit in on Brice's talk with Caldwell, she thought. 'Let them come,' she said.

They took the dogs out then and walked the quiet residential streets behind the condominium, and Felicia marveled, as she had often done in the past, at how fate sometimes took a hand. If the Halburtsons were leaving on Saturday, she told Abby, then she had a perfect reason to go home on Friday, to bid them good-bye. Even her children could understand that.

'I can give you a ride out,' Abby said quickly.

Felicia shook her head. 'No, I don't think so. I don't know when I'll be coming back.

Maybe not until the Christmas holiday season. Some work to do, things to finish up; besides, I hate living in town, and so do my girls.'

She would take Willa, Felicia thought then, and they would stay at the cottage for a few days, at least through Sunday or even Monday. And they would all three get together and have a real talk. But she wanted her own car, wanted to come and go when she felt the need, not be a captive rider. She had no intention of begging at the door and waiting for someone to open it for her.

She really did want to go home, she realized, and she wanted to stay there. Bend was not that far from her cottage; she had friends in Bend, more than in Eugene, actually. And if her children wanted to see her, have her watch her grandchildren grow up, let them do the traveling. More and more often the prospect of giving up the town house altogether and settling down in the cottage was floating up in her consciousness, calling her. She missed the lake, the mountains, the solitude, the freedom . . .

But first she had to see this thing through with Abby and Willa. First things first, she told herself.

★ ★ ★

That night Abby grilled salmon and baked potatoes, made a salad, did a quick stir-fry with broccoli and green onions, and had it all ready by the time Brice came downstairs after changing his clothes. He always did that immediately, took off his suit, hung it up neatly, and put on a sweater and jeans, loafers, his at-home bum clothes, he called them. Cashmere sweater, designer jeans, Italian loafers, she had scoffed the first time he said that.

'There's something I have to tell you,' he said, seating himself at the table without a glance at the food.

'After we eat,' she said firmly. She did not want to hear about his talk with the police yet, and there were things she had to tell him, but after they ate, not before.

The dinner was not at fault, she thought a few minutes later, when it appeared that neither of them had much appetite. She was braced for what she knew would be another ugly scene, and she suspected that he was annoyed that she had put him off as she had. They both drank the wine.

Finally Brice said, 'Good dinner, but I had a late lunch. Now can I talk?'

'Me first,' she said. 'I decided to go out to the cabin on Friday to see Coop and Florence before they take off for California.

They're probably leaving early Saturday morning.'

'I thought we were going together on Saturday.'

'You said that, I didn't. I want to see them, get the key to the boat shed, and then spend a few days at the cabin working on the papers there. And I want to make certain they understand that the deal they had with Dad is still good. He planned to buy their house someday; they counted on that. I'll tell them I'll buy it myself, if they can hold off for six months. They may not want to sell out for years, but they should know the offer is still good.'

He was staring at her in disbelief. 'Buy their house! What for?'

'The same reasons Dad had, to be sure of easy access to the cabin, and to keep the electricity operating without having to move everything.' The electrical service box was on the back of Coop's house; Jud had said he had no idea where they would put it if Coop sold to someone else, and no meter reader would swim across the finger in order to read the meter.

Brice shook his head. 'You're out of your mind! You don't intend to keep the cabin now, not after what happened. You can't intend that.'

'I do intend to keep it. And access to it.'

'Every time you go there, you'll see his dead body, blood, and this nightmare will never end.'

'No, that's not how it is,' she said slowly. 'The happiest memories of my childhood, of growing up are connected with the cabin and the lake. That's what I'll see and remember.'

He rubbed his eyes, then pushed his chair back and stood up, walked stiffly to the sink, where it appeared he was trying to hold it in place. 'You know how I feel about the cabin,' he said. 'It's never been a place where I felt comfortable. You'd do this without talking it over, without even mentioning it first, knowing how I feel about it.'

'Did you talk to the police today?'

He nodded. 'I had to. There's a murderer out there. You have information they need, and they need all the help they can get. Caldwell's coming to town tomorrow afternoon, to the office.'

'And you know how I feel about that,' she said. Then, quickly, before he could respond, she said, 'You'll never have to set foot in the cabin again if you don't want to. I don't even want you to come up this weekend. I'm going to bury my father, and I want to do it alone. You were right, it's time.'

She had expected a yelling match, a

storming rage from him; now she could feel some of her tension drain away as he continued to stand without moving, without speaking. She began to feel that she had hurt him deeply, that she had been unreasonable in presenting her plan as done, something she had already decided alone. Even taking his case to Caldwell was a rational act on his part, she thought without conviction, since she had not told him enough to dispel his belief in an extortionist scheme. Unhappily she drank her wine and wished she could get more without having to cross the kitchen to get it; she didn't want to break into his silence with any motion of her own, not until he had finished whatever he was going through in his mind.

At last he turned to face her, his expression strained and bleak. 'Abby, let's put that aside for a minute. Let's consider an alternative. I know you love the mountains and the lake, the cabin, all of it. But it doesn't have to be that cabin in that place. Let's try something else. I had a call this morning, you even heard part of it, from a guy who's in deep trouble. He has to raise a hundred thousand dollars within the next two weeks, or he's dead in the water, and he knows it. He's really desperate. He owns a house on the coast, a beautiful place, worth at least two hundred thousand,

and he'll sell it for half that in cash now, tomorrow, first thing next week. But it's got to be cash. He offered it to me, and I nearly laughed in his face. Where would I dig up money like that? But he'll make a deal with someone who will hold on to it for a few months, long enough to duck the capital-gains tax, and then make his money back, doubled. Let's buy it, Abby, and for six months try it. You can have your retreat, it's in the forest, with a stream, the ocean nearby, everything you love. After six months if you still want the cabin instead, then we'll sell it.'

'What in the world are you talking about? We can't raise that kind of money, even if we wanted to. Have you seen this house, had it appraised, anything?'

'No, because I knew I couldn't touch it. But you could. I can arrange for a quick appraisal.'

'I can't get that kind of money for months,' she said. 'Now who's talking crazy?'

'You could,' he said. 'You don't realize it, but any bank in town would roll over for you now. You could walk in in the morning and have that money in your account by afternoon.'

'We couldn't even make payments on that kind of loan. It's hard enough to make payments on this house and your car.'

'We'd borrow enough to cover the payments. A hundred twenty-five thousand, keep the twenty-five thousand for payments until we decide. Then we'll either love it and want to keep it, or sell it and double our money.'

'No,' she said. 'No! If he's a crook, let him go to jail. We don't have to get involved, and I'm not interested in doubling money I don't even have.'

'He's not a crook,' Brice said. 'He made a serious mistake, that's all. Let's just apply for the loan, so I have something to tell him, and then go have a look at the property on Monday or Tuesday. But I have to have something to show him, so he won't make that offer to someone else. Someone's going to snap it up. It's an opportunity that doesn't come up often.'

He came back to the table. 'If we look and don't want it, we don't have to take the money out; we'll simply say we changed our minds and don't need it, but if we do want it, the money will be there.'

She didn't remember standing up, but they were nearly eye to eye. She shook her head.

'Is that how it's going to be?' he demanded furiously, his face livid and taut. 'You want it spelled out loud and clear? You're the heiress, you decide what you'll do with your money. Have you decided what my role in your life will be? Will I even have a bit part? You know what you're doing to us? Does it matter to you?'

Staring at him, she felt as if an arctic wind had swept over her. 'You're involved in some way,' she said. 'Are you involved in some way?' Her voice rose, became almost shrill.

He sagged, and turned his back. 'I'm not, but if he goes down, he intends to take me with him. He'll swear he was acting on my advice. Even a hint like that will kill me. I'll be out of the office within an hour, maybe arrested. It's a lie, but that's what he's ready to swear to if I don't find a way out of his mess for him.'

Abby whispered, 'Oh, my God.'

'I'm going up to my study,' Brice said hoarsely. 'I told you the truth. You can do it. Your decision.' He left the kitchen, headed up the stairs.

She sank down into her chair again, seeing nothing before her, thinking nothing coherent enough to recall from minute to minute. She didn't move until Spook nudged her leg, and she realized the dog had been whining to go out, whining for table scraps on the patio. She looked at the salmon, then mechanically scraped it all together and removed the center bone, took the plate to the patio and let Spook out. She stood with her forehead against the cool glass.

At length she moved and started to clear the table, put dishes in the dishwasher. Could she do it? She had no idea, but if he said it was possible, it probably was. He was the one who knew about money. *But he is involved.* She heard her own voice in her head, as if in warning, and she stopped moving, forgetting again what she had been doing.

This had not started today, she thought then, remembering all the hours he had spent in his room at the computer, how he blanked the screen if she opened his door, his sudden outbursts of irritation, how worried he had been for weeks, months even, and not just over year-end business. But if he was telling the truth, if he was innocent and would be implicated in something illegal, and if she could get the money for him, didn't she have to do it? She knew she did.

She bit her lip when she realized that she had used *if* both times. *If* he was innocent, *if* he was telling the truth. And she didn't know.

She poured coffee and sat at the table waiting for Spook to want back in, and saw with surprise that the table was clean, everything put away. She felt as if an invisible creature had come in and done the work for her. A vivid memory surfaced of sitting here with Christina Maas, looking at numbers without comprehension. Christina had said, 'Whatever the figure is, count on half that much by the time the commission comes out and taxes are paid, both state and federal. You'll end up with half of it. And spread over time.'

She wished desperately she had someone she could discuss this with, and knew she would never breathe a word of it. Could a person fill to overflowing with secrets? she wondered. Burst with secrets, swell up and die of secrets, which would ooze out like black leeches . . .

Then, unaccountably, the fight with Jud played once more in her head. 'You didn't learn a damn thing the first time out, did you? . . . You stepped in it with Petrie and turned around and did it again with Brice, and didn't learn a thing.'

This was different, she wanted to cry out. Different!

Spook scratched at the door, and dully she got up and opened it, refilled her coffee mug, started to walk upstairs, as tired as if she had been carrying heavy trays of food for hours.

Inside her room, she stood with her back to the door, gazing at the box that contained her father's ashes. 'You knew all along,' she whispered.

That was nickel-and-dime stuff, she thought then; we've graduated to the big league now. Jud had mortgaged the cabin, bailed out Matthew Petrie, not for him, but for her sake, to get her out of waitressing, get her back in school, but she knew without a doubt that he would not have stirred a muscle, not even a flicker to help Brice now. She remembered his joking refusal to let Brice or his company advise him about finances.

She wondered if Brice had approached him again; if so, neither of them had mentioned it, but the hard feelings on Brice's side had intensified over the past year or two; she had assumed because of her father's affair with Willa, her own fight with Jud, that Brice must have sensed her tension, suspected the cause. But Brice had been the one to suggest a visit in August, surprising her, pleasing her. That was right after the stock market fell drastically, when he first started complaining about his clients and their fears. His fears? That was when something happened, and he must have asked Jud for money the afternoon she had taken a walk with Spook up into the forest, to some of her old haunts, leaving them alone in the cabin.

Suddenly she wished she had not mailed the manuscript, because there was something . . . She went to the closet and brought out the laptop computer that held all of Jud's files, and she began to search the novel sections, those written after August. She had not seen Brice in the novel earlier, looking as she had been for a clue about the mystery of her father's past, but now, as she scanned the pages on the screen, she was looking for Brice in whatever guise Jud might have cloaked him in.

She wanted to weep when she found it.

But what difference did it make if Brice knew last summer that he was in trouble, or just found out yesterday or even this morning? Bottom line, she thought bleakly, he was in trouble.

18

Sometime around midnight Brice tapped on the door and opened it. He didn't enter the room, merely stood in the doorway. She was at the desk, trying to comprehend the many papers Christina had left with her — numbers, contracts, royalty periods, amounts due and when.

'It's late,' Brice said. 'I keep thinking of the things I didn't tell you, and . . . Can we talk?'

'What more is there?' She swiveled her chair around to look at him.

'Can I tell you what happened, what I did?'

She shook her head. 'No, don't.' If he told her, then she would be involved, she thought, and if she became involved, she would have to assume responsibility, not out of choice any longer but out of necessity. 'Do details really matter?'

'Okay. You're right. I am involved. I made a stupid mistake, and then followed it up with a couple more trying to get out from under the first one. But, Abby, I have to tell you why. It's killing me not to tell you why. I kept seeing Jud out there living the life of a hermit, suddenly striking it so rich. Thinking, I owed

296

him this house. You had a car because of him. He even paid your insurance. I was afraid. He could give you all the things I wanted to and couldn't. Then this guy came in, a client, with a tip that he was bursting with.'

Distantly she thought, Someone asks, Can I tell you something, and you say No, don't, and he tells you anyway.

'This guy's son told him the company he worked for was going to go public in a few weeks, get in on the ground floor, double your money in a matter of weeks, then sell. He put in a lot of money, and he's no idiot. All I could think of was that I could make a lot of money fast, pay back what I owed, and then we'd go on a trip somewhere, the two of us, a real honeymoon. And I'd buy you anything you wanted, anything you even looked at twice. I was crazy thinking like that, but that's how it was.'

He cleared his throat, as if speaking were painful. 'All those months, it never occurred to me to hit up anyone, you or anyone else, for money, not until you mentioned the Halburtson place, buying it. It came to me in a flash — if they wanted to sell now, next month, you would borrow the money to buy their house. You could borrow money for us, for you and me. What really scares me isn't going to jail, although that's scary enough.

What really scares me is the thought of losing you.'

He had not moved from the doorway; she had not moved from her chair. He looked like a boy standing at the principal's office, afraid to enter, more afraid to leave, pleading not for sympathy or approval but for understanding. She made a motion toward the papers she had spread out. 'I've been going over all these files Christina left. I need a little time to think about what we'll have and when we'll have it.'

'If you decide,' he said huskily, 'if you think we can do it, I want it all in your name, a loan in your name alone; if we buy the house, in your name. So you won't have cause to worry that I might do something else stupid. But I swear to you, Abby, never again. I've had the shit scared out of me, a pretty bitter lesson, but I have learned it.'

She stood up. 'There's something you have to understand. I don't think of Dad's money as mine, not really. There were things he planned to do, things I have to do for him.'

'What do you mean?'

'Like the Halburtsons. That was a promise. I can't renege on his promises. And there's the school. It's real, and he promised to help financially in the future. Now I have to do it.'

For a moment his face went blank, then he shook his head. 'I do understand. I really do.

298

I know how you felt about him, and frankly I've been jealous ever since I met you. Once I'm out of this mess, we'll make it without a cent of his. You'll see.'

'Tell me one thing,' she said slowly. 'Is there really a house for sale?'

He looked down at the carpet and mumbled, 'There's a place I can get for thirty-five thousand cash. That's real enough. The rest would go to replace what I borrowed. We can apply for the loan, or you can, and on Monday or Tuesday, whenever you get back from the lake, go see it for ourselves. If it's a shack, that's the end of it. I'll go to old man Durkins and tell him what I did, and take my lumps.'

Durkins was the senior associate of the Eugene office; he wore silk shirts and custom-made suits and vacationed in the Bahamas, or the Cayman Islands. 'That's my future,' Brice had said before they were married, talking about his prospects, his future. 'Our future,' he had said. Now he gazed at her for a moment, then said, 'Good night, Abby.' He stepped back into the hallway and pulled the door closed.

She shuddered, remembering something else about Durkins. At her wedding reception, he had patted her arm and said, 'I don't usually give out advice about personal matters, but I told Brice to grab you before someone else did. Glad to see he took it seriously.'

It was a bad night. She studied Christina's figures until her eyes burned, then lay down on the bed, not to sleep, just to rest. Sometime during the night she woke up, chilled, and pulled the bedspread over her, and slept again. She dreamed she was being chased by tigers, that she kept slipping and falling down on a plain covered with little balls of ice. She dreamed that Jud came staggering in from the woods carrying a gigantic rock, that he heaved and grunted with effort, and finally put it down and joined her at the ledge, where they both dangled their feet in the water. He said, 'Honey, go bring that rock over here, will you?' She went to it and lifted it easily: pumice, full of holes, full of air. Laughing, they watched it float on the black water until a giant ray snapped it up and vanished with it.

She heard Brice open her door, then close it softly, and she didn't stir, pretended she was still asleep. She waited until she heard his car leave before she got up. No more explanations, no more talk, no more lies, she thought.

At the kitchen table she started a list of the things she had to get to that day and the next in order to be free on Friday to go to the cabin, where she might be able to think clearly. She had to get the Xuan Bui Institute papers from her car and put them in her backpack at Felicia's house. She had thought they would be safe locked up in her glove compartment, but then she had been thinking only of Brice's searching for something, not of the police, too. And it had come to her during the night that she should bury all of Jud's private papers with his ashes. She would go to an import shop and buy a second box to hold them; it wouldn't be as fine as the mahogany box, but she would get a good one, possibly even one from Bali. Also, she had to be on hand to receive the package from Christina, and sign the contract and get it notarized.

She accepted that if she borrowed against her inheritance, she would have to pay back the full amount in the spring. And when the Halburtsons decided to sell, she had to honor her father's pledge to them. They might make that decision soon, she knew; they were old, and without Jud nearby, no doubt they were very lonely. They would miss him in many ways, not just his companionship; he had helped Coop keep his boat in good repair, helped maintain their house and ramp, had run errands for them . . . And what about the

Xuan Bui Institute? Jud had told Father Jean Auguste he would donate five hundred thousand dollars, spread out over time as he received various payments. Jud's pledge was now hers. She didn't question that; she had never thought of his money as hers, not when he was living, not now that he was gone.

Her father had not believed in borrowing; taking out the mortgage on the cabin must have pained him terribly. Yet, here she was being coerced into doing something he had preached against all his life; spending money she didn't have. Spending his money. Playing with someone else's marbles. 'I'm not being forced to do anything,' she muttered, and realized she was rehearing words spoken by Brice, that he had done it for her, to buy her whatever she wanted, that he had always been jealous of Jud, that they lived in this house because of Jud's wedding gift. She remembered how he had looked, like a sullen child dark with resentment, when Jud had presented her with the sports car, which, Brice said, cost him close to thirty thousand dollars. Brice was making payments on his own car, and would be making them when he traded it in on a newer model, and in fact would forever be making payments on a car. Suddenly she wondered where he had gotten the ten thousand dollars he had put up as his half of the down payment on the house. At the time he had said he saved it up over the years, but how? In school, graduate school ... His parents were not wealthy; they couldn't have given him that much money as a gift. And Brice, she well knew, was not a saver.

She had read that more relationships were fractured by disagreements over money than by sexual problems, and she had to admit there had never been any sexual problems in this household; she and Brice liked sex a lot. Liked it with each other, often. She had always known that their attitudes about money were polar opposites. In spite of Lynne's lecturing, she had adopted Jud's position after all. If you had more than you needed, you found a worthy cause and gave to it. Jud had been wrong about one thing, she thought then; he had said she was getting more like her mother, like Lynne, who had desperately needed security. She knew she had never expected real security in that same sense with Brice; she had said yes because she had been horny. And because they never argued or fought over anything. Never used to, anyway. Simple as that. She had known from the start that Brice was envious of those with wealth, that he yearned for it the way a child yearns for a bicycle like the one the rich kid down the block has. Brice believed money was power and freedom, but who had been freer, her father or Brice?

In vexation she forced herself to return to the list she was making. She should buy a shovel; there might be one at the cabin, but she couldn't remember seeing it in years. Then there was Caldwell. He would see Brice in the afternoon, and no doubt give her a call afterward. Or would he simply appear at the door?

She made a grocery list, enough for several days, a week possibly, in case it snowed and she couldn't get out right away. She closed her eyes, visualizing snow at the lake, the flakes melting silently on the water, vanishing without a trace, without a ripple. The world turning white and black, like a surreal painting or a photographic negative, and the silence. Everything hushed and still. The lake never froze — the water by now was as cold as it got, thirty-eight or forty degrees — but sometimes ice formed at the edges, then broke away, miniature icebergs slowly diminishing; the water looked like India ink then, with incredible ghostly white shadows afloat in ethereal shifting patterns for a short time.

The phone rang, snapping her to rigid attention. Not Lieutenant Caldwell, not this early. It was Felicia. With relief Abby picked up the call and accepted an invitation for lunch with Felicia and Willa. It had occurred to her that Brice might decide to come home for lunch, and she needed more time before they talked again about a loan, the school, a possible house on the coast, or anything else.

★ ★ ★

It was after five when she arrived home; Brice was there already, looking worried.

'I called half a dozen times,' he said. 'What have you been doing all day?' He took a small bag of groceries from her.

She pulled off her jacket and hung it up. 'Shopping. This and that. I had lunch with Willa and Felicia.'

His mouth tightened, but he made no comment.

Sometime during the day she had decided to stop pretending she wasn't seeing both Willa and Felicia. Even if she hadn't lied about it, she had misled him by evasion, and one of them should start being on the level, she had told herself severely. She started to walk to the kitchen. 'Hamburgers okay with you? I don't think I'm up to much more than that.'

'Whatever. It's early. You don't have to start anything yet, and later on I'll help.' He set the

305

bag of groceries on the counter. 'Did the FedEx come?'

'No. I really didn't expect it until tomorrow.' She began to put away the cold things, milk, butter, ground beef. 'I'll sign it and have it notarized and just put it back in the mail. If Christina said it's all right, I'll take her word for it.'

He nodded. 'I dropped in at the bank today and had a talk with Eddie Blankenship. He said if you want a loan, it's in the bag. Just a little paperwork. I brought the application home with me. All you have to do is sign it and take it back. It will be processed and the money transferred on Monday. They can notarize the contract signature while you're there.'

Last night was gone, she thought in wonder. No carryover of bitter words, of her indecision, of separate beds. He really did suffer from short-term-memory-lapse syndrome, she mused. Or maybe not, maybe he enjoyed the syndrome. She almost wished she had it, too. She closed the refrigerator door.

'And Caldwell came by,' Brice said, one matter over and done with, on to another. 'I think they have it pretty much figured out. That guy who flew in to Bend, he must have gone to Portland from California by plane, hopped the flight to Bend, called Jud and got

306

a ride with him to the cabin. That would explain a lot, if he was someone Jud couldn't refuse to see. There had to have been an accomplice, someone waiting for him, but the blond guy brought the ultimatum. So he went over to the cabin, and after he was done there, he waited until daybreak and started hiking back down, and his accomplice met him somewhere on the road. No signs of a car up that road because the accomplice didn't drive all the way up. Nothing else has made sense yet, but that does.'

Slowly she crossed the kitchen to sit down at the table.

Brice was still talking, excitedly, rapidly now. 'That explains so much,' he said. 'Spook wouldn't have attacked anyone Jud brought in with him. There was plenty of time for him to go through papers, get whatever he was after, find the right disk, everything. And Caldwell says there are a couple of places on that road where someone could have turned around to head back out, not in the dark, not at night, but in daylight it wouldn't have been a real problem. The killer might have walked five miles, not a big deal with so much at stake. Then they probably just headed over to Highway 97, and down to California, gone, vanished.'

It was possible, she thought; it sounded

plausible. And Caldwell had suggested a hit man, a contract killer. It was true that Spook would not have attacked anyone Jud had brought home in the rowboat, and Coop Halburtson's dogs wouldn't have barked at anyone Jud met and escorted to the ramp. She rubbed her eyes. Now they would search for a motive, as well as the blond man.

As if reading her mind, Brice sat down and took her hand. 'Abby,' he said in a low, urgent voice, 'you have to tell them what you found out in San Francisco, the name of the priest, about the cashier's checks. That's where they'll find that guy, down in San Francisco, but they don't have anything to go on. You have to tell them.'

She drew her hand away from his, then stood up. 'I'll put on some coffee.'

He turned his chair and watched as she moved around the kitchen. 'You know I'm right,' he said. 'There's nothing you can say about your father that can hurt him now, nothing. And the worst thing you can do, the real sin, is to try to protect his memory and let a killer get off. You have to face it, your father was human, he made a mistake somewhere in the past, and he tried to hide it. But it's not something you have to keep hiding. Even if that priest married him to a Vietnamese woman and there was a child, even if his marriage to your mother was bigamous, it has nothing to do with you, and it can't hurt him for the truth to come out now.'

She had measured the coffee, poured water into the well of the coffeemaker, and now stood with her head bowed, trying to think what next.

'I think you were conned,' Brice said. 'But supposing you weren't, they'll look into it, verify the school story, and get on to something else, some other reason for killing Jud. No harm will have been done.'

Her thoughts were bleak. What they would find out was that Jud had slept with the enemy and gotten her killed, and betrayed his own platoon, his own troops, led them into an ambush that wiped them all out. That was how they would see it, what they would believe, because that was what he had believed ever since that day in Vietnam.

'I feel grimy,' she said. 'I need a shower.' She walked past him, to the hallway, up the stairs, feeling his gaze with every step.

She stood under the shower for a long time. Maybe Brice was right, she had to tell Caldwell what she knew so they would stop wasting time and get on with finding the real motive, the real murderer. They could verify that there was a school, that Jud had given the checks to the priest, and then to the trust fund, and let it stop there without asking why he had done that. They didn't need to know why. Even with that knowledge, she thought then, they might think he had been coerced, that there was a conspiracy. Brice certainly would still think it was a con. Thieves thought everyone stole. Liars thought everyone lied. Con men . . .

She closed her eyes and lifted her face into the water. But he was a con man, she thought. He had conned her thoroughly, lied to her; and he would keep doing it, she added.

She left the shower, dried herself and dressed, and then went to her room and sat at the desk, looking at the box that held her father's ashes. 'I don't know what to do,' she whispered.

She felt like a child confronted with a vast injustice, whose only recourse was to cry, 'It isn't fair!'

19

She was still sitting there when Brice came to tell her he had ordered Mexican, burritos and chiles rellenos; she said she would reheat some in a little while, she wasn't hungry. Still later, when she gathered her gown and robe, preparing for bed, she hesitated, then walked out carrying them.

'Honey — ' he said imploringly from his side of the bed.

'I'm not ready yet. Good night, Brice.'

She sat in the living room for a long time, with a book in her lap; now and then she looked at the words, but they might as well have been in Sanskrit. When she tossed the book down and went upstairs, she stopped outside their bedroom door, then turned to enter her own room to go to bed there.

She didn't want to hear his soft snore, didn't want him to come awake and reach for her, didn't want him to reach for her when he woke up in the morning, the way he often did. Lying in the bed in her own room, she thought it wasn't really revulsion, something akin perhaps, but not that. Because, she thought clearly, if she didn't want to be in the same room with him, within touching distance, if sex went, what was left?

She knew when he got up the next morning, knew when he went down, had his breakfast, knew when he left the house and got into his car. She stood at the window and watched the big silver Buick drift down the driveway, turn, and drift down the street. It looked very cold outside, everything white with frost, and she thought of the times when she had gotten in her fourteen-year-old Honda and let out the brake, coasted down the driveway and then down the street because coasting downhill was the only way it would start when the mornings were very cold. Brice had been humiliated by that car; he had said the neighbors' cleaning ladies all drove better cars than she did, and she had laughed and said at least hers was paid for.

When Brice's car was out of sight, she went downstairs. The newspaper was on the table in the kitchen, and on top of it was the loan application. She ignored both and scrambled eggs, poured coffee, made toast, then found the comics section and read it while she ate. She read Dear Abby, and the medical column, and the section written by teens for teens. She would have gone on to the sports section if Caldwell's call hadn't come before she got to it. She picked up when she heard his voice. He would be there around ten, in an hour.

Caldwell arrived as she was signing for the FedEx package from Christina; she waited at the door for him. The frost was gone; pale sunshine was fading behind a cloud cover now.

'Good morning, Lieutenant,' she said. 'Come in. I was going to have another cup of coffee. Join me?'

'Sure thing,' he said. 'Sounds good.'

Spook checked him out and wagged her tail a little in token greeting, and he grinned. 'Progress,' he said. 'Even in small doses it's gratifying.'

Abby led the way to the kitchen and poured coffee into two mugs, started to put them on a tray, but the lieutenant simply took one from her hand, and sat down at the kitchen table.

'Out here's fine,' he said. 'And I'll take off the jacket, but not too soon. Cold, around twenty-five.' His jacket was sheepskin; it made him look burlier than ever.

Reluctantly she sat opposite him. This was too close. She would have preferred to have more distance between them. He took a sip of coffee. 'Ah, that's good. What kind is it?'

'Celebese,' she said. 'Lieutenant, Brice told me your latest theory about the murder of my father, and it's wrong. I know what the cashier's checks were for, and they had nothing to do with his murder. You'll have to look somewhere else for a motive.'

'You going to tell me what they were for?' He was watching her thoughtfully, his careful scrutiny unsettling.

'A charitable contribution to a school. I'm satisfied about its legitimacy, and I am not at liberty to tell you more than that.'

'That's a lot of charity, Mrs. Connors,' he said.

'Yes, it is.'

'You said *motive*. Let me explain something. I think there's a lot of misunderstanding about police work. Probably television and novels account for it. You see, most crimes aren't mysterious at all. A guy goes into a bank, pulls a gun, or says he has one on him, and walks out with money. No mystery; they even have his picture. So we know who, and what, and how, and we couldn't care less about why. That's for a defense attorney to dig into. When we collar the perpetrator, we seldom even ask why he did it. A prosecuting attorney might make a big deal of it, but it's not our business most of the time.'

'But my father's murder wasn't like most crimes,' she said slowly.

'No, it wasn't. We're still working on the

who and the how. The way we figure, a man like your father must have made enemies along the way; people envied him, a woman was wronged by him, or her husband felt wronged . . . Just the usual human reasons for wanting someone gone from your life. Sometimes the reason turns out to be so petty, it's unbelievable. And most often the guilty party just ups and tells us why he did it after we get him. So that's not a major concern.'

'Then why are you here? What do you want from me?' she demanded. She had steeled herself for a grueling interrogation, hard questions, even anger from him, anything but this chatty tête-à-tête.

'I'd like to know what went on in California,' he said. Then he grinned and made a dismissive gesture. 'Don't get me wrong. I would love to know. But what I really came for was to talk about your father's work habits, and his computer. Okay?'

She stared at him in incomprehension. 'You already know about the missing pages of printout; you know about the computer. Someone turned it off and stole a disk. But your people recovered all the data.'

'And so did you,' he said agreeably. 'That took a bit more than a little knowledge on your part.' He held up his hand in a placating manner. 'Not accusing you of anything. Mind if I take off the jacket now?'

She watched him take it off and toss it down on another chair.

'See,' he said, 'if most people walk in on someone working at a computer, with a stack of papers facedown at their elbow, the logical assumption is that what's on the screen, what's being worked on at the moment, will be printed out and added to that stack. Most people would assume that if you're writing a novel, you start with word one on page one, and go until you reach the end. You know, a logical step-by-step progression, first one, then two, and so on. But what he was working on the night he was killed came from somewhere in the middle of the novel, according to my literary expert Detective Varney; the stuff that was lost when the computer was turned off was stuff he had already written and printed out, and those pages were still in the manuscript. Not where they belonged, mind you, but in among the other sections. The manuscript pages that were swiped, about sixteen, we think, had nothing to do with what he was working on that night, at least not with the material our guy was able to recover. And according to Varney, neither section could have been of interest to a killer. So why the theft?'

Abby found herself nodding. 'She's right,' she said. 'Both sections were innocuous.'

The first section was being rewritten, corrected, she remembered, when the computer was turned off. It was an in-close reminiscence about a boy watching a fish lay eggs, a man, Link, recalling that day, the innocence of boyhood, yearning for its return, grieving its irretrievable loss. The other section, the printout pages that had been taken, had also been on the computer, and another version of it buried in the manuscript pile. It was a funny scene that occurred when the boy, now a preadolescent, tried to figure out if the adult he was talking to was really stupid, or if he was trying to play a trick on him; he couldn't believe the man was that stupid. Later he had accepted that many people were, but that was his first realization of the fact. In both instances Jud had written the passages almost too lyrically, and he had pared the language, sharpened it.

She said, 'Stealing that disk and the hard copy was just to mislead you, make you believe my father had written something that someone knew about and didn't want to be made public.'

'That's pretty much what we decided,' he said. 'But the point is the killer didn't know you could recover that material. We learn the hard way that if we don't save before we turn off the system, we lose whatever is on the screen. Me, if I delete something, I consider it gone forever. Period. You know better. Our computer guy knows better, but how many other people do? We use programs as given, learn the keystrokes, and think we're masters, but for experts like you that's just not true, is it?'

'I'm not an expert,' she said. 'Many people know about recovering data. I just don't see where you're going, what you're after.'

'Okay, okay. Let me ask you this. If you wanted to really get rid of something, how would you go about it?'

She shook her head. 'You could write over it, or reformat your hard drive, or wipe out everything with a powerful magnet.

A strong electrical surge. Probably other ways I don't know about.'

'How did your father do it?' he asked softly.

She felt herself stiffen with alarm. 'What do you mean?'

'See, he didn't use an outline; you told us that and we confirmed it, as far as we can tell. But Varney says some of the parts are so well realized, with dates, places, smells, everything, he must have kept notes. Not on the computer hard drive. So if he used the computer to make notes, where are they?

318

Maybe he wrote them in longhand, in a journal of some sort. Not a notebook, we looked for something like that, not a bound journal, either, but maybe loose among all those other papers. The problem we have is that even if he accused someone of something in the novel, that can't be used as evidence of any sort. Can you imagine our literary expert battling it out with a defense attorney's literary expert, deconstructing a novel in court? So we couldn't use a word of it, no matter what it is, if it's just in the novel. But a journal or a diary? That's different.'

She had to moisten her lips before she could speak. 'You've gone full circle back to motive.'

'Not really,' he said. 'Not really. There could be hard evidence of some sort in a journal like that. A direct accusation, a threat recorded, something. We began to think that maybe we made a mistake letting you take his papers away before we went over them all, but at the time we didn't realize how he wrote, that he wrote about actual people and events, fictionalized a little, but real enough. The problem is that I can't search for those papers, if they exist, you see. I'd have to have cause to show a judge to get a warrant, and I don't have cause. You have a perfect alibi; you're not a suspect. If I opened that FedEx package you got, and found a full confession in it, I couldn't hand it over to the D.A., illegal search, you see. Well, I could, but he couldn't use it. So about all we can do is ask for help.'

She leaned forward, grasping the table with both hands, her voice harsh and low when she said, 'If I found something like that, I'd hand it over in a second. Don't you understand, there's nothing I want more than to see you find the person who killed my father! Nothing!'

'I know,' he said, almost soothingly. 'From all sides what I've heard is how close you and your father were, what a special relationship you had. Some might even say it verged on hero worship. But sometimes, Mrs. Connors, you can be too close to see clearly what someone with a more objective viewpoint might glimpse. That's all I'm saying.'

She stood up. 'If I find anything like that, I'll give it to you. Do you want more coffee?' He kept regarding her with his thoughtful scrutiny; she stared back, thinking, This was his game. Lead you on, let you think he was behind you, supportive, believed what you said, and then spring out like a tiger from a tree. He wanted Jud's private papers; that's what he had come for, nothing to do with San Francisco or a hit man or the theory Brice had talked about — the blond man and an accomplice.

He had strung Brice along at least two times, first the insane idea that Willa had driven up the mountain and back, when he knew by then that no one had done that. And now the blond man. Whose theory had that been, his or Brice's?

Abruptly she turned away and walked across the kitchen for the carafe. He wouldn't have told Brice what he was thinking. No one could know what he was thinking. All traps, meandering paths to the thicket where he would pounce. What had he been after from Brice? Why had he played his game with Brice?

'No more for me,' Caldwell said when she reached for the coffee. 'I'll be on my way. You really going back to the lake tomorrow?'

She returned to the table; he was putting his jacket on. 'Yes. I have a lot of reading to do.'

'Aren't you a little uneasy, the idea of being up there alone?'

'I'll have Spook, and I feel safer at the cabin than anywhere else.' Whether she meant personally, or safety for her father's secret, she couldn't have said.

For an eyeblink he looked surprised, then his expression was back to neutral, friendly even. He reached in his pocket and brought out a card and a pen, wrote on the back of the card, then handed it to her. 'If anything interesting turns up, give me a call. Don't bother with the office number, just call the cell phone number I put on the back. Anytime, day or night. Okay?'

'Yes,' she said.

On the way to the front door he asked, 'By the way, do you know a Robert Langdon?'

'No. Why? Who is he?'

He shrugged. 'His name just came up.'

After she let him out and returned to the kitchen, she sat at the table trying to think what his visit had really been about. Jud's private papers, certainly, but what else? Brice must have told him some important papers might exist, and evidently had told him she was going to the cabin the next day.

For all Brice knew, the only papers she had were the printouts Jud had made; she had not told him about the laptop computer, about installing all of Jud's work on it, how she had found the missing sections. He must assume that she had found only paper copies. She backed up a step. Brice had no idea of the extent of her knowledge of computers, how much she had learned from Jud over the years; she had never talked about those years after it had become apparent to her that he had no wish to go into that part of her life. He could have looked into her desktop computer and would have found nothing of Jud's there; he would have assumed that the papers were all she had, and that among them she had found something that had taken her to San Francisco. She nodded to herself. The theory about the blond man had been Brice's, she felt certain, and he had pointed Caldwell in her direction to find something to confirm it. Lieutenant Caldwell never told you a thing he didn't want you to know, she added silently, but he let you ramble; he had let Brice ramble . . . Why had he wanted her to know the name Robert Langdon?

She was thinking of various things the lieutenant had said: how most people knew the programs they used and little else; how would anyone erase or conceal data? How had Jud deleted his notes?

How had he? She had found nothing on his hard drive to correspond to the very personal notes he had written and printed out, the graphic omniscient record of his life. She narrowed her eyes, visualizing the notes, fanfold papers separated, clipped together, and suddenly she was seeing his loft again, his office, with many discarded, unused computers still taking up space, and remembering: 'Honey, I have something to show you, a new toy.' He had bought a new computer and a new laser printer when he started the last novel, not quite two years ago, and he had made no notes on it. She thought he never made notes once he got into a novel. But that meant the older computer, the last one he had abandoned, might still have them, everything up to that time. She felt almost feverish with anxiety then. If Caldwell thought of that . . . They could still go to the cabin, the crime scene; they could still investigate a new development there even if they couldn't get a search warrant for this house.

She frowned, bringing back what Caldwell had said. He just wanted her help. Did she know a Robert Langdon? They couldn't get a search warrant without cause, and she had an alibi. Slowly she stood up and started to walk toward the stairs. He couldn't get a search warrant without cause, and she had an alibi, she repeated. Then she said, 'And so does Brice.'

At the door to Brice's room, she pointed to the floor and said, 'Spook, watch.' The shaggy dog lay down in the hallway, her ears twitching, accounting for every sound now; if anyone came to the house, came onto the property, she would give warning. Abby went inside the room and sat down at Brice's computer, where the screen saver was displaying silent aircraft in an endless loop.

The first two programs she opened required a password; for the bank account and household accounts, he had used Abby's maiden name. Then, for his Buick account he had switched to his Social Security number, against all advice, she thought when it opened for her. That number also opened a financial file with stock market reports. She wasn't interested in any of them, but was testing only, finding his method for passwords. His office accounts did not yield to either of the earlier ones. She leaned back in the chair thinking. His mother's maiden name was probably it. Brice was methodical, everything on record, all the tax records, utilities, car, everything neat and orderly, and uncomplicated. He would have used something easily remembered and would not have made a note about it. Had she ever heard his mother's maiden name? She couldn't remember.

She got up and walked down the stairs, thinking. The phone was ringing and she stopped to listen; when Brice's voice came through asking her to please answer, she continued to the foyer, picked up the FedEx, and went back upstairs. She opened the package in her own room and spread out the contract copies on her desk, then went back to his computer.

She was recalling their wedding, his relatives who had attended, an aunt and uncle, his mother's brother from Idaho. Roger . . . 'Call me Uncle Rog,' he had said jovially. 'Welcome to the family.' Someone had introduced him and his wife — Wanda, that was her name — to Jonelle. Brice had introduced them. 'Jonelle, this is my aunt Wanda and uncle Roger Laurelton.'

Laurelton. Too long. She tried Laurel, and the program opened the office accounts file. She blinked at the screen; the file had opened to a list of names, clients, she assumed, scrolling until she came to the name Robert Langdon. She clicked on that one and knew she would not be able to make sense of what she was seeing: Shares In, Shares Out, Capital Gains ST, Capital Gains LT . . . She couldn't, but others could, she thought then, and hurriedly got up and went to her room to get the laptop from the closet, where it was inconspicuous among several other suitcases stored there. She took it back with her and found Jud's continuous save program, made a copy, and installed it on Brice's computer, under a file she thought of as FAILSAFE and coded beyond recognition; anything deleted or any changes made would automatically go to that file, and it would be hidden from anyone who didn't know how to look for it.

Then she studied the information on the screen. Apparently the Langdon account had started in January, this year, with a deposit of five thousand dollars. Shares had been bought in a company with a ticker tape name that meant nothing to her. She compared this account with those preceding it, and a few following, and they all looked alike to her eyes. Some with more activity than others, but with the same type of activity. The Langdon account had grown very large over the next months, then had plunged steeply in July.

Meaningless, she decided. So why had Caldwell wanted her to know that name? Who was Robert Langdon? There had to be something else, she decided, and exited the program.

But the fact that Caldwell had brought up the name and she had found it on Brice's computer had to mean something, she told herself, even if she didn't know what that something was.

She was scanning his directory when Spook made a low growly noise. Abby exited the program, and went into her own room and a minute later when Brice yelled up the stairs, she said, 'I'm here.'

Brice tapped on her door, then opened it enough to put his head in. 'I called and no one answered. Have you been out yet?'

'No,' she said, not turning around to see him. 'Caldwell came and stayed a long time, and the contract came. I decided to look it over before I signed it. I'll have to buy an envelope, I guess, but I'll make a label.'

'You want me to go with you?'

'Of course not.' She glanced at him. 'Oh, Caldwell asked if I know someone called Langdon. Robert, I think. Robert Langdon. Do you know him?'

Brice frowned, gazed past her a moment, then shook his head. 'Never heard of him. Who's he?'

'I don't know.' She looked down at the contract again and saw that her hands were shaking. Quickly she began to gather the copies together.

'I've got a couple of things to check out, then I'll take off,' Brice said. 'You have that loan application?'

She nodded, and he backed out and closed the door.

Waiting for him to leave the house, she made a label, and wrote a note to Christina, put the copies of the contract back in the envelope they had come in, and then simply sat with her eyes closed. Whatever he was doing took over half an hour, something an expert like her could have finished in five minutes, she thought savagely, but he did finish at last, and returned to her door.

'Honey, I have a client coming in about ten minutes, so I have to dash back to the office, but I won't stay long. You should be back about the same time I get home, and let's spend the afternoon and evening together. Let's plan a vacation for next summer. Someplace really dreamy.'

'I have a dozen more things to get done today,' she said sharply. 'I have a headache, and I'm feeling mean and irritable. You get something to eat when you're ready; I'll get something before I come home. I'm not in the mood for vacation planning.'

'That bastard Caldwell,' he muttered. 'Did he give you a hard time?'

'Yes,' she said. 'He did. He gave me a hard time. Now leave me alone.'

★ ★ ★

She watched from the upstairs window again until his car was out of sight, then she hurried to his computer and brought up his office accounts file. The client list now went from Lanier to Laughton. No Langdon.

The rest would have to wait until he was

asleep, she decided uneasily. He could shake off a client and return anytime. She went to the bedroom and packed the few things she would need at the lake, not willing to do it later when he would probably be there watching, talking, trying to get to her one way or another. As an afterthought she got out a larger suitcase, put the laptop in first, then her clothes on top of it. She carried it out to the van and put it in the back with her groceries. And finally, taking Spook with her, she left the house, with no intention of returning until after eight, maybe even nine. No more talk, no more explaining, cajoling. No more anything now.

Down the hill, driving toward town on Willamette, she saw his Buick coming her way. He had gotten rid of his client in record time, she thought, and pretended she didn't see his wave as they passed each other.

Well, he would have all afternoon without interruption to hide whatever he needed to on his computer; later, she would have most of the night to find it again.

20

She did her errands: the bank, post office, a long walk with Spook along the river front, the library for an hour, then to Felicia's to collect her backpack.

'I can't stay,' she said to Felicia. 'Too much to do. Thanks for holding this for me.'

'Abby, what's wrong?' Felicia asked, peering at her closely. 'What's happened?'

'Nothing. Nothing. I just feel . . . Too much to do, I guess. I really have to go. I'll be in touch this weekend sometime.' She nearly ran from the condominium. She couldn't talk to Felicia right now, and she knew she couldn't have faced Willa when she came. She would know in an instant that something was very wrong. They had planned to spend time together, the three of them discussing the novel, putting real names on the fictional characters. How could she stand being around anyone now, what could she say? Oh, by the way, this character Buster, actually he's my husband, an embezzler, a thief, and a liar; pass the butter, please. Better to leave them both wondering, she thought unhappily, starting the van once more. Then, driving, she

331

didn't know where to go next, how to kill three more hours.

In the condominium Felicia was pacing, thinking, pacing, worrying, until she finally went to the phone to call Willa.

* * *

It was nearly nine when Abby pulled into her own driveway, more exhausted from her aimless wandering in the mall for hours than she could have been from doing any work she could think of.

When she entered the house, Brice was in the foyer waiting for her. He reached out with both hands and she backed away.

'I'm tired, and I'm near the point where I might start screaming and throwing things,' she said, hanging up her jacket. She could hear the truth in her words, in her voice, and when he stopped moving toward her, she thought he probably could, too. She faced him. 'I need, I really need to be left alone for now. I'm having a hard time accepting that my husband is an embezzler, on top of losing my father. Maybe after a few days of solitude at the lake, I'll be able to deal with things better, but not right now. I'm going to take a bath and go to bed. If I wake up very early, I'll just take off.'

'Abby, God, I'd do anything to have a second chance, to undo things. Anything. Going to jail would be easier than seeing you like this.' He looked agonized, a muscle twitching in his jaw, fists clenched at his sides.

She walked past him, started up the stairs. 'I don't know when I'll come home. Monday, Tuesday. I'll call first.'

She took a bath, went to her room and set an alarm clock for two-thirty, and went to bed. Later she knew when he came in to look at her, and she knew when he went to their room and went to bed. She dozed, came wide awake with a start, and dozed again. She hit the OFF button of the alarm at the first sound of a buzz.

Soundlessly, without turning on a light, she got up and slipped on her robe, crossed the hall to the bedroom door and listened. He might have heard the alarm, soft as it was; he might be awake, also listening. When she heard his gentle snore, she backed away and went into his room.

She didn't waste a second getting into his computer, starting her search in the FAIL-SAFE file, where everything he had deleted was waiting for her. She stifled a groan when she saw that in addition to the Langdon account there were three others from his office. She didn't stop to examine them, but moved on down the list of deletions. Games. Of course, he couldn't bear the thought of being ridiculed for playing adolescent computer games; he would have taken them off. She would examine them also, she decided; it was easy to label something whatever you wanted, try to hide it behind a false name. She moved on. A lot of bookmarks from the Internet; she started down the list to visit each one, find out what it was about.

A chat group about sports cars . . . A page from a car broker's Web site, price quotes . . . An understated page about yachts, luxury vessels that would sleep forty on their trip around the world . . . She sighed and moved on . . .

Minutes later she stopped moving altogether, stopped breathing, even her heart tried to stop, with heart quakes, sharp jumps that shook her body; it found its rhythm again and she could breathe.

Inflatable canoes. A page of inflatable canoes. Collapsible to backpack size, inflatable in minutes, with compressed air in seconds, seven feet long, twenty-seven pounds, under three hundred dollars . . .

Order forms for mail, phone, e-mail purchases. Or visit the showroom in Seattle.

She was numb, no feeling in her hands or feet, her legs were gone . . . She felt the room shifting, tilting, and pressed her head down on the keyboard. When she pushed herself upright again, the screen was garbage, and she began to shake.

Out! Get out! Now! Almost as if someone else had marched in and started issuing orders, the words came to her. She exited the program, stood up, paused at the door only a moment to listen, then ran across the hall to her room. *Get out! Get out!*

Fumbling with clothes, she dressed as fast as she could, grabbed the mahogany box, motioned to Spook, and left the house. She coasted down the driveway, down the street to the intersection with Willamette, and only then started the engine, but she knew minutes later that she had to go somewhere, had to stop and think. She didn't even know where she was; no familiar landmarks, no familiar storefronts, hardly any other traffic. It was four-thirty in the morning and she had to go someplace where she could stop the chaos of her mind, stop and think.

Ahead she saw a sign for an all-night restaurant, a doughnut and hamburger place, and she pulled in.

'Honey, you look like you've been on the road for a long time,' a middle-aged waitress said when Abby sank down into a booth. 'You want coffee?'

She nodded. That was exactly right, she thought; she had been on the road for a long time.

Finally she began to sift through the blizzard of thoughts. Call Caldwell. And tell him what? That Brice had surfed the Internet, looked at yachts and sports cars and inflatable boats. She remembered phrases Caldwell had uttered: hard evidence, good defense attorney, cause for a search warrant . . . He suspected Brice, she thought then, but he couldn't prove it. She could hear another voice in her head, like a distant echo: *No! No! Brice had an alibi. He wouldn't have done that! He couldn't have killed my father!* But that was what Caldwell's visit to her had been about, to get her help in finding evidence he could use against her husband.

'When you want something to eat, just holler,' the waitress said, placing coffee in front of her.

He had an alibi, she thought. He couldn't have gone to the cabin. He wouldn't have done it. Flesh of her flesh, body to body, his hands on her, hers on him. He couldn't have done it! Although the coffee was bad, it was hot and the jolt of caffeine was welcome. Against her will, she found herself visualizing that day a month ago, what Brice could have done.

336

When she leaves for the museum, he follows her out quickly and is on the road before nine, in Portland by eleven, in the motel minutes later. He goes to his room and orders lunch from room service, takes off his jacket, takes papers from his briefcase and spreads them on the bed, then tips the bellboy lavishly when he brings the food. So he'll remember.

No motive, she told herself, just what he could have done.

He hangs the DO NOT DISTURB sign on the door, clears off the bed, turns down the covers, probably packs up the sandwich to eat later, and takes a nap. That must have been his reason for going to Portland so early when their meeting wasn't scheduled until three in the afternoon. Time to take a nap.

He could do that, take a nap whenever he lay down, fall into sleep like a child.

From three until nine-thirty or ten he is with his associates.

It was before ten, she thought; the other times he had gone up to the meetings, they had broken up before ten and he had arrived home by midnight at the latest, even if he had told the police it had been after two. Why hadn't she contradicted him? Because it had seemed irrelevant then. The group had been together for hours; there would have been little reason to linger for more hours over dinner. Maybe none of the others had even noticed precisely when they separated.

By ten, and more likely before ten, back in his room, he orders a large pot of coffee, and when the bellboy brings it, another big tip, more papers spread around, the bedspread in place, hiding the fact that the bed has been slept in already, wet towels in the shower, soap tossed in the shower. Then, moving fast, change clothes again, pick up papers, pack up, put the coffee in a thermos, or simply dump it out, throw the bedspread on the floor in a heap. Everything used, everything normal. A few minutes at the most. The sign still on the door. He doesn't take it down when he leaves.

Three and a half hours to the lake, at the minimum, the lieutenant had told her. They must have timed it. He could have arrived at the lake by two. Florence Halburtson said that Coop usually got up between one and two, but they had not looked at the clock. How long to get from the car to the water? To inflate the canoe? Ten minutes, fifteen? In a real canoe it would have taken only minutes more to cross the finger and get to the cabin, but an inflatable one wouldn't be as swift, she felt certain, and Brice wasn't an expert. Fifteen minutes?

He gets out of the canoe, says something to Spook, and she doesn't bark; she knows him. He goes inside the cabin and locks the dog door, gets the gun from the drawer, and the minute Jud appears at the bottom of the stairs, he shoots him.

Abby shuddered, spilling coffee. She mopped it up with paper napkins. Did he call him? 'Jud, I have something to show you.'

He runs up the stairs, grabs sheets of paper from the stack, removes the disk, and turns off the computer, then runs back down and out. Ten minutes in all? Fifteen? Back across the finger. How can he know where to go ashore again? Coop's light would carry to the first low spot above the water, but dimly. He could have tied something to the tree roots, something that would have reflected the light, served as a guide. He steps out of the canoe, pulls the plug on it to let the air out, and hurries back to the car. The canoe will finish deflating while he drives.

She shook her head. It would have taken at least an hour from the time he arrived at the lake until he left again. There wasn't enough time for him to go back to Portland, and then drive to Salem and get there by seven-thirty. He had to have stopped to change his clothes; he wouldn't have gone through the woods, out in the canoe, and back in his good suit and shoes and not leave a trace for a sharp-eyed detective to notice; he needed time to hide the canoe in the trunk; everything he did would have added minutes. She grasped at the fact; there wasn't enough time. The police must have gone through the same kind of reasoning; they must know there simply wasn't enough time.

'He didn't go back to Portland. He drove directly to Salem,' she said under her breath. Two and a half hours. She knew how long that took; she had done it in an old car, in heavy traffic, and in no particular hurry.

He had plenty of time, she thought bleakly, time enough to stow the canoe in the trunk, shave, change his clothes, freshen up.

Caldwell knew that, she realized, but there must have been witnesses in Portland who would swear he had spent the night in the motel. The maid, the bellboy. No one knew when you checked out of a motel; you used a credit card, and the next morning you got up and left. He had kept a log of a trip to Portland and back, miles, gas, everything, and he had receipts for lunch, coffee, breakfast in Salem. Business trip, tax deductible, he had explained to the sheriff: he always kept a careful record.

The inflatable canoe on the Internet wasn't enough proof to counter his records, possible witnesses. He might even claim he had thought about ordering a canoe for her, for Christmas.

The waitress refilled her cup, and Abby shook her head, nothing to eat.

Another memory surfaced, and she narrowed her eyes recalling it. He said he had gone to Jud's lawyer's office to ask about the cashier's checks, and she had accepted that without question. But it was a lie, he would have known the lawyer wouldn't tell him even if he knew. He must have gone to find out what the two different waiting periods meant, six months and thirty days. She could imagine the scene, Brice sincere and puzzled, asking on her behalf what they meant; they had been in shock, without any understanding of the legalities before. And he found out, she told herself, that she couldn't even borrow against the estate until after the thirty days had passed. Until then nothing was hers legally. That explained the loan coming up now, to be finalized exactly thirty days after Jud's death. It would have been impossible sooner.

She thought about the four accounts he had deleted, and wished she had paid more attention to the numbers, the figures. How much did he have to put back before the auditors arrived? Evidently, at least a hundred thousand had to be in place next week sometime. His desperation was real. But what if there was more?

Would he push her for more loans in the coming weeks? And if she balked, refused, there was no possibility that he could raise more money unless she died. And, she added slowly, she couldn't die too soon, not before Sunday.

She had signed the loan application, reassured that since it was in her name, she would have time to think it through at the cabin, and that he couldn't touch it if she changed her mind. But if she died and the money was in her account, he would inherit it as well as Jud's estate. It would all be his. He could borrow in his own name, hire a good defense attorney, if it ever came to that.

But it wouldn't come to that; Caldwell needed hard evidence and he didn't have any. He didn't have enough to show cause for a search warrant.

Her stomach was churning, and abruptly she felt she was going to be sick, she would throw up here at the table. She jumped up and nearly ran to the women's room, and stood in a stall taking deep breaths with her eyes closed.

She was spinning a theory, she told herself, exactly the way Brice had spun theories, each one more incredible than the last. He was a liar and a thief, but a killer? Hurt and betrayed, outraged, she had taken a theory past belief without a thing to go on except the fact that he had looked at inflatable canoes and had tried to conceal it. She should have stayed home, she thought then, looked further.

She left the stall and stared at her reflection in the mirror over the sink: gray-faced, wild-eyed, almost unrecognizable. She shook her head. 'He did it,' she whispered.

She remembered what Matthew had said when they were splitting up, and he had begged for another chance. 'You win a little, lose a little, and it's a game, just fun. Then you lose a lot and you try again, to get it back, because you know your luck will change again. It always does. You feel lucky this time, really lucky. You have to keep trying to win it back because that's the only way you'll ever come out ahead. Luck. I know better now. I've learned my lesson.' But he hadn't learned anything. He had taken the rent money and tried again.

Brice was in too deep. Time had run out. His luck had run out, just as Matthew's luck had run out. Her father had said she didn't learn a thing the first time, and that was wrong, she thought, remembering the bitter fight they had had. She had learned never to try to come between an addict and his fix. The addiction would win every time. What she hadn't learned was how to recognize an addict in the first place; they came in many guises.

She dashed cold water on her face and dried it, and when she looked at herself in the mirror again, a little color had returned to her cheeks, and a hard glint was in her eyes. 'You married the same man twice, idiot. And this time there's no one to bail you out.'

She knew now that in heeding that voice of command in her head, she had done the right thing, the only thing possible: run. If Brice had seen her, if she had confronted him, he would have done something drastic to the computer, gotten rid of everything, finished covering his tracks. But as long as he didn't suspect anyone could find what he had hidden, it would be there next week, next month. And she desperately needed time alone, time to find a way to prove what she knew. Caldwell couldn't do it, and unless she did, Brice would get away with the murder of her father.

21

At ten-thirty on Friday morning Felicia pulled into the Halburtson driveway. Where it split, one part going down to the boat shed and carport, and the other around the front of the house, she followed the one to the front door. Willa was in the passenger seat, composed but very pale. Felicia patted her leg.

'We won't stay long, a few minutes only,' she said. There was an explosion of sound, a shot that echoed and reechoed around the lake and cliffs. Almost immediately there was another gunshot. 'Good heavens! What on earth . . . ?'

Coop's dogs bounded up through the woods at the side of the house barking, and the poodles in the backseat barked excitedly in response.

'Stop that nonsense,' Felicia said crossly, getting out of the car. All the dogs stopped barking, and now she saw that Spook was there; Abby had arrived already.

Willa got out more cautiously than Felicia had done, and the three big dogs came to sniff her, accepted her, and escorted the two women to the door, which Florence was opening.

No one said Florence was fat; they said that she was stout, or that she had put on some weight, or that she was heavyset, but in fact at forty to fifty pounds overweight, she was fat. She wore her gray hair in a braid coiled on her head and looked like an aged Brunhild. Holding a conversation with her was a trial, Felicia had decided long ago, because Florence seldom finished a sentence, and her thoughts seemed to jump from one subject to another in a manner that suggested she was paying little attention to what she was saying. It wasn't her age, or the onset of Alzheimer's, or anything else ominous taking a toll; she had always been like that.

Florence embraced Felicia warmly, then tentatively embraced Willa, who appeared just as tentative about the gesture. Another pair of shots sounded, fainter now that they were inside the house.

'Who's that shooting?'

'Coop. Take off your things. I'm making muffins . . . '

'What on earth is he shooting at out there?' Felicia demanded as another shot sounded. 'If he hasn't hit it yet, he isn't going to.'

'Nothing. He isn't shooting anything. Huckleberry, the last of them. Cleaning out

346

the freezer. Abby's with him, and they'll be cold . . . Is there snow in the pass? We might hit it down around Klamath Falls. And coffee . . . You have our key, don't you?'

Felicia and Willa took off their coats and put them down on the sofa, then followed Florence to the kitchen; she was rambling on, but Felicia decided to wait for Coop to come in and tell her what was happening.

This was a good house, she reflected, built back around the turn of the century, when finishing details had been important and craftsmanship counted. Hickory wainscoting, oak and mahogany floors that had turned almost black with age but were as beautiful as they had been when the house was built, high ceilings and tall windows with wide window seats. The kitchen floor was inlaid linoleum in a speckled pattern, fifty years old or more, waxed to a high polish. Florence and Coop had raised three sons in this house, and when the boys had grown up, married, moved away, they had come home often with their children, and the house accommodated all of them. The rooms were big; there were four or five bedrooms on the second floor, and a partly finished attic; and all the rooms used to get filled with laughter and fun-loving children and their parents. Now the grand-children had their own children, and the visits

347

had become more and more rare. The big old house seemed preternaturally still and lonesome. Then Felicia heard what Florence had been rambling on about: Abby intended to buy the house.

'... what she'll do with it. I know what Jud planned some day. An art colony.'

Willa was nodding sadly. 'He would have done it eventually. I told him I'd teach courses, and Abby probably would, and maybe Felicia would do workshops on illustrating children's literature ...' She looked at Felicia. 'He thought maybe he'd talk to you someday about being the administrator, when it was closer to the time to start. He didn't want anything to do with paperwork, he said.'

Florence began talking about the meter man; the meters and the service boxes were side by side on the back wall of this house. 'Coop had to show Abby the electric boxes and circuit breakers ...' Felicia always thought that was the real reason Jud wanted the property, not only to keep the ramp but because it would have been a problem to move the electrical service if strangers bought the house. An art colony, she mused, that was more his style. It would have been for Willa and Abby, of course. She walked to the back door and gazed out. Florence took muffins from the oven; they smelled wonderful.

' . . . no fuses anymore. Isn't that strange? He'd come in with a bucket of huckleberries, and sit there at the table and wait for me to make muffins . . . '

Abby and Coop came into sight on the path from the back of the boat shed. She was carrying a shotgun. The dogs romped around them as they came up the path, apparently deep in conversation. She nodded at something he said. From the kitchen door Felicia couldn't see the ramp or the cabin, the boat shed was in the way, but out in the other direction she could see some of the lake, black water today. Some days from here it looked azure. It all depended on the sky, the cloud cover, whether the sun was bright . . . She turned away from the door.

When Abby and Coop came into the house, her face was fiery red from the cold, and Coop had a blush on his nose and cheeks, but hardly noticeable; his skin was so weathered and brown he seemed almost impervious to weather.

Abby was surprised to find Felicia and Willa in the kitchen. She looked at the shotgun she was holding, and said with a shrug, 'Coop insisted that no one can stay around here without a gun of some sort, and the police still have the rifle. He was showing me the difference between shooting a shotgun and a rifle. I may never be able to use my right arm again.'

'See,' Coop said in his deliberate way, 'you don't have to hit anything. I never did, and I never intended to; a shot in the air will do the trick. It will scare off whatever might be prowling around, and if the first shot doesn't do it, you want to shoot closer, at the dirt in front of the critter. That's going to do it.' He was peeling off layers of outerwear as he spoke.

Abby had taken off her gloves, but that was all. Now she went to Florence and hugged her. 'Remember, write — let me know how your trip was, how you both are. And don't worry about me. Coop's good old gun and Spook, that's all I need.' She hugged Coop, who looked slightly embarrassed but hugged her back. 'If she forgets to write, it's your job. Thanks for the use of the gun and the lessons.'

She looked at Felicia and said, 'We've had a long talk already, and I have to get started on things. I'll call you in the next day or two. Now I'm off.'

Florence pressed a paper bag of muffins into her hand and walked to the door with her, then stood there watching for a time. When she turned to the room again, her eyes were filled with tears. 'Now, you two can stay for a bit, can't you? All those warm muffins . . .'

Willa nodded, and Felicia, who had been watching Abby, sat down abruptly at the table, and she thought with certainty: she knows. Abby knows.

★ ★ ★

She had turned the heat down too low, Abby thought when she entered the cabin; it was freezing cold inside. Trying to ignore Spook, who was racing around looking for Jud, she adjusted the thermostat and, without taking off her jacket yet, checked the kerosene supply for the oil lamps, the way Jud always had done after an absence of a few days. Abby hadn't remembered to do this when she brought Christina here, but today she was methodical about checking out the cabin, making sure it was prepared for any emergency. Outside, she looked over the supply of firewood, neatly stacked and covered with a tarp. They usually burned wood for heat and didn't rely on the electricity; Jud had said the exercise of collecting firewood and cutting it up was an absolute necessity for him, and besides, wood heat was best. After she carried in wood, she unloaded the boat and took everything inside, stowed away the groceries, cleared an end table and put the mahogany box on it, and finally hauled the boat to a higher ledge; the lowest one had several inches of water on it now. She started a fire in the woodstove. Soon the cabin would be warm enough to turn off the electric baseboard heaters and she would take off her heavy jacket and boots. She made coffee and sat at the table, gazing at the lake, and now let herself think about Brice.

Ever since she left the restaurant in Eugene, she had shied away from thinking about him, about what she should do, what she could do; instead, she had planned her next few days, apportioned time, so much to reconnect the old computer and reformat the hard drive to obliterate everything on it, so much for the paperwork upstairs, so much for deciding what to keep, what to give away, what to put in the box she had bought, what to do with all the material Christina couldn't use . . . Each day would be filled.

Driving, she had almost stopped and turned back to Eugene; she should change her will, she had thought suddenly; then she had continued driving. She apportioned time enough to write a new will in longhand, and even planned how to keep it safe until a later date. She would mail it to herself in care of Felicia. It would be dated, of course, and the canceled stamp would be proof enough. She had learned how a lot of Jud's money would be used, the Xuan Bui Institute, but what had he planned for the rest of it? Coop Halburtson had given her the answer when she told him and Florence that she intended to buy their house when and if they decided to sell, exactly as her father had planned. And Coop had told her about the art colony, the first she had heard of it. The colony would be for Felicia and Willa, and her, of course, she added. Coop said that Jud thought the world needed educating about how to read, and how to see clearly, and an art colony would be a step in that direction. Right, she told herself. It would be.

Realizing she had shied away from thinking about Brice yet again, she forced her mind back to him. There weren't any guidelines for her situation, she thought bitterly. Call Caldwell and say, My husband killed my father. And he would say, But we can't crack his alibi. Tell Brice to his face, You killed my father. They would yell at each other, and the following day it would be as if she had said nothing. Wait for him to try to kill her. He might put it off for a while, she thought, but eventually it had to be done.

She put herself in his place, trying to think his thoughts. All that money, the trouble he was in — there wasn't any other solution. He couldn't wait out the six months, and she probably couldn't or wouldn't borrow enough to cover all his debts. Also, she must suspect him, or she wouldn't have walked out.

She stopped her chain of thought and considered that. Of course, she would leave him; he was a liar and a cheat, a thief, an embezzler, and now she suspected that he had become involved in day trading. He scorned the idiots who got hooked on video poker, the lottery, slot machines; he was far too intelligent for those brainless games. He understood stocks and bonds; he could beat the system, and he was lucky. Would all that have been enough to make her walk out? She didn't know. In him she had found what she had been looking for: peace, a good and satisfying sex partner, someone to share the hearth and home . . . They might have worked something out, since after her disastrous first marriage, she had been desperate to make the second one work. But he had killed her father. She thought this icily, without any doubt, with as little feeling as if she were considering the probability of sunshine in summer, or rain in winter.

Then, remembering that she was trying to think like Brice, she went on: if she suspected him, sooner or later she would tell the police, and once they became really suspicious, they would start a full-scale investigation at the office, one that would uncover irregularities. Self-preservation was instinctual, a duty that had to be undertaken, regardless of how repugnant it appeared. Poor Brice, forced to kill his wife. How he would suffer, because he really did love her. But if it had to be done, why wait?

Not Friday night, too soon. Probably not Saturday night. He couldn't be certain when the Halburtsons would leave. Besides, everyone said Jud died on Friday night, but it had been on Saturday morning actually, another day to wait. Best to avoid even a remote possibility of the technical problem of when the thirty days ended. Sunday night then, after midnight. Their neighborhood was very quiet on Sunday nights; he could slip out and back in without being seen. Two hours both ways, a snap. Row over in his little collapsible canoe, do what had to be done, and get out. He would have an alibi, of course.

Almost gently she reminded herself that she didn't really know; she could be as wrong as he had been with all his theories. Her gaze came to rest on the shotgun she had placed on the table along with a box of shells Coop had given her. All she had said to Coop was that she regretted the rifle the police had taken away. It had been enough. If it hadn't been, she would have asked if she could borrow it.

She worked on the discarded computer first: disconnected cables, reconnected others, brought up the systems information, then a file or two. She had been right. Everything written before twenty months ago was still on the hard drive. She hesitated, but only briefly; what was the point in printing out anything else, just to bury it? She reformatted the disk drive, returned all the cables to their rightful places, and it was done.

In the afternoon she sorted papers, separated out stories from private matters. The box she had bought to hold his private papers was filling, and she worried that it might not be quite big enough. It was a poor companion to his box, but the best she had been able to find. The wood was pale, intricately carved, just as the other one was, but it had been carved for the tourist trade, and that made a difference.

No longer reading every word, she found the work of sorting was going faster than she had thought it would. When she grew tired of reading, she roamed the cabin, fingering objects that he had liked enough to keep. There weren't that many, although there was a ton of books. A mantel clock that was wrong as often as it was right; he had had to reset it frequently, but he had liked it, and paying much attention to the time had never been one of his virtues. She checked it against her watch and reset it. Several framed pictures of her at different stages, a baby, first-grade age, teenager, a more recent one of her swimming in the lake . . . On the dresser in his room a framed studio picture of Willa; she was radiant and lovely in it. Next to it a carving from Bali, a white bird, possibly a crane. For years it had been attached to a piece of driftwood, then it had been broken off the base, and he had made a frame to hold it. The frame was very simple; the bird hung from the top by a nearly invisible nylon string, free to move in all directions. He had glued the frame back onto the driftwood, as white as the bird. She touched it and it swung to and fro. It was so lightweight, so beautifully balanced, it responded to the most gentle breeze.

On his desk was a paperweight she had given him for Christmas one year. She shook it and watched rainbows form, become elongated, and finally settle into a blue base. She had saved her allowance for more than a month to buy it, she remembered, and moved on.

That night she wrote out a new will, and although she kept it as simple as possible while making it clear that she intended it to replace the one on file with Brice's attorney, it took her hours to finish. She kept forgetting something, or making a mistake in the wording and had to start over again and again. No corrections, no errors; it might have to stand up to a challenge in probate court. She burned each discarded draft in the woodstove and she burned a lot of them before she was satisfied. On Saturday she would row across the finger and put it in Coop's mailbox, raise the flag, and know it was done. Over the weekend she would have to remember to ask Felicia to hold a letter she was expecting until she collected it.

★ ★ ★

On Saturday she found a piece about Willa; she started to read it, then put it down. It was too personal, too private. How Willa had blushed at what he had written in the novel, how much more she would blush if she saw this. That afternoon Abby finished sorting; everything left could be seen by anyone who cared to look, and her pale box was filled all the way. She closed the box and locked it with a tiny key, and then said, 'Tomorrow afternoon.'

She made a cheese omelette and salad, and as she ate she thought again of what Jud had written about Willa; abruptly she put down her fork, and went to the phone to call Felicia. They should all three attend his funeral, she thought. The three people he had loved, who had loved him, they should all be there.

When Felicia hung up after talking to Abby, she regarded Willa with a searching gaze. 'She wants us to go with her to bury her father,' she said. 'Tomorrow.'

Willa had been pacing restlessly most of the afternoon, gazing at the lake, pacing again, unable to sit still more than a few minutes at a time. Now she exhaled a long breath and nodded.

'And afterward, we'll tell her about Brice,' Willa said. 'We'll bring her back here with us.'

Felicia shook her head. 'Afterward we'll have a wake for Jud. I'll make us some dinner and we'll eat over there with her.'

Willa started to protest, and Felicia said softly, 'She knows. We don't have to tell her anything. She knows. She isn't likely to come back with us.'

'Then . . . She can't just sit over there not

knowing what he might do. He might show up tonight, tomorrow, who knows when? She can't just sit and wait for him to come. That's crazy!'

Originally Felicia had thought that when they told Abby what they believed, she would be shocked, disbelieving, horrified, and finally accepting. Then, she had thought, they would all come to the cottage and decide what to do. But seeing Abby with the shotgun, knowing her, recognizing the change in her expression, she had thrown out all the planning. Abby already knew, and she was making her own plans.

All night she had worried the problem of what to do, what Brice might do, what Abby was planning. He had gotten away with it the first time, and however he had managed then must seem the likeliest way to get away with it again. But not before midnight on Sunday, not before the thirty-day grace period. And since he didn't know for certain when Abby would return to Eugene, he probably wouldn't trust waiting until Monday night.

Now she said, 'Willa, please sit down. I've given this a lot of thought, and here's what I think we can do. First, nothing's going to happen tonight; the thirty days aren't over yet. Tomorrow night we'll hole up in the Halburtson house and keep watch. We'll take turns, one of us rest on the sofa, one keep watch. You can see the start of the driveway from the dining-room window, and if he shows up, we'll call Abby and tell her to hide in the woods. She might get a little cold, but that's all, and she knows those woods the way you know your own house. That won't be a problem for her. And we'll call the sheriff. So Brice will go over and find the house empty, and come back across the finger. But we'll disable his car, let the air out of the tires, and the sheriff will come and get him and find whatever evidence they need to keep him.'

Willa sat at the table considering it, and finally nodded. 'But I'll try to get her to come back with us, or to let me stay there with her. Something might go wrong, and she'll be alone. Maybe we're wrong and he won't come at all, or he has different plans in mind. An accident in their house, something like that.'

The image of Abby holding the shotgun was in Felicia's mind again, but she nodded. 'Yes, we'll try to get her to be reasonable, but I don't think we should mention Brice yet. She's working things out for herself and needs a little time to finish.' Then very briskly she said, 'I hope and pray I'm wrong, and nothing will happen this weekend or ever. If nothing happens, we'll have our talk with her on Monday, but for Sunday night, we'll keep watch over her, just in case. Now I have to go to Bend and do some dinner shopping, and buy a long rope. We won't dare show a light in the Halburtson house, and we'll need a guideline to follow to the carport to get to his car. You want to come along?'

They went shopping, and afterward they drove to the Halburtson house and took the rope around to the back, where Felicia tied it to the porch rail, and then strung it along the path, wrapping it around a tree here and there as she went. At the boat shed she stopped and tied it.

'This is enough,' she said, surveying the boat shed, the carport off to the side, the boat ramp down below. 'The light from the ramp will be enough for the rest of the way; it's just that first section that's too dark.' She looked at the cabin across the finger; smoke was curling out of the chimney, lights already on in the upper part reflected palely on the black calm water. Later, when daylight failed, the reflected light would be an illuminated path.

22

No one talked as Abby led the way up the drive, then onto the ruined road toward the bridge over the north finger. Willa carried the box of papers, Felicia the shovel, and Abby the box with her father's ashes. It was very quiet in the woods that early afternoon, little wind, no frolicking dog; they had left Spook in the cabin, and the forest creatures had been stilled by the arrival of intruders. It wasn't very cold.

After crossing the bridge, Abby turned toward the lake; there was no trail, but she knew where they had to go, and although it was not a strenuous walk through the woods, she kept the pace slow, afraid that Felicia would tire. When they stopped, the north finger was in sight, grumbling and hissing its way over and around rocks and blowdowns on its way to the lake, which was in view below.

Mindy's grave looked different; a flat black obsidian rock had been placed on it. Jud had been here, Abby thought; he had repaired damage done by an animal or a storm.

She and Willa took turns digging, and

363

during her rest periods she gazed at the tall trees, mostly pines, not very big through the trunk but elongated, reaching for light; through the silvery gray-green needle patches of pearly gray sky shimmered, and down below, the black lake was a reflecting pool. Underfoot, centuries of pine needles carpeted the earth, sound-absorbing and resilient; trees felled by the most elemental of all foresters told their own stories, bore witness to the time lines of their history. Those most recently struck down were still cloaked in thick russet bark; then the mosses claimed the tree trunks, brilliant greens and grays, and the multihued lichen, white, red, yellow . . . Burrowing creatures inhabited the decaying trees, cave dwellers deep in the inner recesses. The crumbling bark became foothills to the cave dwellings; then the trees were no more than dark mounds with one last visible act to perform — nurse trees to seedlings, preserving the species. And finally even those mounds sank back into the earth, leaving places on the forest floor where the earth offered less resistance to whoever trod upon it. Here and there, like sculptures, black obsidian rocks rose, some fractured and faceted, some polished by years of tumbling, artless art. Abby thought this was the most beautiful place in the world.

When the grave was ready, she placed the box of papers in first. Neither Willa nor Felicia had asked what it contained. Then she put the mahogany box in the grave, and for a moment stood gazing at it silently, saying good-bye. Willa took a gold chain from her neck and placed it on the box, and Felicia added a small figurine. Abby and Willa took turns filling in the grave, and then all three gathered rocks to cover it, protect it.

His funeral, Abby thought: silent, reverential, fitting. It was done. His secrets were buried with him for all time.

★ ★ ★

Back inside the cabin, Abby put another piece of wood on the fire, then said, 'I have cheese, snack food. Let's have it now. Tea? Coffee?'

'Nope,' Felicia said. 'I bought two bottles of a very nice wine, fumé blanc. And a duck. He used to drop in and say, 'You'll never guess what flew into the car on my way home from Bend. A duck. Maybe I can make us some dinner.' And, of course, I'd make dinner. He did love duck. And he always brought in a bottle of fumé blanc to go with it. Between the two of us we drank it all.'

Abby smiled faintly and went to the refrigerator to find the cheese. In the novels

Link's aunt Sookie had made duck for the boy, then the man. She had always known that Felicia was Aunt Sookie, she realized: his mother, companion, confidante.

'Too early to start the duck,' Felicia said, rummaging now in the refrigerator with Abby. 'Ah, here it is. Pâté.'

They sat at the table, looking out over the lake, nibbling, sipping wine, and then Willa said, 'He brought a duck in to my house once and asked if I knew how to cook it. I said no but I was game, and he said so was the duck. Anyway, I got out my handy-dandy cookbook and followed instructions to the letter, and we ate it, but afterward all he said was, 'Never mind.''

They all laughed. Willa gave Felicia a fond look. 'I didn't know at the time what the competition was. I never tried it again.'

'I used to try to make chili the way he liked it,' Abby said. 'But no matter how much chili powder or red chilies I put in, he always added more at the table. So this one time I decided to get it right to start with, and doubled the amount I usually used, then added even more. He came in while it was simmering, and I was off in the woods or something, and he must have thought he'd fix it himself and added still more red chili flakes. When we sat down, I waited for him to sample it, looking forward to his surprise when he found it was okay for once. He nearly choked on the first bite. He let out a yell, and gasped, 'Milk! I need milk.' He drank a glassful, and then he looked at me and said, 'Abby, you're an overachiever.''

They sat and told Jud stories, smiled and laughed, drank wine, and lapsed into silence now and again. After one of the silent periods, Felicia shook herself. 'I'll get that duck started,' she said.

When she went to the kitchen, Abby and Willa followed and watched her preparations. Her secret, Abby thought, was that she braised it first in a mixture of wine and water, with garlic, ginger, a leek, a carrot . . .

'We'll let it simmer awhile. What goes with duck is mashed rutabagas, brown rice, and a salad. Should have red vine-ripened tomatoes, but forget that this time of year. All tomatoes are good for now is to look at.' When Willa and Abby offered to help, she shooed them away. 'Later I'll take the duck out and set it to the side and strain the broth and chill it down, so I can get the fat off the top. Used to keep it for making biscuits, but I gave that up.' She glanced at Willa and Abby. 'You girls like biscuits?' They both nodded. 'Calories be damned! Cholesterol be damned! Biscuits, with duck fat. Best thing there is for making biscuits while the oven's so hot from finishing the duck, crying out for biscuits.'

Watching her, Abby smiled; then, looking past her, she saw out the kitchen window that the ramp light across the finger had come on. Beyond the reach of pale light the world was as dark as the black lake. She emptied the wine bottle into their glasses and raised hers in a semisalute. 'Calories be damned,' she repeated.

Felicia finished the duck by covering it with a paste she made from a little broth, mashed leek and carrot, more ginger, more garlic, and a dollop of orange marmalade, then put it in the hot oven. It came out half an hour later crackling golden brown all over; the biscuits went in, and she finished mashing the rutabagas, tossed the salad, then surveyed the table, gave it a satisfied nod, and said, 'Let's eat. I'll get the biscuits in about one more minute.'

It was a beautiful and delicious meal, and for a time no one spoke. Then Abby asked Willa, 'How much detail did you and Dad go into about an art colony? What made him think of such a thing in the first place?'

'You,' Willa said after a tiny sip of wine. No one was drinking much wine now, a sip from time to time was all. 'I'm afraid I had been bitching about some committee work I couldn't get out of. He asked me what a girl like you could do with an advanced degree in art history. You know the answer: work in a museum, do restoration or authentication, teach. He said you chose to work in the museum instead of being a T.A., and that said something.' Willa smiled faintly. 'He knew the kind of work you're doing, hauling and crating, hanging a show, taking it down, more hauling and crating . . .'

'I might like to teach,' Abby protested, 'just not like they'd want me to.'

'That's what he said, that you'd be a fine teacher if they gave you your head, and that what you needed more than anything else at this point was to travel and see some real art, and then he started talking about an art colony. Established artists who need space and quiet now and then, students who are there because they want to learn something, maybe an occasional Elderhostel.'

She looked at Felicia, still pink and flushed from her kitchen duties, with her curly white hair curlier than ever. She looked like Mrs. Claus, after a good nutritionist had worked the elf over for a year, trimmed away every excess pound.

'He said,' Willa continued, speaking now to Felicia, 'that you needed a really good reason

369

for staying here at the lake because your kids were driving you up the wall, pressuring you to move to civilization and act nice. And, by God, an art colony would be a fine reason, if you would agree to take any part in such a crazy idea.

'I said I'd give up my position, go on part-time, and divide the year, half here, half in town, the best of both worlds . . . '

Abby's mind was drifting: the Xuan Bui Institute in Vietnam near her village, the Jud Vickers Art Institute here by his cabin, his lake. How excited he must have been.

They talked about the art colony throughout the rest of dinner. Abby made coffee, and later she and Willa cleared the table and washed the dishes.

Then Felicia said, 'Abby, thank you, child, for letting this day happen, for letting us be here. Thank you. Now, we should be going.'

Willa clasped Abby's hand fiercely. 'Come with us. We'll toss a coin for the cot; the winner gets the sofa. Please, Abby, come with us.'

Abby shook her head. 'I'm glad I realized in time that I didn't want to be alone today, that you both belonged here, too. But now I have to be alone. For a while.' She hugged Willa and kissed her cheek. 'Thanks, Willa.' Then she drew away and embraced Felicia.

'And you. I can't thank you enough. I love you both so much.'

Then very briskly she said, 'Now get bundled up. It's going to be a cold ride across. Felicia, you must be exhausted, all that hiking, cooking, shopping. You have your gloves?'

They all pulled on waterproof boots, heavy jackets and hats, gloves, and left the cabin. Abby told Spook to stay, to watch, and obediently the dog lay down with a low whine.

'I won't linger on the other side,' Abby said, steadying the boat for Felicia to step in. 'Too cold.'

It was very dark, the woods and sky a black wrap that started somewhere beyond comprehension and came to the edge of the boat; only the lights from the cabin and the light from the ramp existed in such overwhelming darkness. A faint breeze had started at the surface of the lake; higher up it was brisk enough to rustle the pine branches, whisper in the needles. That and the faint slap of the oars sliding in and out of the water were the only sounds.

At the ramp Willa helped Felicia out of the boat, and then pleaded with Abby. 'If you won't come with us, let me go back with you, spend the night.'

'Another time,' Abby said. 'Take care of Felicia.' She pushed off and started to row.

For several seconds the two women on the shore watched her, then Felicia took Willa's arm and said, 'Let's get to it. Come on.' They started up the path to the carport; when they got there, Felicia looked once more at the water; Abby was gone, out of sight, past the reach of the ramp light. On the other side of the finger the cabin glowed like a beacon.

Felicia and Willa got into Felicia's car, and she started the engine and backed out carefully. At the fork in the driveway she turned and drove to the front of the Halburtson house, then farther, and stopped between two pine trees, a spot where the car would be all but invisible to anyone who didn't look hard for it. Silently they got out and walked back to the front porch; Felicia used a tiny penlight to find the keyhole, unlocked the door, and they entered the house to start their vigil.

23

Abby reentered the cabin and locked the door. She checked the wood supply, unnecessarily; she knew there was plenty inside, more than enough to see her through the night. Spook was pathetically happy to have her home again, and she ruffled the dog's fur, then unlocked the dog door. Later she would lock her inside. After taking off her heavy jacket and boots, she picked up the shotgun and the box of shells and took them to the table and very methodically loaded the double-barreled gun.

The answering machine light was blinking, she realized. Someone had called in the short time she had been out. It was Brice. His voice sounded strange, thick, the words slurred: 'Abby, pick up the fucking phone! I know you're there. Please. Please pick up.' She stared at the telephone. Was he crying? 'Abby, please. I'm begging you. Tell her, Eddie, tell her I'm begging.' His voice broke, and a moment later, in a steadier, more measured, even deliberative manner, he said, 'I'm at Eddie Blankenship's place. I'll be here for a while. If you need me . . . What's your number, Eddie? What's your fucking number?'

He was drunk, she thought in amazement. Drunk, at Eddie Blankenship's house. He was repeating a number, enunciating each number too clearly, too precisely. 'Call me, sweetheart. Call me.'

She felt weak with relief suddenly. He couldn't drink and almost always stopped with one drink, one glass of wine. The only time she had ever seen him drink too much had been at his birthday party when he turned thirty. He had passed out on the couch and had slept for hours, through the party, through the noise of music and laughter, through good-byes hours later, through the night. She had covered him up and left him on the couch. After that he had been teased mercilessly by his friends. Cheap date, they said, what a cheap date. Eddie Blankenship had been at the party, she remembered. And tonight Brice was at his house, drinking himself into a stupor.

She started to replay the message, and midway through she whispered, 'I don't believe it.'

He was putting on an act. There must be others around who knew he couldn't drink, and he was putting on an act for them. Setting up an alibi. Using her to set up his

374

alibi. Someone would take him home and put him to bed, and presumably he would be out cold for the rest of the night. Respectable people would testify to that: a banker, his wife, people whose words would not be doubted. She disconnected the phone from the wall jack.

Eddie lived a few blocks away in their neighborhood, at the top of the hill; their house was midway down, and how Brice wanted a house at the top of the hill. By the time he achieved it, Eddie would have moved to Spyglass Hill, or some other even more elite neighborhood, and then Brice would not be able to rest until they could move there, too. She looked at her watch, a quarter to ten. He would make it look good, another fifteen minutes or half an hour, and then Eddie would take him home, probably take off his shoes, watch him pass out on the couch the way he had done before. He wouldn't arrive at the lake for at least two and a half hours. If he came, she added.

If she was wrong, he wouldn't show up at all. But if she was right, he would be there sometime after twelve, probably closer to twelve-thirty or one, or even later. On Sunday nights most lights in their neighborhood were off by eleven. He might wait until eleven or a little later to start.

Unhurriedly she resumed her preparations. On the back wall of the kitchen, the refrigerator was in the corner next to three feet of counter; there had been wall cabinets above it at one time, but Jud had taken them down and put in a sliding window, for light and air, he had said, but actually in order to sit at the table and be able to see out over the finger. Then came the sink, with another window, more counter and cabinets, and the stove. The worst possible kitchen design; Lynne had complained about it often, but for one person or even two people, it was fine. Abby cleared the counter between the refrigerator and sink, put the toaster and dish drainer on the other side and placed the shotgun on the side where they had been. She considered the box of shells, it should be within reach, but not in the way. She put it near the splashboard under the window. Caldwell's card with his cell phone number went by the telephone in the living room. She made a pot of coffee and filled a thermos, placed a mug nearby; she hated the plastic cup on the thermos. The binoculars, she remembered, and got them from a drawer to take to the kitchen. Scanning the opposite side of the finger, she found the rock she had picked out as a focal target, and when it was perfectly clear she put the binoculars down, close to the edge of the sink. A glass in the dish drainer, where, if she knocked it over fumbling in the dark, it would not crash into the sink; any sound at night carried, she knew. No noise. No light. No shadows at the window.

She brought in a rattan chair and placed it by the counter, but when she sat down, she realized she was too low; she couldn't see the lake well, couldn't see the ledge, only across the water. Two cushions made it exactly right. She surveyed the scene, unlocked the window, and then turned off the lights in the cabin. Rehearsal time.

There was more light than she had thought there would be. The glass panel in the door of the woodstove glowed with firelight. Standing at the window with that glow behind her, she might be seen. Regretfully she decided to turn up the thermostat, let the fire die out. The light from outside also illuminated the cabin dimly. It would not reveal her, but it would be a spotlight on him when he came ashore. No rehearsal was needed, she realized; she could see all the items she had arranged. She stood up, then paused, gazing at the water beyond the window.

Although only a few inches deep, the water on the ledge looked bottomless, an abyss; it was responsive to the breeze, restless with shifting patterns under the soft light from the house. Would he wear waterproof boots? She doubted it. He had never been here at this time of year; he didn't know that the ledge would be covered, that his feet would get soaked with the icy water, his fine Italian shoes ruined.

It was still early, just eleven. Without turning on a light, with no need for more light, she went to the stove and poked at the wood to make it burn faster, be done sooner. Afterward she sat in the living room. Newly energized, firelight flared brighter than ever; fire shadows danced on the walls.

If he didn't come, if she was wrong about everything, then what? She didn't know. But no matter what else, she knew she could never live with him again. In her mind she had seen him plot the murder of her father and carry it out; she knew he was capable of it, and she believed he had done it. But they might never be able to prove anything.

Uneasily she got up and while there was still enough light, although it was fading at last, and went to the pegs in the kitchen, reached into her jacket pocket, and pulled out her penlight. She wouldn't need it in the kitchen, she now realized, but when she used the bathroom she would, and even now she needed it to see the thermostat and set it.

Having turned off all the lights, she felt a great reluctance to turn them back on.

She checked the door again, and latched the dog door, and finally she sat down in the rattan chair in the kitchen. Poor dumb Spook, without a clue, sniffed her legs, nuzzled her hand, and finally lay down at her feet with a sigh.

If he didn't come, Abby started again, she would leave tomorrow. What if he really had a foolproof alibi? If he really had not committed murder? She would go home, pack some things, and hole up someplace. Go to Salem? Talk to Caldwell? She had to do that, but when? Not before Brice's hard drive was copied onto disks. If he had left a trail, it was on his computer. She had to start there. And if his alibi couldn't be disproved, what? Give Brice a chance to admit what he had done at the office, make him go to Durkins and confess and guarantee restitution, starting with the money she was borrowing? She realized she was considering giving him the same chance her father had given her first husband: confess, pay up, and get out. Brice would have to agree to go into some other line of work before she turned a cent over to him; he could never manage anyone else's money again. That would be like putting a pedophile in charge of a day-care center, or a diabetic with an insatiable sweet tooth behind a candy counter.

It was almost laughable, trying to imagine Brice accepting such an ultimatum from her. She would tell him she had changed her will first, or better, leave him a note saying that she had done it. She bit her lip. When should she talk to Caldwell?

The idea of accusing her husband of murdering her father made her stomach hurt, made her spinning thoughts spin even faster, out of control. She knew what she had to do, but she couldn't find a sequence. Everything had to be first. She took several deep breaths and started over. If she went directly to Caldwell, what could she tell him? *Brice made his motel reservation only after I reserved the cottage at the coast, and that was at his urging, to go that weekend.* Brice would deny it. *He stayed home that morning because my father called and wanted me to come out, and Brice had to make sure I didn't do it, that I would go on to work, and then to the coast.* His word, her word. *He went to three meetings in Portland before that one, and each time he got home by midnight; there was no good reason for him to stay over that night.* He already had explained that away.

Embezzlement, the need of money, supplied a motive, and Caldwell wasn't interested in motives, only means. That left the canoe, and possibly the gun, but where were they, if he had them at all? He could have flown to Seattle, bought the canoe with cash, flown back home with it the same afternoon. Would a salesman remember him? And he had kept it somewhere. Not at home; she might have seen it during one of her sporadic cleaning frenzies. He wouldn't have risked it.

She stood up to stretch, afraid tension would make her legs start to cramp, make her hands cramp. She reached across the counter and slid the window open. A faint rubbing sound was the only noise it made. She picked up the shotgun and cradled it against her shoulder, against a big bruise that throbbed painfully at a touch. Coop had said if she intended to practice a bit more, she should pad her shoulder with a towel.

Maybe he really was drunk, asleep on the couch. Maybe he had wanted to come out here and found he couldn't do it, and had started drinking instead.

She lifted the shotgun and sighted the restless black water at the end of the ledge, where he would come ashore, and she said under her breath, 'I can go this far, but could

I shoot him? Actually shoot him?' She didn't know the answer.

She had visualized how it would be, but she had no image, no idea what would follow tomorrow, the next day, next week; everything beyond tonight was a blur.

He would not be holding a gun — he would need both hands to manage the canoe, to get it up onto the ledge. The gun would be in his pocket. Her shot would be a complete surprise; he would stagger on the ledge, slippery under the water, fall backward into the icy water, another systemic shock. He might struggle up, try to get back on the ledge, and she would shoot him again, knock him back again, and while he struggled, she would have time to reload and to shoot as many times as he got to his feet and tried to reach her. But it would be like shooting an unarmed man, lying in ambush and killing an unarmed person. Coop said the buckshot wouldn't kill a bear, and probably not a cougar, but it wouldn't do them any good, either. She had visualized Brice climbing back into the canoe, fleeing, and then she would call Caldwell and tell him that Spook had wakened her, that she had seen someone coming ashore and shot him. They would find Brice, wounded, bloody, soaking wet, find the gun, find the canoe, and it would be over.

She shook her head violently. If she shot him, he would die from wounds, loss of blood, hypothermia. He would die. Shaking, she put the shotgun back on the counter and closed the window. Could she do it?

★   ★   ★

In the Halburtson house Felicia shifted on the sofa and looked at her watch: twelve o'clock. Although she had not slept, she had rested; now it was Willa's turn to stretch out and try to relax. She felt stiff and creaky when she stood up, but by the time she reached the dining-room window and touched Willa's shoulder, she felt fine again. They had positioned a comfortable chair by the window, and Willa had taken a throw from the living room to cover herself. No matter that they had turned up the thermostat and the house was warm enough, keeping the night watch was chilling, as Felicia well knew. She wondered how many nights she had sat up with a sick child, and shook her head. Many, many times.

'Go get some rest,' she said softly as Willa stood up and stretched.

'I doubt that I'll sleep,' Willa said, just as softly, as if they both were afraid their voices would carry out into the black night. 'If you see his car lights, come get me. And only two hours, then my turn again.'

'I know,' Felicia said. 'I know. Go rest now.'

★　★　★

Abby sipped hot black coffee and wished she had left some cheese out, but she wouldn't open the refrigerator to get any. The cabin would be flooded with light. She should have thought of something she could do in the darkened cabin while she waited. Like Madame DeFarge, knit and watch, knit and wait. She stood up, stretched, sat down again and again, but still felt twitchy all over.

Suddenly, on the opposite shore, a shadow moved in front of the ramp light. No longer aware of her restless legs or her nervous hands, she snatched up the binoculars, slid the window open, and searched the ramp area, and then she found him.

Brice was putting a tiny canoe into the water.

She could see him clearly, black cap, black coat that she had never seen before, a peacoat, the kind sailors wore, black pants. He got in the canoe and started to paddle; the canoe was faster than she had thought it would be. Very soon it would pass out of the light from the ramp, into the black space, and then it would reappear in the light from the cabin. She put the binoculars down and picked up the shotgun.

★　★　★

When Felicia saw the headlights turn in at the Halburtson driveway, she stood up and silently put on her heavy outer-wear: jacket, scarf, knit stocking cap pulled down nearly to her eyes, wool gloves. She checked to make certain the cell phone was in her pocket, then she made her way through the dark house and out the kitchen door without a sound. On the porch she felt for the rail and the guideline she and Willa had placed there.

Using the utmost caution, she descended the three steps down to the bark mulch trail; then, keeping her hand on the guideline, she followed the trail to the back of the boat shed. There was a glow beyond the shed, but no light on the path; she never let go of the guideline. She stopped at the shed and watched Brice inflate a rubber boat. He had a canister of compressed air; it took him only seconds to finish. Across the finger, the dock light beckoned, a warm yellow light road.

As soon as he was in the boat and had started to paddle, Felicia retraced her steps back to the house. She had to warn herself repeatedly not to rush, not to risk a fall, not to lose the guideline. She could not see her hands, or the line, or even the house.

Finally, back on the porch, she felt for the door, then continued to feel her way across the rear of the house, past the window, and to the electrical service boxes. She took off her gloves now and felt for the switches. The bottom one, the biggest one, was the one she needed. She found it and threw the switch, then repeated the act with the service box next to it. The glow beyond the boat shed vanished. The glow from across the finger vanished, and the night was darker than ever.

She found the stairs again and, as before, keeping a grasp of the guideline, she returned to the back of the shed. Now she had her other hand on the cell phone. If he had a flashlight, a light of any sort, she would have to call Abby, warn her. She did not believe he had a light; the dock lights were sufficient. She waited.

★ ★ ★

Before Abby could position the gun against her shoulder, the ramp light went out, the light at the back of the cabin went out, and there was only the black night.

Spook made a low growly sound, a deep

386

rumble in her throat. 'Be quiet,' Abby whispered. 'Spook, watch.'

What was he doing? What had he planned? Maybe he had a light of some sort in the canoe. She shook her head. A flashlight wouldn't be of any use to him, not unless he followed the black shore all the way around the finger to the ledge. That would take a long time. But if he didn't have a light, or if he had a night-light of some kind, she wouldn't be able to see him when he came ashore; she would have to rely on Spook to warn her, rely on her own ears to warn her. She didn't move, listening, watching for the beam of a flashlight to come on, go off. It was so dark, nothing was visible — no sky, no water, nothing.

She had begun to feel drowsy, but adrenaline and the cold air had roused her, and now fear raised her to an even higher level; she could hear her own heart, Spook's every breath, the whisper of water on basalt . . .

Then she heard the sound of a paddle slapping water, and again . . . It got louder, nearer; he was beating the water, not sliding the paddles in. The sound began to fade again. Drawing away? Or had he begun to master the technique? She leaned against the counter to get closer to the window, and she heard it again, the splash of a paddle hitting water, but it was faint, farther away.

He was lost, she thought then. Out there in the dark, lost. She didn't move, listening.

After a long silence, during which she hardly breathed, straining to hear, she lowered the shotgun to the counter and rested her hand on Spook's head; the dog's ears were stiff, her hair bristled, her whole body was rigid, listening, on watch. If Brice came this way again, Spook would know, and through her Abby would know. She didn't move again for a long time.

Then she heard a faint cry from far away; it sounded like the scream of an owl. Slowly Abby reached out and closed the window. If it had been closed before, she wouldn't have heard the cry, she thought distantly. She sat in the rattan chair and started to shiver.

★   ★   ★

Across the finger Felicia was standing at the back of the boat shed, also listening, and she too heard the cry that could have been an owl. Slowly she began to make her way back to the house, using the guideline rope as before, blind in the pitch-black night. She reentered the house without a sound and returned to the dining room, the comfortable chair by the window, where she sat down and pulled the cover about herself without removing her heavy jacket, her gloves, or the stocking cap. She was aching from the cold and she knew that without electricity, the house would only get colder.

24

'It's time,' Felicia said, touching Willa's shoulder. The young woman was sleeping, huddled in a tight mass, with a blanket up to her nose; the house had become refrigerator-cold overnight. Felicia was still dressed in her heavy outdoor clothes, her face flushed with cold. 'If we're going to get to the cottage before the park ranger drives through, we'd better be on our way,' she said.

Willa yawned and sat up.

'Let's put that chair back where it belongs, and while you straighten up things in here, I'll collect that rope, and we'll be off,' Felicia said. Together they moved the easy chair back to the living room, and afterward Felicia went outside quickly. The sky was lightening, but the woods were still very dark, with shadows dense and impenetrable. She needed her penlight to see the circuit breakers, restore them to their proper places. Then she followed the guideline to the end of the boat shed and gazed at the cabin across the finger; the pale light looked warm, soft yellow against black. At this side, the ramp light was enough so that it was a matter of seconds to undo the rope and start back to the house, coiling the rope as she went.

They finished up in the Halburtson house quickly, went out and got into Felicia's car, and she backed out from between the two pine trees, turned, and headed toward the road. At the spot where the driveway branched, she caught a glimpse of Abby's little black car down near the carport. Willa's eyes were closed, and Felicia didn't say a word. She drove to the cottage.

'It was a bust,' Willa said tiredly when they got out of the car. 'But I'm glad we did it. Are you okay?'

'Fine,' Felicia said. 'I'm fine.' She opened the cottage door, where they were greeted by the two excited poodles. 'As far as the rest of the world is concerned, last night we drove home, talked awhile, then went to bed. Not a word about anything else. Agreed?'

'Of course,' Willa said.

'You should go on to bed now, get in a few hours of real sleep at least. I'll let these idiot dogs out and as soon as they come back in, I'll go to bed.'

Willa was already peeling off layers of clothes as she headed toward the bedroom they had been sharing. There was a sofa made up for a bed in the room, and Felicia's twin bed, one easy chair with a lamp nearby on an end table, and a chest of drawers. Enough.

While she waited for the dogs, Felicia stood at the kitchen window gazing out over the lake that was slowly defining itself, re-creating itself from darkness, form out of chaos. Presently the poodles wanted back in; she opened the door for them, undressed, put on a warm flannel gown, and went to bed.

In the cabin, when the light came back on and she could see what she was doing, Abby put things back in their place, then huddled on the couch, shivering hard. She should go to bed, get some sleep, she knew, but she leaned back, pulled one of the gaudy throws around herself, and after a long time fell asleep.

★ ★ ★

At nine Felicia woke up; then, putting on her robe, she went to the kitchen to look at the lake, at what was happening out there. On shore were two sheriff's cars, a truck, and a rescue-team ambulance. A few people were being kept back by a deputy — curious campers, she guessed. In the water she saw a six-man rowboat, with men grappling for something. She was glad they hadn't sent a diver down; the water was too cold to put anyone through that. She went to rouse Willa.

They stood side by side watching for a moment, then Willa said faintly, 'We have to call Abby. He must have gotten to the lake somehow.' She looked and sounded terrified.

'Did you see any car lights?'

'No! But he must have gotten in!' She ran to the phone and punched in numbers, and after a few seconds, her face ashen, she said, 'The phone's disconnected or something. I'm getting a recording.'

'I have her cell phone number,' Felicia said, and hurried to find it in her address book. Her hands were shaking.

Willa placed the call, and on the fifth ring Abby answered groggily. Willa slumped down into a chair. 'Listen,' she said, 'something happened out on the lake last night. The sheriff is here and a lot of men are looking for something in the water. I think you should come over. Drive. Don't come by boat.' She listened a moment, then said, 'We didn't, either. No one.' When she hung up, she looked old and tired. 'She didn't hear or see a thing during the night.'

Felicia nodded. 'Thank God!' She was putting on her heavy jacket and stocking cap. 'I'm going to talk to the sheriff,' she said. 'Ed Grayson. I've known him all his life. Why don't you make coffee?'

She wanted to intercept Abby before the

sheriff got to her, or one of his deputies turned her away. Abby would see the little black car; she might not be able to get around it without scraping it, in fact, and she would know what they were looking for out there. Felicia let herself out and walked toward the ramp area and the sheriff.

'What's going on, Ed?' she asked when she drew near him. He was a slightly built man with a mustache far too big for his face. He was very proud of that mustache; he seemed to think it made up for a fast-receding hairline.

'Morning, Mrs. Shaeffer,' he said. 'Reckon there's been some kind of accident out there. The park ranger spotted a little boat hung up on the rocks and called us, and here we are. I put in a call to the state troopers, 'cause that lieutenant — Caldwell? — he said if anything unusual happened out here, he should be called. And that's all I know.'

She nodded. It probably was all he knew. She pointed to a small blue canoe on the shore, partly deflated. 'That was out there?'

'Yep. Damnedest thing I ever saw. Rubber canoe, who would have thought of such a thing?' He shook his head in wonder.

They stood gazing at the canoe for a time. Out on the lake the men continued to drop the grapple over the side of the boat, and pull

394

it up. Then Felicia saw the van appear on the park road that edged the parking area, and she waved to Abby to stop. 'It's Abby,' she said to the sheriff. 'Jud's daughter. I thought since she was at the cabin alone, maybe she should come on over and stay with us for a time, until we know what's going on out there.' She went to meet Abby, who was still in her clothes from the day before and who looked as if she had been up all night. She was pale down to her lips. She drew even with Felicia, stopped, and rolled down her window.

'My car is in the driveway over there,' Abby said in a low voice. 'My car, the Supra, it's in the driveway.'

'Maybe you'd better tell the sheriff that,' Felicia said. 'It looks like someone had an accident last night, maybe fell out of a boat, something like that. Let's tell him about the car, and then we'll go on to the cottage and get warm.'

Abby stared at her, a long, searching look; she started to say something, but abruptly turned away and swallowed hard. Then, not looking at Felicia, she nodded. 'Yes, I should tell the sheriff,' she said.

Sheriff Grayson nodded politely when Felicia and Abby drew near. 'Why don't you ladies go on to your place,' he said, not unkindly but clearly wanting them not to linger.

'She saw her car in Halburtson's driveway,' Felicia said. 'Her own car. She drove Jud's van over from Eugene.'

He looked past them at the van, then at Abby. 'Anyone in it?' His voice was different, harder now.

She shook her head, her gaze fixed on the big rowboat on the lake. She was as pale as death.

'Take her back to your place,' the sheriff said to Felicia; it was no longer just a suggestion. 'I'll send one of the boys over to see about the car, keep an eye on it until Lieutenant Caldwell gets here.'

★　★　★

They sat at the table by the back window. Felicia made toast and spread butter and jam on a piece and put it in Abby's hand; she took a bite, then put it down. Willa put coffee in her hand; she sipped it, and put it down.

They saw Caldwell arrive, followed by another state police car, and soon after that a man drove stakes into the ground and strung a crime-scene tape. Caldwell and the sheriff stood together, watching the rowboat; the onlookers stayed behind the tape. Two more state cars arrived, and Detective Varney appeared, talked with Caldwell, then left again with several men.

The men in the rowboat dropped the grapple into the water, rowed the boat a foot or two, drew the grapple up, dropped it again. Now and then the grapple appeared to be snagged on a rock or something, and the men had to reverse their direction, maneuver to free it again, then they resumed their search.

At twelve-thirty they stopped moving forward, and began to pull up the grapple line slowly, three men struggling with it, until they got it out of the water. The mass they pulled into the boat was shapeless, black, big, and dripping water.

Felicia took Abby's arm and drew her away from the window as the men began to row toward the boat ramp.

Half an hour later Caldwell came to the cottage. Felicia met him outside on the front stoop. Caldwell looked tired, and he looked very angry.

'It's Brice, isn't it?' Felicia said. He nodded. 'She knows, Lieutenant. She saw her car, and she has been putting things together for herself. She knows.'

'You told her your suspicions about him,' he said harshly.

She shook her head. 'Yesterday we buried

her father; Willa, Abby, and I buried him up in the forest. We had dinner in the cabin, the three of us, then she rowed us across the finger and we came home. Brice's name was never mentioned all day. I haven't said a word to her about him. But she saw her car over there. It certainly wasn't there when Willa and I left. She knows.'

He started to move past her, toward the door; she caught his arm. 'Was he carrying the gun?'

'There was a forty-five in his pocket,' he said, still harsh, still angry. He pushed the door open and entered the cottage.

Abby, seated at the table, watched silently as he strode across the studio with Felicia at his side. Felicia pulled a chair close to Abby's and took her hand.

Caldwell drew in a breath, then said, 'Mrs. Connors, there's no easy way to tell you this. We've just recovered your husband's body from the lake. I'm sorry.' He sat down across from her. Abby bowed her head and didn't move again, or make a sound. 'Can you answer a few questions?' Caldwell asked after a few moments. She nodded.

He asked questions, and Felicia held Abby's hand as she answered. She might have been holding an ice sculpture, but Abby's voice was steady, if faint. She told Caldwell about the shotgun that Coop had insisted she take and about the call from Brice, then, startled, remembered that she had not reconnected the phone. Willa looked at Felicia, agonized, and Felicia knew what she had to be thinking: even if they had seen the car lights, they wouldn't have been able to call Abby in time. They would have had to come back to the cottage to look up the cell phone number.

'So his message is on the tape?' Caldwell asked.

'Yes. I thought he was at Eddie's house, passed out. He couldn't drink really.'

Finally Lieutenant Caldwell stood up. 'I'll have to have that tape with his message,' he said. 'And the shotgun. Are you going to stay at the cabin now?'

'No,' Willa said quickly. 'I'll go with her to get her things and then take her home with me. She can't stay up here, or at her house.'

Abby didn't protest. Instead, in a voice that had become even fainter, she said, 'Lieutenant, if I give you permission to search my house, the computers, whatever you want, do you still need a search warrant?'

He regarded her steadily for a long time, then shook his head. 'No. Let's go to the cabin now,' he said. While Willa and Abby were getting their jackets on, and Willa collected the few things she had brought to the cottage, he stood looking down at the small fantastic models on the worktable; then he asked Felicia, 'You going to be here later on?'

'Yes. I'll be here.'

★   ★   ★

Dusk was gathering before he came back, no longer angry looking, but tired. Without waiting to be asked, he took off his jacket and sat at the kitchen table. 'She went back to Eugene with Ms. Ashford,' he said. 'She said she'll be back and forth a lot in the months ahead.'

Felicia nodded and poured coffee for them both and sat opposite him, also looking out. No one was on the lake now: no boats, no onlookers on shore. A fine rain had started to fall.

Without glancing her way, the lieutenant said, 'We were checking out everyone who drove a Buick to that Portland motel the night Connors stayed there. A tourist was willing to swear he saw him leave before seven that morning. What he saw was a silver Buick and a man in a dark suit, but he would have been hard to shake unless we found another Buick, another driver. And we were running down everyone who bought a collapsible canoe or boat of any sort west of the Rockies during the past few months. We had that narrowed down to two possible customers, one's off to Alaska or someplace, the other used a pseudonym: Robert Langdon. We were doing that before you called me with your theory about Brice Connors. Plodding, laborious work.' He sighed heavily.

'But you let him come out here with a gun,' she said bitterly.

'I had people keeping an eye on him,' he said. 'What they saw was Connors drive to the Blankenship house, park at the curb, and go in. Later a car came from the garage with two people, neither one was Connors; it left and then came back with just the driver, Blankenship. Connors had been in the backseat, lying down, according to Blankenship. He and a friend took him home and dumped him on the couch, and he was out cold, they thought. Blankenship took the other guy home, and went back to his own house. Our guy was still watching the Buick.'

'And Brice slipped away in Abby's car,' Felicia murmured. 'With a gun in his pocket and a canoe in the trunk.'

He nodded, almost absently, it seemed. Still not looking at her, he said, 'The sheriff thinks he had a few drinks, came out with the

401

gun, maybe to harm her, and then was overcome by remorse, and turned away from the cabin, maybe headed for the break and miscalculated. The little island is just about all under water, invisible, and he rammed into it. He couldn't free the canoe from inside, so he climbed out and slipped into the deep water. The shock of ice water, the heavy clothes he was wearing, they kept him from climbing back out. That's how your sheriff has it figured out.' He glanced at her. 'I keep thinking of what you said early on, that you'd like to see the murderer with an anchor tied to his feet and dumped into the deepest water.'

She had to think back a moment, then she shook her head. 'I said something like that to the young lady detective, not to you.'

'Like I said, Varney's young and pretty, and a good detective. After a couple of days she'll drive the little sports car back to Eugene. She'll like that.' He finished his coffee, then eyed her speculatively. 'You believe he suffered remorse?'

'Of course not. You have to have a conscience to suffer remorse.'

'Conscience. Guilt and conscience. Real driving forces, aren't they? One or the other — both — can ruin a decent person's life for all time.'

Felicia stood up and went to a cabinet. 'I'm

going to have a drink, Lieutenant. What I can offer is scotch and water, or wine. Are you on duty? Or do you want one, too?'

'Scotch and water,' he said without hesitation.

She put ice in glasses, added scotch and filled them with water, then sat down again. 'Did you ever track down that blond man?'

He nodded. 'Weeks ago. It was like you said, a family matter.' He picked up his glass and tasted his drink. 'I read once,' Caldwell said after the first sip, 'that if you're lost in the forest, you should sit still and let searchers find you, or you just wander in circles. I suspect the same thing's true if you're rowing around in the dark, you just row in circles until you run into something.'

He drank again. 'That's good,' he said. 'Just what I needed. You ever go down in a cave?' He didn't even glance at Felicia, didn't wait for an answer. 'You get down in it and the guides turn off the lights, and for the first time for most folks, they experience real darkness. The total absence of light. The old saying, you can't see your hand before your face? True. You can't. City people don't know what that means, not really. Low dense clouds, no light to bounce off them to light up a little of the landscape, total darkness, that's how it must be out like this. Like being deep in a cave.'

He gave her an oblique glance, then looked away again. She didn't move. 'I keep wondering how and why Connors ran up onto the little island like that, far enough to make it necessary to get out of the canoe to free it. Seems to me he would have been paddling along, not very fast in that little rubber canoe, not fast enough that his forward momentum would have carried him up onto the rock before he felt a bump, enough to back off. He could have felt a bump, reached out, expecting to be at the ledge back of the cabin, and felt the rock, pretty much like the lowest ledge behind the cabin. Couldn't have seen it, or he would have known he was off course. He could have reckoned he had reached the place he was aiming for and climbed out, pulled the canoe out, and stepped backward, into the deepest part of the water. And once he was in the deepest water, that's all she wrote.

'Of course,' he said reflectively after a moment, during which Felicia didn't stir or make a sound, 'it wouldn't have been that dark, not with lights on both sides of the finger. The utility company says there was no outage, nothing like that last night. And the circuit breakers, the main switches in the electric service boxes, they're all okay. I checked. Even checked for fingerprints;

nothing but smudges.'

She didn't say a word. Across the way the tops of the trees were black against the gray sky, but already the base of the trees, the basalt, the lake were merging, becoming one. Soon the trees would be one with them, and there would be only the enveloping darkness. She loved this time of day, when everything merged and became one.

'I keep thinking of Abby Connors up in that cabin alone with her dog and a loaded shotgun,' Caldwell said. 'She's what, twenty-eight? A long life ahead of her, fifty years, sixty? A long life.' He finished his drink, put the glass on the table, and stood up. He gave Felicia one of his thoughtful looks. 'Would she have shot him?'

For a long time Felicia didn't speak, but finally she stood up also, and said, 'Yes.'

He nodded. 'I'll be running along now. Thanks for the coffee, for the drink.'

'Lieutenant,' she said, going to the door with him as he pulled his jacket on, 'is the case closed now?'

'Paperwork to clean up, reports, wait for auditors' reports, a bit of tidying up to do, but as far as I'm concerned, it's closed.' He opened the door, then looked at her once more. 'You take care, Mrs. Shaeffer.'

25

On Tuesday Abby went to her house to meet Lieutenant Caldwell and get a receipt for whatever he wanted to take away, and she knew that Willa had been right; she could not stay in this house a single night. She would have to come back later and pack her belongings, and then she would turn it over to a real-estate agent, and never come back.

While Caldwell and his team made their search, she listened to the answering machine messages, two from friends that she skipped over, one for Brice that she skipped, and then Harvey Durham, Jud's attorney, was speaking.

'Mrs. Connors, will you please give me a call at your earliest convenience. Following the instructions of your father, I am to deliver a letter to you in person on Monday.' The call had been placed on Friday.

She closed her eyes in relief. Harvey Durham would know what to do about a funeral, about Brice's parents, about the house. She sat down in the living room to wait for Caldwell to finish. His team had already taken out some clothes, papers,

406

Brice's computer; when he entered the living room, he was holding keys. 'A mini-storage place,' he said, 'and his car keys. Duplicates. We found another set in his pocket. Have you decided what to do about his car?'

She shook her head.

'I'll have someone bring it around and put it in the garage.' His cell phone rang and he answered, turned away, speaking in a voice too low to catch. When he looked at her again, he said, 'Mr. Connors was carrying the gun that killed your father. They just phoned in the results.'

★ ★ ★

Now she was in Harvey Durham's office, and the attorney was deeply shocked. He was in his sixties, with unruly white hair, a paunch, very pink cheeks. He held her hands and led her to a chair as if afraid she might collapse as she told him what had happened at the lake, and that Brice had killed her father.

He would arrange everything, he assured her; he would get in touch with Brice's family, arrange to have them take care of the funeral; of course, she should not attend; he would take care of the house and car, meet with Brice's attorney . . .

Then he said, 'Your father gave me explicit

directions some years ago, three years ago, my dear. I am to shred a document in your presence, and deliver to you a letter.'

Three years, she thought numbly, before he and Willa had gotten together, but after Abby and Brice were married. That was when he had added the thirty-day contingency clause to his will, a year after she married Brice. She nodded and watched as the attorney fed a manila envelope into a shredder that turned it into confetti. Then Harvey Durham handed her a sealed envelope.

'I'll leave you alone for a few minutes,' he said, and walked from the office.

Slowly she opened the envelope and took out several sheets of handwritten papers.

Hi, honey,

I'm writing this letter on the assumption that for whatever reason, we won't have talked about these things when you receive it.

'She was a child, and I was a child in our kingdom by the sea.' Her name was Xuan Bui, she was seventeen years old, I loved her, and I killed her.

They sent me to Bali, to a hospital. One day as I bicycled around the island with two other patients, we came across an old man on the beach, carving something. He was as brown and wrinkled as a walnut, and the wood he was carving was driftwood, bleached bone-white. He motioned for me to join him and I did. The other two men began to walk along the shore, looking for shells, but I sat near the old man, neither of us speaking for a long time. Now I could see that he was carving a bird with outspread wings, one foot already drawn up for flight, but the other foot still attached to the driftwood base. Each feather was detailed, the ruffled breast feathers parted by the wind, the wings taut and strong. Then he stopped carving and said in perfect English, 'She is still bound to the earth, she is not released yet.' He handed the piece to me. He got up and walked away, so ancient, so frail and small, he looked unreal. The other two men returned and asked where I had found the carving; all they had found were a few worthless shells. I said the old man had given it to me, and they said there had been no one with me. I had sat there by myself while they walked. They had checked now and then; we were all considered to be suicidal, you see, and not permitted to go out alone. One of them must have reported to the doctor that I was delusional, and the following week they sent me home, booted me out of the army. Go home and be crazy was the message I got loud and clear.

You've seen the bird, Abby. It's real enough. Was he? I don't know to this day. I went home and was crazy for a long time. I met your mother in San Francisco, and at first, seeing her from the back, I thought it was Xuan Bui. Her hair was long and black, straight to her waist; she was slender . . . Three weeks later we were married.

I did your mother two terrible wrongs, Abby. I married her when I didn't love her, trying to substitute her for someone else. And I failed to provide for her afterward. I never blamed her for leaving me. The wonder is that she didn't do it many years sooner, the day she came to know that I couldn't love her.

I knew I had to do something, something important to me, and I couldn't find what it was. I tried to write, I read, I meditated. All useless. Then I saw a woman drown out by Siren Rock, and it was as if everything in me shattered, and when it grew back together, I knew.

I had to write the novel, a long novel. Now three volumes are done, and there is one more to do. They will make a great deal of money, and I will build a school in

Vietnam. I was responsible for the destruction of a village, and the death of a lovely young girl. Maybe I can redeem myself. The school has been started, and as more money comes along, it will grow. It is called the Xuan Bui Institute.

You will have wondered what I did with the cashier's checks, and now you know. One other person knows, and he has helped me through every step. He is very old and I'm afraid he won't live to see it all completed. Because his health is failing, we have set up a legal trust, the Xuan Bui Institute Trust Fund, in the Bank of America Trust Division in San Francisco, and that is where I deliver the checks.

In the unlikely event of a fatal accident — the plane crashes, the boat sinks, lightning strikes — I have instructed Harvey Durham to deliver this letter to you thirty days after my death. And you should also know that if, God forbid, your death should have followed before the thirty days have passed, then all the money due me would have been sent straight to the institute trust fund. Since you are now reading this letter, the thirty days have passed, and you will have had time to start down the very difficult path of recovery from the merciless grief of the death of a

411

loved one, and Harvey by now will have destroyed, unopened, the second part of this document.

Honey, please understand that this letter is in no way a demand on you. It's meant only to inform you so you won't worry and speculate about the checks, as I know you would without hearing this from me. I failed you in the same way I failed your mother, by not providing adequately too many times, and I am sorry, and yet your unquestioning love never wavered, and for that I am truly grateful. I don't believe the sins of the fathers are visited on their children. You have no obligation to repay my debt, and I would never try to dictate from the grave. Whatever I leave is yours without restraints, without strings. But you should know what I did, what I'm doing.

My truest wish is that one day I'll burn this letter and you will never see it. But, Abby, since you are reading it, know this: I have been blessed twice. I have loved and been loved by a woman who was heroic, and I was given a magical child. My two loves. My life has been blessed.

One last bit to ponder. A puzzle without an answer, a cosmic riddle. The day I finished Siren Rock, I felt a freedom I had not known before, a release, as if I had *been in restraints that I could not identify, could not find, could not escape. And on that day when I picked up my lovely bird, it came apart in my hands, set free from its driftwood trap. The bird is for you, Abby. Be whole, my darling, be free, be unhurt. I love you.*

She read the letter twice, then slowly folded it, returned it to the envelope, and put it in her purse. She crossed the office to stand at the window, seeing nothing outside, looking instead into the past, her father in Vietnam, Brice lost on the black lake, her mother's tears . . . She had been weeping for her lost child, not her lost husband, Abby understood now.

And she was seeing the final scene from her father's last novel. The man Link, exhausted, defeated, was staring at the mud bath, slowly undressing. He never had believed a word of the myths that had arisen about the mud bath, its power to heal, to cleanse, or to cling as a stench that could not be washed away, but still he hesitated. Finally he moved forward, and up above the big hot spring he saw the woman he loved, holding a large white towel, waiting for him. He stepped into the mud bath.

Abby was startled by the voice of the

attorney; she had not heard him reenter the office.

'Are you all right, my dear?' he asked hesitantly.

'Yes.'

'How can I reach you, if the need arises?'

'Willa Ashford will know where I am,' Abby said. 'I have to go to Seattle, stay with my mother for a week or so. Willa has her address and phone number.'

When she left the office and walked out to her car, the words were in her head: *Be whole, be free, be unhurt.* 'I'll try,' she said under her breath. 'I'll try.'

THE END

Other titles in the
Ulverscroft Large Print Series:

FIREBALL

Bob Langley

Twenty-seven years ago: the rogue shoot-down of a Soviet spacecraft on a supersecret mission. Now: the SUCHKO 17 suddenly comes back to life three thousand feet beneath the Antarctic ice cap — with terrifying implications for the entire world. The discovery triggers a dark conspiracy that reaches from the depths of the sea to the edge of space — on a satellite with nuclear capabilities. One man and one woman must find the elusive mastermind of a plot with sinister roots in the American military elite, and bring the world back from the edge . . .

STANDING IN THE SHADOWS

Michelle Spring

Laura Principal is repelled but fascinated as she investigates the case of an eleven-year-old boy who has murdered his foster mother. It is not the sort of crime one would expect in Cambridge. The child, Daryll, has confessed to the brutal killing; now his elder brother wants to find out what has turned him into a ruthless killer. Laura confronts an investigation which is increasingly tainted with violence. And that's not all. Someone with an interest in the foster mother's murder is standing in the shadows, watching her every move . . .

THE READER

Bernhard Schlink

A schoolboy in post-war Germany, Michael collapses one day in the street and is helped home by a woman in her thirties. He is fascinated by this older woman, and he and Hanna begin a secretive affair. Gradually, he begins to be frustrated by their relationship, but then is shocked when Hanna simply disappears. Some years later, as a law student, Michael is in court to follow a case. To his amazement he recognizes Hanna. The object of his adolescent passion is a criminal. Suddenly, Michael understands that her behaviour, both now and in the past, conceals a deeply buried secret.